IT'S BEEN A LONG, LONG TIME

READERS LOVE BERYL BLUE, TIME COP!

"Time has met its match in Beryl Blue!" – Lea Kirk, *USA Today* bestselling author of sci-fi romance

"Beryl Blue, Time Cop is an exciting start to Janet Raye Stevens's new series. Combination time travel, action with futuristic tech, suspense, and romance. Clever dialogue and emotion sucked in this reader immediately. I couldn't put down this book and look forward to the next installment." – Susan H. Vaughan, author of *Genuine Fake*

"A perfect blend of historical fiction, a bit of sci-if and wonderful romance. A really fun read, I can't wait to see what next is in store for Beryl. If you like historical fiction with a little romance, then this is a must read. I cannot recommend it enough." – Goodreads Review

"This is outside my typical genres... But I loved it! There is so much action going on from the first page to the last. Beryl is a spunky and smart heroine all the way through. I had so many emotions following her journey. I'm excited this is going to be a series and can't wait to read the next book!" – Amazon Review

ALSO BY JANET RAYE STEVENS

Beryl Blue, Time Cop—Book I

Feisty librarian Beryl Blue is hurled from 2015 to WWII, tasked with stopping an assassin from killing a soldier and changing history forever. She soon finds herself falling for the assassin's target, sexy, stubborn Army sergeant Tom "Sully" Sullivan, who makes it abundantly clear he can take care of himself. The future is toast unless Beryl can figure out how to stop a killer, protect a man who refuses to be protected—and keep her heart intact.

A Moment After Dark—A WWII paranormal mystery

Addie Brandt considers her ability to predict the future a curse. She hides from the world, tending the dead in her family's funeral home. But when her power of second sight shows her a terrifying future event, an attack on a US naval base in Hawaii, the horrific vision is too big to ignore and she sets out to raise the alarm. Can she stop the tragedy in time? Will anyone listen?

Cole For Christmas—A contemporary holiday romance

An event planner getting over a bad breakup, a chef who was left at the altar. Recruited to save a Christmas Eve wedding during a blizzard, the last thing on their minds is new romance —but they can't say no to the mistletoe.

IT'S BEEN A LONG, LONG TIME

A BERYL BLUE, TIME COP NOVEL

JANET RAYE STEVENS

GREAT BROOK PUBLISHING

Printed in the United States of America

First printing, 2022

ISBN: 978-1-7373103-6-5

To the inimitable Lauren Sheridan, sounding board, champion mouse wrangler, and listener of ideas, no matter how outlandish. Thank you for being a friend.

1
———

Montpelier, the state capital of Vermont. A place so small I could stretch out my arms and my fingertips would be over the city limits. Home to a top-notch culinary school, and not much else. At least, nothing else to tempt a time tourist to fork over a lot of cash, step into one of Time Scope, Inc.'s rattletrap time travel machines, and find themselves popped out here on a cold winter's night.

Nothing except the date, that is. December 31, 1999.

If anyone had asked, gee, Beryl, what are your plans for New Year's Eve, I certainly wouldn't have put chasing a time runner determined to blow up Montpelier's electrical grid at the top of my list. A real jerk of a perp, too. A guy who thought it would be just dandy to terrify the good people of the city by killing the juice at the stroke of midnight and sending the city into a full-on Y2K, end-of-the-world, chaotic panic.

Why? Because with the lights out and security systems down, Walter Solon figured he could waltz into the city's two jewelry stores and smattering of art galleries and pick the places clean.

As simple as that. My time runner was a time-traveling thief.

Walter might have succeeded in his nefarious scheme if his wife hadn't contacted Time Scope's HQ and warned of her husband's plan. Oh, she hadn't dropped a dime out of the goodness of her heart. Wife was all-in on Walter's plot until she stumbled upon intel that dear husband planned to cash in his ill-gotten gains, then ditch her and take himself, his mistress, and his new wealth to someplace off the grid. Away from wifey and mortgage and life's other responsibilities.

"We need to catch up to him," my boss and lead time cop on this mission Jake Tyson said as we raced up a side street. "We need to stop him. We don't want people to panic."

I held back a snarky *thank you, Captain Obvious.* I mean, as time cops, catching people was our mission. Keep calm and stop the temporal perp. Secure the timeline. But one look at Jake's extremely solid jaw clenched in determination, his forehead crinkled with worry, his thick, jet-black hair spiked and tangled, and I bit my tongue. He teetered on the verge of panic himself. If we didn't catch this thief, the electricity would wink out all over the city. And five people would die.

I picked up my pace, my shoes slapping on the slushy pavement. "Jake, look over there. He's veered off."

Over to our right, a flash of oversized cargo pants and a neon green fanny pack—thank you, dreadful 1990s fashions—disappeared around a corner. We darted after the guy. Something big and metal hurtled at me. Walter had flung a trash barrel into our path. The oldest feint in the book. Runaway teens in Roman times had probably chucked trash cans at pursuing centurions to trip them up and slow them down.

You'd think I, Beryl Blue, savvy time cop, would've been onto such a ploy. Nope. I stumbled into the metal thing and went flying. I squeezed my eyes shut and prepped for a belly flop into the slush. Instead, I landed with a bounce, not on hard pavement, but onto something only a fraction softer.

Jake.

He'd thrown himself under me to break my fall. He'd broken protocol, too, as well as about a zillion Time Scope rules related to pursuing and extracting a temporal criminal. Eyes on the prize, no detours, no matter what. Me tripping and flailing and belly flopping was a *no matter what* of epic proportions.

Jake's arms circled my waist. His warm breath panted on my face, scented with the triple-synth-latte and cinnamon bun we'd split in 2132, before we'd stepped into the glorified car wash bay known as the Temporal Oscillator and landed back here. His totally '90s costume of flannel and baggy jeans under a Tommy Hilfiger jacket disguised the lean, mean six-foot physique underneath. His muscular thighs and equally solid chest pressed against me. His to-die-for laser blue eyes gazed into mine with an expression that defined intense.

Not to mention hot. *Way* hot, to quote a 1990s phrase.

Now, it'd been a long time since I'd been in such an intimate position with a man. Exactly two years, to be precise. Two years since Sergeant Tom Sullivan and I had quite literally knocked Army boots in the basement of a

Belgian town hall in December 1944, with the Battle of the Bulge about to erupt outside. Nearly two years since I'd last seen that big, gruff redhead.

Point is, it'd been a long, long time, and damn it all, my body reacted despite my brain ordering it not to. My heart was already racing. My breath caught and my belly launched into an excited salsa dance, followed by the Macarena. A sweet flicker of desire I couldn't deny.

"You fell for me," Jake said, waggling eyebrows as dark as his hair.

That cheesy line demanded an eyeroll. Jake may be all muscled and confident and almost breathtakingly pretty, but he was full of the most groan-worthy dialogue I'd ever heard.

"Uh, he's getting away," I said, composing myself. "You can probably let go of me now."

He held me a moment more, an odd look on his face, then he snapped back into action. The professional time cop at work. He shoved me off him, sprang up with the grace of a gazelle, and sped away, as if the tumble and close personal contact had never happened. I scrambled to my feet with much less elegance and chased after him.

Our temporal perp had bolted in the opposite direction of the power substation. With us in pursuit, Walter saw his Y2K plan crumbling and raced off toward the Winooski River instead, most likely hoping to find cover where he could hide. We sprinted after him, rounded another corner and he'd vanished. No echoing footsteps. No shadows to follow. No sign of that neon fanny pack.

"Where is he? Did he time skip?" I whispered, bending forward with my hands on my hips, trying to catch my breath.

"I don't think so." Jake squinted into the darkness. He'd barely broken a sweat. "He doesn't have a Kicker, or even a TDC Junior."

He'd gone all Captain Obvious again—Kicker and Junior were time cop slang words for the Temporal Displacement Catalyzer, the portable time travel devices we used to skip around in time.

Suddenly, a figure swooped down from above and landed behind us. He clocked Jake on the head with what appeared to be a lead pipe. Stunned, Jake's legs folded under him like a paper accordion. He hit the pavement with a wet thud.

My blood went cold, but before I could turn and raise my weapon, Walter Solon grabbed my ponytail. He jerked my head back. My scalp screamed in pain. I *knew* wearing that scrunchie to finish off my *Clueless* meets the Spice Girls outfit had been a bad idea. I deployed *Self-Defense for Girls 101* and stomped down on the perp's insole then kicked back, connecting with his family jewels. He yelped and released my ponytail as if it had burst into flames.

I spun around and armed my weapon, a sleek, silver metal rectangle that looked like a TV remote, called a Cack .22. It powered up with a whine. Solon's eyes widened in fear. He flung his fanny pack at me. I hopped back and the bag hit the ground with a clank of tools the man had no doubt planned to use to disable the substation.

He took off. I aimed in his general direction and mashed the cack's trigger. The weapon shuddered. A bitter smell, like burning acid in a thunderstorm burst into the air, followed by a sizzling pulse of electricity that shot from the weapon and drilled into the fleeing man's back. He screamed, his body twitched, and he fell nose first to the ground.

Barely blinking, I rushed over to Jake. "*Please* don't be dead," I cried.

"I'm not dead," he muttered. He winced as he sat up and touched a big lump on the side of his head. "It just feels that way."

Relief flushed through me. I reached down to help him to his feet. Took a little effort for him to stand. His usual tan complexion had turned pale, and blood matted his hair.

"Oh, man, you're a mess, Jake. You're going straight to Doc Carroll when we get back to the future."

"I'm fine," he said with true grit then peered closely at me. "What about you? Are you okay?"

Seriously? *He* was the one with a bump the size of a melon on his head. "All good, never better."

He flashed a rueful smile then went to check on our unconscious time perp, squatting beside him. "I guess you decided not to kill the guy."

I scooped up Walter's fanny pack and came up beside Jake, squinting in annoyance. He knew me better than that. I'd only stunned the man, as I had every time-runner I'd had to shoot in my two years on the job.

Punishment enough, frankly. The cack had only two settings, *stun* and *kill*, and believe me it came as no surprise to discover the woman who'd invented this weapon was a *Star Trek* fan. The stun setting shot a stinging electrical pulse that singed every nook and cranny of a person's body. Hurt wicked bad. I didn't know that personally. I only had Jake's word for it. I'd stunned him once, long ago. Oh, he deserved it, but seeing the way he'd writhed in agony when I'd zapped him, well, I did *not* want to think about what the kill setting would do.

And I'd vowed never to find out.

With one exception.

The only kill I wanted on my record when I retired from the glamorous time cop life was Oliver Bishop. The rogue time traveler who'd murdered my parents. When I finally tracked him down.

Jake winced in pain from his injury as he rolled Solon over and yanked him to his feet. The man's eyes spun like pinwheels, and he offered no resistance as Jake cuffed him and recited a long list of Time Scope rules Walter had violated during his larcenous jaunt through Montpelier.

"In short," I said when Jake finished talking what seemed like hours later. "You shouldn't have gone rogue, Mr. Solon. You threatened the timeline and you're in big trouble. Especially with your wife. Be glad you're gonna be locked away for a long time, because if we turned you over to her, you'd be in for a world of hurt."

The Temporal Oscillator Cocoon, what Time Scope called the blue light and rock and roll tornado that blasted us about in time, shunted the three of us directly to a free-standing arrival port in the detention block.

Jake took one of Walter's arms, I took the other and we half-carried, half-dragged our prisoner to the booking station just off the jump bay. Solon wobbled a bit. Okay, he wobbled a lot. His legs were as unsteady as the Scarecrow in *The Wizard of Oz*. Getting stunned by a cack, or even a zap from the smaller version of that weapon known as a stinger, will do that to a person.

Jake and I filled out a ton of paperwork via commpad touch screen, then sent the report to some magical cyber beast known as the Interface. Where it went from there, I had no idea. I only knew my job was done.

I dropped off my '90s gear at wardrobe on the thirteenth floor, gave our costuming guru Gerry Aguilar a high five, then changed into my everyday clothes, comfortable jeans and an *Orphan Black* tee shirt that had been disappeared from my closet in 2015 and time jumped to the 2130s.

Just like what had happened to me.

Two years ago, I was a broke and aimless twenty-four-year-old librarian-in-training living in 2015 in the sleepy Massachusetts town of Ballard Springs. Until time travelers from the future, Jake and Glo Reid, head of Time Scope's time cop division, had dropped in on me and plucked me out of my time. *Extracted* me was more like it. Not that I had a choice, with my options being go along with them and become a time cop or stay in my own time and die a ridiculously ungraceful death.

I chose the not-dying option, thank you very much.

Making that choice had been the easy part. The hard part was the rigorous test Jake and Glo had put me through first. They'd time skipped me back to 1943 and threw me and a burly, redheaded Army sergeant named Tom Sullivan together, hoping I'd be willing to kill anyone who'd threatened Sully's life. After several false starts, detours, and a lot of complaining, I'd passed the test.

Falling in love with Sully hadn't been part of the plan. *That* I'd done on my own.

Ready to head home for a well-deserved nap, I met Jake in Time Scope's parking lot. Yeah, there were still parking lots in 2132. This lot was chock full of surface vehicles on the lower level, and on the upper tier, the long-haul commuters from Mexico, Canada and the West Coast had parked their personal flight craft. I usually took a Slide home but didn't relish the rush hour butt-cheek-to-butt-cheek squeeze of public transportation, so when Jake offered me a lift, I readily accepted.

I hopped into the passenger seat, the door snapped shut, and Jake's car glided into traffic with barely a bump or rattle. I use the term *car* loosely. More like a box with four steel wheels and tinted windows to shut out UV rays. The TCV, Total Control Vehicle, the twenty-second century's personal mode of transport, was all electric, computer operated, totally hands off, and timed to move with the rest of traffic. Pretty amazing to a woman raised in the gridlock era. Though I couldn't help but think if someone hacked into the system, it'd be a total *Grand Theft Auto* meets Stephen King's *Christine* horror show.

"How's your head?" I asked shortly after we set out.

"Superficial." Jake dimpled. "Dr. Carroll says I'm fine. As I told you."

"I'm glad you had it checked out. You could just as well have been *not* fine." Take that from someone who knew how dangerous a bump on the head could be. As in, fatal. On Monday, May fourth, 2015, at exactly eleven in the morning, I was supposed fall off a ladder and crack my head on a stepstool while at work—and die. At least, I would have if my heroes Jake and Glo hadn't intervened.

Our conversation switched from Jake's noggin to the usual on-the-surface nothing stuff we always chatted about. Office gossip, the silliness of the Y2K panic, 1990s fashions, the surprising spike in time tourism to Pompeii pre-Vesuvius blowing its top. No feelings, no probing each other's hopes and dreams. My choice or Jake's, I wasn't sure, but except for an occasional question about my adjustment to life in Futureworld, we never went very deep.

But tonight, a tension threaded his voice that heightened my own anxiety. He didn't look at me as our vehicle glided along the streets of the west side, not even a glance. Something weighed on his mind. My brain raced. Did he have new intel on Oliver Bishop, the man who'd murdered my parents? My anxiety doubled. If he knew something, would Jake even share? He was a man who loved keeping secrets, particularly from me.

I'd been able to piece together only a few details about Bishop. He'd worked for Time Scope in the early days, until he'd stolen a Kicker and fled into the past, where he'd killed my parents, for some reason that probably made perfect sense in his warped mind. He'd blasted them with a cack when we were out on a Sunday drive then went on his merry way, leaving six-year-old me in a burning car. I would've died if not for Jake. He'd been hunting for Bishop through time and had caught up to him too late to save my parents, but in the nick of time to rescue me.

We reached my place, a grey, granite apartment building that stood thirty stories tall, nestled among dozens of other apartment towers of equal height and construction. The TCV slid sideways into a parking slot, restraints that looked like T-Rex claws clunked into place around the tires, and the doors popped open.

The evening was cool for May, filled with the scents of Futureworld's version of spring. Flowers, wet soil, and clean, pollution-free air, tinged with an almost antiseptic smell. Jake followed me inside my building. Unusual. The few times he'd given me a lift, he'd walked me to the front door, said *see ya* and left. Tonight, he seemed determined to take me all the way up. Not that there was any need for that kind of chivalry. After two years as a time cop, I was fully trained and could take out an attacking horde with my pinky.

But I didn't discourage him. I thought it a quaint, old-fashioned gesture. Reminded me of Sully a little.

The elevator spit us out on the nineteenth floor. Overhead lights popped on as we walked down the tiled hallway. He didn't say a word and my curiosity deepened. He *must* have news about Oliver Bishop. News he wanted to share, privately.

I pressed my thumb to the keypad on my apartment door and heard the telltale click of the lock disengaging. I also heard the immediate meow of my Maine coon cat, Jenjen, from inside. Not a *welcome home, human, I've missed you* kind of meow. More like, *get in here and feed me, two-legs, before I poop on your bed. Again.* Jenjen had *never* forgiven me for that rocky trip through the Temporal Oscillator to bring him here from 2015. Ingrate.

"Someone's hungry," I said.

Jake grinned, giving me a fine show of his dimples. They softened his chiseled features, made him look like a real boy rather than one of those impossibly perfect androids in every sci-fi TV show or movie ever made.

Made him look kind of vulnerable, and wicked nervous, too.

"Before you go in," he said, taking a deep breath. "There's something I have to say."

I eyed him warily, my heart thumping for a different reason now. All that tension and long pauses weren't about Bishop at all. This was about something else altogether. The thing he'd been dancing around since I'd met him. The thing I'd been dreading. Anticipating a little, too.

"Beryl, I was thinking, maybe we could—" Inside my apartment, Jenjen meowed like a fiend then scratched the door as if digging a trench. Jake's eyes narrowed in exasperation, and he raised his voice to be heard over the din. "Anyway, I was hoping, maybe if you have time... I thought maybe we could go to dinner. Maybe tomorrow night, maybe?"

That was a whole lot of maybes. I'd think he didn't want to go to dinner with me at all except I knew, had known from the beginning, that he definitely wanted more than dinner. He'd not only waited a decent interval for me to mourn for Sully, I suspected he'd waited to get beyond his own hurt as well. The mystery woman he would never talk about, the woman he'd loved and lost. I'd asked about her, more than once, and his only reply had been a terse, "It's over. Long ago."

That nicked at me, the way he closed up. Wouldn't even tell me her name. I only knew he'd been involved with someone, and something had ended it. Was he now ready to move forward? Was I? I still loved Sully and still hurt from losing him. Could I finally accept the fact that he was not only in the past, but he *was* my past and I had to move on?

And if I could move on, did I want to do that moving on with Jake? Once, my answer would've been an emphatic *no*. Two years ago, I'd wanted nothing more than to kill him. To be fair, he'd set me up to make me want to kill him, to *have* to kill him or I'd be dead myself. All part of the test to prove I was time cop material. Back then, my fury toward Jake for tricking me had raged like the bitter winds of a nor'easter and I'd vowed to have nothing to do with him.

Now? When I thought he might be dead back in Vermont, I'd panicked. Jake may be annoyingly secretive and kind of bossy, too, what with quoting Time Scope's rules and regulations until I thought I'd upchuck, but I'd grown accustomed to his face. I liked him. He'd done so much for me. He'd saved my life. He was my mentor, teacher, the most upstanding guy I knew in any century. With the exception of Sully.

But did any of that mean I wanted for us to be more than friends?

Jake sighed. Heavily. "I'll take this awkward silence to mean no."

"Yes. No," I said, and his face fell. "I mean, no to tomorrow. I'm going bowling with Glo and Alice tomorrow night."

He cleared his throat. "What about Thursday?"

"Can't. I have a shift at the library, working the desk until we close." When I wasn't occupied bopping around in time saving history, I put in a few hours each week at the district's west branch library. Becoming a librarian had been my life's goal until I'd fallen into the time cop job, and Jake had made both of my careers happen. He'd made *everything* happen, even my tiny apartment and Jenjen's journey to 2132.

Beyond the door, the aforementioned cat shrieked, as if in danger of imminent starvation. Jake adopted a stoic look and nodded like my saying no to a date with him twice wasn't a big deal.

He turned to go when I heard myself say, "B-u-u-u-t... You didn't ask about Friday." He brightened. "I'm free Friday night. How about then?"

He suddenly seemed two feet taller, and, oh my, the dimples. He really had a nice smile.

"Great. Friday night. Great." He suddenly leaned in, as if going for a kiss.

Nope. The idea of kissing Jake was tantalizing, but also terrifying. A bridge too far. With a hurried "good night," I skittered into my apartment, slamming the door shut behind me.

Seeing me, Jenjen leapt up onto the kitchen counter and let out a howl that shook the windows. I wanted to howl too. Had I just done that? Accepted a date with Jake? When Sully still occupied a large portion of my head and heart?

I knew I should put him behind me, firmly and completely, since I could never see him again. At least, I was determined to do my best *not* to run into him again. If Time Scope had read the temporal tea leaves right, Sully's destiny was to die, saving me. Not clear how or when except it would happen sometime post-World War II. If I wanted him to live a long and healthy life—and oh, how I wanted that—I had to stay away from Sully for good.

But that didn't keep me from missing him.

After I fed Jenjen so he wouldn't die, I wandered across my apartment to look at the pictures I'd hung on the wall near my overstuffed bookcase. Not a long trip—my place was pretty small, even for a studio. I skirted the coffee table and the matching armchairs that Jake had arranged to be delivered when I'd moved in, homing in on one particular photo in an antique wooden frame. The only picture of Sully I had, taken at a nightclub in 1943, when I'd hung out with him and some of his men.

I reached up and touched the glass over the black-and-white picture. I wore a cute, 1940s-style dress, Sully looked handsome in his uniform. I sat on his lap, and he had his strong arm firmly around my waist. I gazed at his rugged face, his thick hair cut short, granite jaw softened by the Cary Grant-style dimple in his chin, the happy smile that replaced his usual scowl, and my knees literally went weak.

How could I get over him if just looking at his picture still did that to me?

"Oh Sully, *what* am I going to do?" I knocked my forehead against the wall in frustration. Way too hard. "*Ouch!*"

"Beryl Blue, are you injured?" my apartment's Interface asked in a courteous, mildly curious voice. "Shall I call for medical assistance?"

I answered with another maybe—if a trip to the ER could mend a broken heart.

2

The coffeemaker hissed and spit as my triple-synth latte gurgled from the machine into my cup with "So many books, so little time" written on the side. Glo had given me the cup for my birthday, or maybe Christmas. Or maybe both, seeing as how I was born on Christmas Eve, and she probably figured she could kill two birds with one stone. Ah, the woes of a December birthday baby.

My coffee cup and I crossed the conference room to my usual spot at the long, polished table. I sank into my chair and plopped the mug in front of me, ready for the weekly security team's department head briefing. Not that *I* headed up any departments. An honor I did not want, and Time Scope knew enough not to bestow. My presence at these meetings came down to my status, Special-with-a-capital-*S*.

I took a sip of my triple-synth. Followed by my usual grimace of disappointment. The stuff tasted like caffeinated mud. It *always* tasted like caffeinated mud, so why did my taste buds hope this time it would be different? What did they expect from synthetic java? Coffee in Futureworld was as rationed as when I was kicking up my heels with Sully in 1943, thanks to the twin demons of crop blights and climate change. Just like back in the war years, a fast and furious black market sold real coffee at high prices, but no way would the penny-pinching Time Scope pony up the cash to buy some illegal brew for the staff.

So, coffee lover me had to suck it up and drink brownish mud.

I leaned back and picked up my commpad, a cross between a phone and a tablet that offered all the delights of the infoverse at the merest touch. I sipped warily while I scrolled through the myriad books on my device, mostly novels. There had been a lot of great books written in the century I'd lost when I jumped ahead to now and I diligently applied myself to catching up on them all.

A colorful cover caught my eye, and I pulled up a romance called *Party Girl*, about a lively corporate party planner and her quest for love in the modern world. Imagine my surprise when I discovered that both real books and corporate party planners still existed in my new era. And that people still called women over the age of eighteen a "girl."

Jake breezed in precisely one minute before the meeting's go time. He barely looked my way. The man could be as emotion-free as a robot when he wanted to be. Not me. My anxiety picked up and so did the nauseous nerves that had gyrated like a pole dancer in my belly since last night. Had I done the right thing saying yes?

Glo settled in a chair next to me. "You ready to get your butt handed to you tonight?"

I put my commpad aside. "What's that?" I asked, beyond distracted.

"Are you prepped to lose tonight? You know, bowling."

I laughed. Gloriana Evelyn Reid, director of the security department's time cop team, was chill about most things but bowling. Well, any kind of game. A petite, light-skinned Black woman in her mid-thirties, with a toned, muscular body, angular jaw, and close-cut black hair, Glo was the most competitive player I'd ever met.

Not that she had to work hard to beat me. I'd never bowled, so I didn't know how. Especially not this century's version of the game, all virtual reality, except for the grody shoes. I'd only been in a bowling alley once, way long ago, with my parents and another couple, a blonde and her date, a guy named Curly.

Glo pulled a pair of pink reading glasses with a cat's eye frame from her beige jumpsuit's breast pocket and put them on. She swiped through a number of documents on her official, super-secure, industrial strength commpad, loaded with so many bells and whistles it made my device look like a burner phone in a cheesy spy movie.

"Look at this bad hombre," she said, tilting the screen toward me.

A swirl of pixels rose from the screen and formed into a 3-D hologram of a cowboy, circa 1880, creased ten-gallon hat, bandana, handlebar mustache, chaps. Actually, what a dude from the twenty-second century thought an Old West cowboy looked like, but too clean to be authentic.

"He's running wild in New Mexico, in 1889," Glo said. "I want him back. Do you want the job?"

I weighed the pros and cons. Cons, horses. Not a fan, not even a little. I mean, beautiful creatures and all, but a city girl like me preferred her transportation to have a relatively stable place to sit and a seatbelt. Pros, I'd never been to New Mexico, and it was a sure bet they had real coffee back then.

"Sure, sign me up." She tapped a button and my commpad pinged as the mission info downloaded. I glanced at Jake, across the room, talking with Lu Diallo from the tech security team. Jake poured himself a cup of that triple-synth abomination. I looked back at Glo, still scanning through files. "Glo..." I lowered my voice to a whisper. "I've gotta tell you something. Jake asked me to dinner Friday night, and I said yes." I ran my finger around the rim of my cup, fixated on the movement. "Am I doing the right thing?"

She pulled off her glasses and gazed at me for a couple of years before answering. Felt that way, anyway. I squirmed under her stare.

"Only you can decide that," she said finally.

My heart sank. That was the problem, I couldn't decide.

Glo picked up on my fears. "Just be sure you're sure. Jake may act like he's steel plated, but there's a wounded guy in there, still trying to heal."

Something Jake and I had in common. "Tell me about her, Glo." I dropped my voice so low Glo tipped toward me, straining to hear. "What happened? He looks like he's taking a knife to the gut each time I even get close to the subject."

"Not a subject for here or now, Beryl." She sat back in her chair and sighed. "Plus, it's complicated."

Really? The most evasive excuse ever devised by the gods of linguistics. Of all the phrases that should've gone the way of the dinosaur and basic cable by the year 2132, *it's complicated* topped the list.

I didn't get a chance to grill her for more, because Director of Security Devon Soares bustled in, and the meeting began. A tall, barrel-chested man with thick and wavy chestnut hair like mine, only cut much shorter, Devon had golden brown skin and a nose so large even Cyrano de Bergerac's eyes would pop. He wore the same style of beige jumpsuit as we all wore, the Time Scope required uniform. Not having to buy a work wardrobe gave me more money to spend on leisure clothes, but I sometimes missed getting gussied up for work.

Devon got right to it. "Holmes." He pinned a willowy young woman in his dark-eyed gaze. "Question. What are the three unshakeable rules of time travel?"

Elspeth Holmes squirmed. "Uh, don't threaten the timeline, don't tell anyone about the future, and—"

"Don't call attention to yourself," Devon snapped, finishing for her. "Your mission to stop a time runner in 1440 went well enough but be more alert next extraction. *Especially* if you're in such an unenlightened time period. You were slow to punch the Kicker for your return. You could've been seen. Worse, you could've been caught and arrested on suspicion of witchcraft."

Holmes muttered an okay, sounding mortified by the reprimand. New on the job, she had no idea how easy

Devon had been on her. His bellow hovered only a hitch above normal, not dialed up to eleven like with others he'd berated.

Devon tapped his personal commpad, a giant thing as big and cumbersome as my first laptop. He squinted at the document that rose from the screen then glanced at me. Briefly. "Montpelier's still in one piece, I see."

He moved on to the next report without another word. I held back a sigh. I wished Devon would yell at me like he did everyone else, but I doubted that would ever happen. He resented that Special-with-a-capital-*S* me had been dumped on him like an unwanted relative and had given me the cold shoulder since I'd come on board.

While Devon went on to lambaste victim after victim, I pushed my cup of mud around and surveyed the conference room, looking everywhere but at Jake. A little too bright, a little too warm and stuffy, a few people nodding off, a boardroom like any other in any place throughout history. Except for the personal flight craft tooling by outside the twentieth-floor window. How those mini airplanes didn't all bash into each other was anyone's guess and an air traffic controller's nightmare.

Next to me, Glo stiffened. I followed her gaze through the glass windows into the hallway. Alice Ly hovered near the door. A slim woman of Vietnamese and German descent in her early forties, with shoulder-length brown hair, a straight fringe of bangs, and the only person worse at bowling than me, Alice bounced up and down like her feet were made of springs.

She glanced at me then gestured to Glo, who excused herself and strode from the room, all calm waters and granite jaw set with resolve.

I gripped my coffee cup so tight I thought it might shatter. As Director of Research and Information, Alice led a large staff who pored through historical events for any ripples or anomalies that might mean time tourists gone rogue or attempting to mess with the timeline. Including Oliver Bishop. Alice had been hunting for that time-traveling murderer's temporal location since long before I'd come on board.

"Don't leave me hanging," I whispered to Glo when she returned a few seconds later and took her seat. "Does Alice have a hit on Bishop?"

Glo answered with an almost imperceptible head shake, leaving me to stew for the rest of the meeting. Alice remained in the hallway, fidgeting as much as I did.

After Devon had chewed out his final victim, the meeting wrapped up and my colleagues hurried from the room, heading for fight training or extraction assignments.

"Devon, wait," Glo said as he hefted his commpad off the conference table and stood. "Jake, you too. Beryl, will you stay?"

She had to ask? I wouldn't budge if the place suddenly flooded and Noah's ark was my only ride out of here. Devon sank into his chair again. Jake came up beside me and Alice bounded into the room, her expression radiating excitement.

All eyes settled on Glo. "This goes nowhere, Devon. Not to corporate, not to the board. No one else can know." She paused long enough for Devon to nod a reluctant okay. "Ms. Ly has made an interesting discovery," Glo said, looking right at me.

"You found Bishop? Where is he? What era? When do I go get him?"

By that I meant, when did I get my chance to kill him. Funny, I never used to be this bloodthirsty. In fact, 2015 me had been a coward, afraid of heights, mice, and her own shadow. Not anymore. Once I'd found out about what Bishop had done, I'd set my mind on payback.

"It's not him, Beryl," Glo said, quickly bursting my revenge bubble.

She eyed Alice, who picked up the tale. "There's this artifact, a suitcase, maybe two hundred years old." She tapped a long fingernail to her commpad and a holographic image of a vintage, cream-colored, box-style suitcase swirled up from the screen. "It was found in a storage area of the Ballard Springs Public Library."

My Bishop fury fizzled, replaced with confusion and a lot of curiosity. The library in Ballard Springs? The library where I'd worked in 2015, in the town where I'd grown up. The town Jake and Glo's test had taken me to. Where I'd met Sully. My mind reeled.

"What's inside?" Jake asked. Ever practical, that man.

"They didn't open it," Alice said.

Really? I would have had that thing opened in two seconds flat. Then again, patience was the least of my virtues.

"Why not?" Devon demanded.

"They're waiting for permission from the owner."

I snorted a laugh. "Are they planning a séance to get in touch with them?"

Both Alice and Glo stared at me and after a second, Jake did too. Glo got that *uh, duh* look on her face she always got when I should totally get the point. A point I usually missed by a mile.

"What? Someone tell me, please."

Alice cleared her throat. She was the designated driver, apparently. "The person they're looking for is you, Beryl. *You* own that suitcase."

THE PUDDLE JUMPER slid into a docking bay at the Ballard Springs flightport an hour later. Jake, Alice, and I got off then rode an elevator down fifty-four flights to the ground floor of a building that hadn't existed in 2015 when I'd called this quaint little Massachusetts town my home.

But the library had been here.

Excitement and anticipation gripped me as our contracted TCV cruised along streets that were familiar yet different, heading for my beloved library. We passed restaurants and cafes and shops selling the usual things, clothing, jewelry, stuff for kids. No banks since money was all digital now, but movie theaters still existed. Well, at least one, on the corner of Main and Elm Street, playing a holographic version of *Casablanca*.

Our vehicle hooked around a corner and the Higgins Memorial Library came into view. An expansive new wing of chrome and glass gleamed in the late morning sun, but the rest of the place looked the same. The original building, a four-story Victorian gothic built in the 1860s, had aged like a fine wine. The honey-gold granite had weathered and faded to a dull brown. The dormer windows that had once jutted out of the pitched roof like pointy arrow-heads had been removed, replaced with clear glass panes that looked into the top-floor storage area.

My throat tightened, seeing my library for the first time since Glo had popped in on me and dragged me kicking, screaming, and complaining into Futureworld. The library I'd visited dozens of times as a child with my parents. Where I'd toiled and bickered with my coworkers more than a hundred years ago. Where I'd fallen in love with Sully in 1943, and where I'd yearned to return ever since.

"You okay?" Jake asked as the TCV rolled up to the door.

I thrust my feelings into a deep, dark hole in my brain and shut the door, something I'd been damned good at long before I'd stepped into Beryl Blue, Time Cop's shoes. Losing my parents at the age of six and getting shoved into foster care after my grandmother died when I was fifteen had taught me to run from anything even remotely connected to tender emotion.

Until I'd met Sully.

"I'm fine," I bit off, more to reassure myself than Jake. "Let's get this over with."

Steeling myself, I followed him and Alice up a familiar flight of time-worn stone steps, trailing my hand over the iron bannisters. The door creaked open, and we entered the spacious front room that looked almost exactly as I remembered it. Dark paneled walls, arched windows, a high ceiling with suspended globe lights, and the second-floor mezzanine in the back. A gazillion smells rolled toward me, mahogany, steam heat, and that oh-so-familiar scent of *books*—binding glue, mustiness, a whisper of vanilla.

Though, to be honest, I may have imagined the smell, since the place housed way fewer books than in my time. A few shelves dotted the room, interspersed between tables and chairs and meeting spaces. A school group huddled around a console in one corner. In another corner, a health clinic had been set up next to what looked like a training session. Lots of information being delivered and services to the community rendered, a library and librarians doing their jobs as they had for centuries.

The library director, a balding, slender white guy, greeted us in the lobby and introduced himself as Floyd Fontaine. That ancient adage, everything old is new again, applied double for baby names in this time period. All those grandpa names we millennials snickered at were mighty hip in 2132, including monikers like Cuthbert, Aloysius, Adeline, and, yes, Floyd.

Despite the hipster name, Floyd's library director officiousness was as timeless as book return dates and overdue fines. He made me show six forms of ID to prove I was Beryl Blue, owner of the mysterious suitcase, before he'd let any of us get a glimpse of it.

Floyd led us across the main room and into the new wing. Thoughts of Sully hit me in an aching wave as we passed under the mezzanine, the spot where I'd gazed into his eyes and tumbled head over proverbial heels in love, though I hadn't realized it until much later.

"We found it in the history room," Floyd said, filling us in on the suitcase saga as we climbed a flight of stairs and turned down a hallway lined with offices. "We think it's been there since the nineteen fifties at least. One of the staff discovered it behind boxes of late-twentieth-century artifacts. There's an odd collection in that room, I must say. *Babysitters Club* paperbacks, a videotape of an ancient television show called *I Love Lucy*, some bug-eyed creatures called Furbies, and a cotton shirt advertising someone named Pearl Jam. Ah, here we are."

We stopped outside Floyd's corner office. He thumbed a keypad, the lock clicked open, and the door retracted into the wall like something out of *Star Trek*. We stepped inside, and by *we*, I mean Alice, me, and Jake, after he shoved Floyd back with a brusque, "Beryl needs her privacy." The door whisked shut, leaving the library director fuming outside.

"That is one *ugly* piece of luggage," Alice offered, aiming her commpad's camera at the small suitcase on Floyd's desk and activating the record function.

I would've agreed with her if my voice hadn't abandoned me, taking all rational thought with it. I'd thought the suitcase pretty damn homely the first time I met it—when Glo had sent me to Ballard Springs with it in 1943.

The flood of memories, both sweet and bittersweet threatened to drown me, so I put aside the past and replaced it with questions. Foremost being, how had the suitcase ended up in the library?

Jake answered that question with a shake of his head. "I have no idea. Our team retrieved the suitcase, *your* suitcase, after your visit to Ballard Springs."

Visit? Ladies and gentlemen, Jake Tyson, king of understatement. That so-called visit had changed my life.

"It's a paradox," Alice said, zooming in on my face.

I frowned into the camera. "Please do not use that

word in my vicinity," I scolded. Wrapping my head around the reality of time travel had been tough enough. Trying to digest the whole contradictory, dual timelines, multiverse creating paradox thing put me in a no-good, rotten, foul mood every time.

I moved on to my next question. The most logical one. What was inside? I crowded Jake out of the way and leaned in. An off-white color, the boxy suitcase had brass clasps on either side of the braided handle and the Amelia Earhart brand name stamped on a metal plate below the lid. Could this bag have something to do with Sully? Alice had learned he'd settled in Ballard Springs after the war. Could he have somehow gotten hold of this bag, perhaps put a message for me inside? My belly whirled in excitement at the thought.

Only one way to find out.

"Beryl's about to open the bag," Alice said, her voice both hushed and excited, like a host on one of those TV ghost hunters shows. "No one's laid eyes on what's inside for a hundred and fifty years or more."

I shot her a *cease-and-desist* look and reached for the clasps. Took a few tries to open because the tarnished snaps were somewhat sticky after all these years, but they eventually gave way with a reluctant *pop*.

The hinges creaked as I gently lifted the cover. I bit the inside of my cheek and leaned in closer. Jake peered over my shoulder. Alice focused her camera on the interior, lined with faded red satin, and harboring another mystery. Several mysteries. A pair of vintage Army dog tags, a matchbook for a nightspot called *Chaisson's Fun & Frolic* with half the matches gone, a small gold key, a yellowed newspaper clipping, and a single earring, a convincingly real diamond in a delicate pear-shaped style I suspected could be worth a pretty penny, as Grandma Blue liked to say.

The metal dog tags clinked as I picked up the chain. They were cool to the touch and in pretty good shape considering their age. I focused on the raised letters and numbers stamped onto each rectangular tag, both dreading and hoping I'd see Sully's name. Instead, the tag read Fred Pattinson, along with his service number and religion.

My heart sank, but really, these dog tags being Sully's would've been a *giant* coincidence straight out of a Dickens novel.

I exchanged the tags for the earring, which sparkled in the light, then examined the key, engraved with the number sixty-three. I squinched my forehead, hoping the newspaper clipping might shed some light on these mystery objects. I picked up the paper and spread it out, causing bits of newsprint to break off and sprinkle over Floyd's desk like snowflakes. Alice, the historical preservationist dedicated to conserving all things old and delicate, moaned as if I'd just run over her puppy.

I aimed an apologetic grimace her way then skimmed the paper, a news report dated July 27, 1946. Under the headline, *Vets Brawl Erupts at Popular Bar*, was a grainy, black-and-white photograph of dozens of men in 1940s style clothing, fighting. Apparently, a long heat wave and short tempers had triggered a fight outside a place called the Slipknot, in the seaside Massachusetts town of Point Bailey.

Beside me, Jake let out a startled grunt.

"What? What is it?" I asked. "Why do you look like you've seen a ghost?"

"Because he is a ghost." Jake sliced a look at Alice. "Cut the recording. This is off the record from now on."

She did as he asked then gazed at Jake as expectantly as I did.

"This man." He lightly tapped the paper, indicating a man in the upper right corner of the photo.

"Is it Bishop?" I asked hopefully.

He shook his head.

"But you know him."

"I do."

I tapped my foot. Terse might be Jake's middle name, but I was in no mood to drag the answer out of him syllable by syllable. "Jake, please, who is he?" I demanded.

"He's a clue, I think." He straightened and focused on me with an eager gleam in his eyes. "We need to get back to headquarters. I think we have our first solid link to Oliver Bishop."

3

"Does this mean we might actually have a lead on that bastard?"

Devon looked up from the newspaper clipping Alice had placed in a plastic sleeve to prevent further decay. His gaze bounced around the office, from Glo to Alice and, bypassing me, to the man of the moment, Jake, who nodded, stoically containing his excitement.

As soon as we got back, we'd gone straight to Alice's expansive suite of offices. Devon now sat at her desk, the rest of us gathered around. Normally I loved visiting Alice's digs. I felt more comfortable here than anywhere else at Time Scope's HQ, mostly because I was as much a relic as the collection of old newspapers, magazines, books, folders filled with papers, and all the other documents of world history Alice kept strewn about.

But today, this moment, I had no interest in any historical stuff, except for what we'd found inside that suitcase. I fidgeted like a kid waiting in a long line at the john, bursting with curiosity. "Will someone please tell me who the guy in the picture is?" I blurted. "And what does he have to do with Bishop?"

Jake gave Alice a *you're up* glance. She leaned over Devon's shoulder and tapped her commpad. The man in the newspaper photo came to 3-D life in the middle of her desk. Much clearer, and in color. A white man in his late thirties, he had sandy blonde hair, a broad chest, an amiable but bland and forgettable face, and brown eyes set too close together, giving him a sly, *I'm up to something* expression.

"This is Niels Rasmussen," Alice said. "He worked at Time Scope about twenty years ago, in the early days of time travel. He was assigned to the same team as Oliver Bishop. They worked on the development of the temporal skip technology, the oscillator specifically. Around the time the company took ownership of the tech, Rasmussen disappeared."

The others nodded as if that was old news. Everyone but me. I frowned at Glo, then at Jake. Especially at Jake. This was info I'd never heard before, though I'd asked often enough. How could they have kept me in the dark like this?

"Rasmussen disappeared? Why?" I asked. I'd stick around and bask in all the glory if I had anything to do with inventing time travel, but then, that was me, still smarting from my younger years of little praise but heaps of criticism and yearning for approval deep down.

"There was an accident in one of the labs," Alice said.

"A fatal accident," Jake added, his expression darkening.

Alice nodded. "Yes, sadly. The accident put the project

back many months and took a toll on the development team. We don't know why Rasmussen time skipped. There's been no ripples or changes in the timeline. Perhaps he left simply to put some space between himself and the tragedy."

Whoa. That had been quite the info dump. The history of time travel's creation was well known, sanitized and polished and wrapped in a pretty bow by Time Scope's PR department, but info on the scientists who'd developed the tech, not so much. I'd always thought the secrecy around the team had been to protect their privacy, and the gazillions they'd earned off their invention. But now that the words *fatal* and *accident* had debuted in the conversation, I suspected the story had many more layers.

Which led to many more questions burning on my tongue. "What kind of accident was it? Who died? Was Bishop involved? Was it before or after Bishop time skipped? If the two men went on the run around the same time, is there a connection?"

Alice didn't answer. She stared down at her comm-pad. Jake shifted from foot to foot. Glo wouldn't meet my gaze.

After about thirty hours of uncomfortable silence, Devon cleared his throat. "That information's classified, I'm afraid."

It's classified. As in, common knowledge to everyone in the room except me.

I lost the tiny shred of patience I'd clung to since opening that suitcase. I'd had it with all this secrecy. I'd learned precious few details about who Oliver Bishop was before he'd gone on a murdering spree in the past, and now that I'd gotten some crumbs, everyone clammed up. Probably because the Bishop debacle had been a corporate scandal of monumental proportions.

In the aftermath, Time Scope had revamped its entire security apparatus. Now, all time tourists and employees needed their DNA mapped and coded, so anyone who skipped through time could be tracked, tackled, and transported home should they go rogue. This prevented shitheads from killing their own grandpa and other mayhem that could mess up the timeline and create the mother of all paradoxes. With the added benefit of cutting down on the company's liability.

The downside? Temporal perps with crime on their mind could get hold of the same DNA tracking tech and easily evade Glo's time cop crew. That's where I came in. A woman plucked out of time, an untraceable whose DNA had never been entered into Time Scope's or anyone else's data files. I could sneak up on temporal perps without warning.

In short, I was special. But not special enough to be told more than the barest minimum about Oliver Bishop's motives. Not special enough to get past that solid, *it's classified* wall.

"Here's the good news," Glo said, breaking the strained silence. "We know where Rasmussen is, and we know when. *Exactly* when. We can extract him, bring him home, and finally get some answers about why he skipped. And about Bishop. Get a lead on the man's location."

I brightened, but only a little. No guarantee Glo or anyone else would tell me what those answers were.

"I can be ready in one hour," Jake said, turning toward the door.

Devon raised a hand. "Hold up. You're not going."

Jake's jaw snapped shut like an alligator snatching a golfer off the ninth hole.

Glo scowled. "What the hell, Dev? We've been after Bishop for years. You know Jake's our best man to bring Ras in."

"He is," Devon conceded. "But I want Beryl on this mission."

Jake muscled up. "No. Too dangerous."

I flashed Jake a frown. Too dangerous for me, or for Sully? Alice had conducted a thorough scan of Sully's timeline in the post-war years, a timeline full of ripples and uncertainty. We knew only one thing for sure. He was going to die, and I would be there when it happened. With Rasmussen brawling and raising havoc on the Massachusetts coast in 1946, a mere seventy-five miles from Ballard Springs where Sully lived, I'd be too close for comfort.

But Devon didn't know that. He didn't have a clue about me and my connection to Bishop. All he knew was Jake had IDed me as someone skilled whose timeline was about to end, the perfect candidate to bring to the future to work for Time Scope. The only time Jake and his secrets had worked in my favor.

"Think it through, Devon," Jake said. "Beryl's not ready for a job like this—"

"Then why did you extract her if we're not going to use her? You fought tooth and nail to bring her on as a DNA ghost. You know we only choose ex-military for that, not out-of-timers. I didn't want her, but I went out on every limb there is to allow her extraction because *you* insisted. You tested her in that time period. She's familiar with the nineteen-forties era. Let's put her to the test." He turned and eyed me full-on. "Let's see what you can do."

Gee thanks, Dev, for making me feel so wanted.

Jake's jaw clenched in a fine display of anger, but he gave in. "Alright. We'll both be ready to skip soon."

"No. I don't want you blundering around there. If Rasmussen is our link to Bishop, you might be recognized. We might lose our target and lose any chance we have to capture the man. Did you forget what happened last time?"

A slap in the face, but kind of true. Bishop had slipped away from Jake, who'd come on the scene seconds too late to stop him from killing my parents, and barely in time to pull me from the burning car. Or so the story went. I suspected there was a lot Jake hadn't told me about the day my parents died and why Bishop had targeted them. A lot Jake hadn't told anyone, except maybe Glo.

Devon put his foot down, ending the debate. "Beryl goes. Alone." He seized my gaze again. "This mission's yours. Do the job, bring Ras back, you might just get your questions answered." He pushed his chair back. "Get the historical details from Alice, get to wardrobe, and get to work."

I gave him a firm, *challenge accepted* nod. He stood and puffed out his chest. I half expected him to add a *harrumph* as he and his linebacker shoulders disappeared through the office door.

AFTER A FLURRY of activity and a little over an hour later, I was ready to go.

Alice had loaded the necessary historical and GPS data into the TDC Junior, the computer-slash-time machine I wore strapped to my wrist, with an era-appropriate gold basketweave-style watchband. Our costumer, Gerry, had put together a 1946 summer wardrobe in record time, including my adorable traveling outfit, a blue A-line skirt, flowered blouse with cap sleeves, and a pair of low-heeled, lattice-front sandals with special cushioning in case I had to break into an unexpected sprint. As usual, I left my hair alone. It despised being told what to do, anyway. Just like me.

I entered the security department's dedicated transfer station, where time cops quantum-leaped back and forth to the past in search of rogue time tourists and troublemakers.

Alice, Glo, and Jake came to see me off. We walked together down the row of temporal oscillators, or time coffins as I preferred to call them, based on their shape and claustrophobic interior. The whole mob of us stopped at bay T-2, already powering up to take me to the past.

Turning to my friends, I twisted the braided handle of my Amelia Earhart suitcase, the original, non-rusty suitcase that I'd toted around when I met Sully two years ago and had been in storage ever since. Devon had insisted I take it with me. I wondered if that would be creating a paradox within a paradox, but he shut the thought down fast.

"How do we know you didn't bring the suitcase there in the first place?" he growled.

That didn't explain how the suitcase ended up in the Ballard Springs public library, but whatever. I did not want to get into a paradox debate with a guy who knew tons more than I did about the subject.

Alice gave me a hug. "Just so you know, I did another check on Sully's life while you were in wardrobe. I saw no blips or ripples connecting him to Point Bailey. Not one hundred percent certainty, but the chances are, you won't run into him."

I nodded and turned to Glo. No hug from her. I hadn't expected one. "Watch your back," she said. Cliché advice she always offered before a mission, but I took heed of her warning.

She and Alice faded back, leaving me alone with Jake. No hug from him, either. Just a scowl and a thoroughly miserable, "*I* should be going on this mission, not you."

I thought he should go too. Alice's *chances are you won't run into him* had done little to reassure me. My nerves stretched as tight as the girdle I'd been forced to wear when I'd first met Sully. Traveling to his timeline and in such close proximity was tempting fate. And as Grandma Blue liked to say, fate was an ironic bitch. Some grandmas were all sugar cookies and knitting and sparkly sweatshirts with cats on them, mine was all whiskey and salty language. As cynical as the day is long in Norway in June.

"You got everything you need?" Jake scrubbed a hand over his face. "You've got your zapper charged and ready?"

Zapper. An old-school time cop word for our electronic pulse weapons, the cack and the much sleeker stinger, which I'd opted to bring on this mission. A small firearm that fit into my palm, the stinger looked like a ray gun from a 1950s sci-fi movie.

"Got it right in here." I patted my suitcase. "I can take care of myself, so don't worry."

"I'll try not to," he said, by which he meant *not even possible*. He worried about me morning, noon, and night, it seemed. Way too much. "Be careful. Don't trust anyone, and don't get angry. You get sloppy and make mistakes when you're angry."

"You're lecturing," I teased. Not that I didn't occasionally need reminding to be cautious.

He gave a soft smile, minimum dimpling. "Raincheck on our dinner date?"

I doubted he even knew what raincheck meant. It was a Sully-era word that had gone out of fashion long ago. "Sure thing."

On impulse, I hiked up onto my toes and kissed him. A quick peck, nothing lingering, but long enough to taste his warm, perfect lips against mine. I stepped back, and without another word, I dove into the temporal oscillator and slapped the button to close the coffin door. It clanked shut with an ominous thud, trapping me inside.

My heart hammered, from the closed-in feel and from that fleeting kiss. And what it could mean. Jake had built some mighty daunting walls around himself with his secrets, but not as solid as my own emotional barriers, grief and longing for another man. I didn't know if it was possible for either of us to break through those barriers and move on, but I began to believe we could try.

Maybe.

4

The temporal oscillator wailed as it powered up. The chamber's walls reverberated, undulated, then melted. An optical illusion. After so many trips, I knew that. The time machine wasn't melting, *I* was. Not a comforting thought, but reality. A swirling cloak of cerulean blue light encircled me. Hot prickles danced up and down my skin. I bit back a shriek that tried to roll up my throat.

I hated the power-up, but not as much as I despised the next part. The full-on temporal skip. Tiny knives seemed to slice my veins and drill into my pores. My stomach reeled from the machine's intense shake and shimmy, like a roller coaster ride through a pinball machine. Not to mention the squish of my atoms dissolving then stitching themselves back together, and the final nerve-snapping yank as time and gravity jerked my body into the past.

The temporal tornado spit me and my luggage out in the center of a circle of lilac bushes, in the backyard of a tall, Victorian-era cottage with an enclosed widow's walk on the roof. I sat on the ground a moment, waiting for the dizziness to fade, then crawled out of the bushes and stood. I wobbled a little before I got my balance. Used to be, my atoms took forever to settle after a time skip, and I'd have vertigo for hours. Now, after only a few seconds of heavy breathing, I was good to go.

I picked up my suitcase and followed the wraparound porch to the front of the aptly named Seaside Inn, situated near the end of sandy road, a few feet away from the ocean. If all went well, I'd tackle Rasmussen tonight outside the Slipknot bar and whisk him back to the future. If something went wrong, which, please, pretty please, don't let anything go wrong, I had a place to stay, chosen by Alice herself, until I could figure out an alternate plan.

I climbed a flight of creaky wooden steps to the front door. The salty scent of the Atlantic carried on a hot, late afternoon breeze, along with the comforting sound of the waves pounding the shore in a steady rhythm. A long row of wicker rocking chairs were lined up like airplanes ready for takeoff along the porch. A slim, elderly Black man with tufts of hair that framed his face like clouds snoozed in the rocker on the far end. I suspected he'd been in that chair since Teddy Roosevelt charged up San Juan Hill.

The screen door squeaked as I entered a brightly lit and cloyingly humid front room, reminding me of the rooming house where I'd stayed when I first met Sully. An apple-cheeked woman with steel-gray hair pulled up into a bun librarian-style took my two dollars for the weekend and handed me a key.

The stairs creaked like a haunted house as I climbed to the third floor and entered a small room with a bureau, a spindly chair in the corner, a side table, and a double bed with a wooden, but solid-looking headboard. The windows had been thrown open and the frilly white curtains billowed as the sea breeze pushed in.

I stepped to one of the windows and took in the view. At the end of the street, a path cut between scrubby rose bushes toward the ocean. Sailboats bobbed on the water, and several people strolled along a rocky beach. To the left, houses crowded together at the shore. To the right, a long stretch of sand that curved in a half moon for a mile or more toward the south end of town, where the beaches and entertainment were. And my quarry, Niels Rasmussen.

Beyond that, due west a bunch of miles, was Sully. When Alice had discovered he'd moved to Ballard Springs after the war and become a cop, I hadn't asked if he'd married or had a family. I didn't want to know. I only knew he'd lived his life. Or *would* live his life as long as I stayed away from him. So, no matter how much I ached to take a detour from my mission and go to him, I wouldn't.

I turned away from the window to unpack my few belongings, then stowed the suitcase in the closet and got ready to go. I stuffed a small clutch purse filled with cash into one of my skirt's pockets and my zapper into the other. No cumbersome purse or handbag for me. I wanted my hands free and nothing to get in my way if I encountered trouble. That's why I insisted on pockets for all my mission costumes.

The day was fading as I left the inn. The elderly man

in the porch rocker had woken up. He eyed me with curiosity as I crossed the porch to the stairs, but a true New Englander, he kept his questions to himself.

I had a few hours to kill before my date with Rasmussen, so instead of taking the faster streetcar, I decided to hoof it from my seaside retreat to the downtown area. It was still pretty hot, so I took it slow and after a while the neighborhood of quaint seaside houses that seemed to have weathered a thousand storms gave way to office buildings, restaurants with nautical décor, and a number of hotels.

I picked up the *Point Bailey Times* at a newsstand, then found a place to grab a bite to eat, a classic lunch-car diner tucked between a Woolworth's and a mom-and-pop grocery store. I ordered fish and chips. What else would one eat when by the sea? I devoured a generous portion of fried cod that tasted heavenly, and so did the coffee —*real* coffee—I ordered with my meal, despite the heat.

The sky reddened with sunset and soon, night fell. The streetlights outside the diner popped on. Because of blackout restrictions, lights along the shore had been muted during the war. Now, they blazed like a boss, as if making up for lost time.

I lingered over my third cup of coffee and skimmed the newspaper. Most European nations had just begun to pull themselves out of the rubble of war, the Equal Rights Amendment had been narrowly defeated in the Senate, and a French designer's scandalously tiny new two-piece bathing suit was making a sensation. Dubbed the bikini, the swimsuit had been named after the Bikini Atoll where the US had conducted its first nuclear tests earlier in July.

At ten, I drained the last drop of my coffee, left the newspaper behind, and set out toward the Slipknot. Occasional flashes of lightning flickered across the humid night sky. Heat lightning, Grandma Blue used to call it, silent flares that seemed somehow more ominous than a crashing thunderstorm.

I reached Main Boulevard, the entertainment center of Point Bailey. Hordes of people in lightweight summer wear strolled the sidewalk, checking out the restaurants, bars, arcades, and nightclubs open for business. Detroit was just getting back to work on civilian vehicles, switching from war work, and shiny new Fords and Pontiacs tooled down the street. The romantic song "It's Been a Long, Long Time" wafted out of an arcade, doing battle with the roar of conversation and laughter and the ringing bells of pinball games within.

The air literally thrummed with energy and an immediacy that made me ache for Sully. Even the reek of cigarettes and clouds of smoke hanging overhead and puffing from every building I passed reminded me of him. Not in a good way. The man had a pack-a-day Lucky Strikes habit, despite my nagging him about the dangers of smoking. A melancholy wave washed over me. I wished I could see him and nag him now but knew that was impossible.

I put my longing aside and focused on my mission as I arrived at the Slipknot, a one-story clapboard building with neon signs advertising Black Label beer in the windows. I hung back and kept my eye on the door, a flimsy thing that squawked open dozens of times as men staggered in and out. Rasmussen wasn't one of them.

A few more minutes passed. Those three cups of

coffee kept me alert, but also got me thinking of checking my TDC junior to find a bathroom nearby. Thinking only. The junior's holographic GPS might be ho-hum common in my future time, but I'd never expose such sci-fi tech to the general public of the past. With portable transistor radios still a few years away, the flashing images and annoying sounds that would shoot out seemingly from my wristwatch would probably scare these 1946'ers to death.

The Slipknot's door banged open, and I straightened. Something was happening. And right on time.

A horde of men in summer casuals spilled out of the bar, as if they'd all been kicked out at the same time. They pushed and shoved as tempers flared. Voices hiked up, something about General Patton and Bastogne. Finger pointing and chest thumping ensued. I braced for the powder keg to go off.

My pulse raced when I spotted my quarry, Niels Rasmussen, wending through the mob. He wore a powder-blue suit, white Panama hat, and a benign expression that morphed to anger as he pushed up to two other men. One of the guys, built like a bulldog, had a nasty scar that sliced his face from ear to chin. The other was smaller, with stringy hair. The three men exchanged words I couldn't hear through the noise of the crowd. Nasty words, from the look of it. Words Rasmussen did *not* like. He shoved the bulldog away and backhanded the other man so hard the guy's lip split and he flew backward and banged into the wall of the building.

Yikes. So much for the scientist who'd fled into the past to nurse his wounds after a workplace accident. This guy had a temper.

I pushed the questions about what the stringy-haired man had said that set Rasmussen off aside. Their fight wasn't my business. Corralling my target was. I eased my stinger from my skirt pocket and held it at hip-level, moving through the mob. Though really, would I even risk firing at the guy and hitting an innocent bystander? The struggle to explain a laser pulse burn to a 1946 ER doctor would be almost as difficult as explaining to Devon and Glo why I'd discharged my weapon on a crowded street.

Rasmussen suddenly stiffened and swung his gaze my way. His eyes widened. I swore under my breath. He'd seen me—and made me as a time cop.

I rushed forward, determined to get to him before he bolted.

A thin man in a baggy gray suit came out of nowhere and slammed into me. The force shot me into a big guy in a tee shirt, who flew into another man, and they butted heads with a *thwack* that reverberated across the pavement. The sound was like a gunshot starting a horse race. The mob exploded. Fists flew and so did profanity as two dozen men hurled themselves into the fight with deadly conviction.

A white-hot flash lit the night, spilling over the brawlers and making them look like ghosts caught in a macabre dance. Not heat lightning this time, but the flare of a camera's flashbulb. The newspaper photographer taking the picture I'd find in my suitcase nearly two hundred years from now.

I kept moving. I cut around two men grappling with each other like high schoolers at a wrestling match, and both of them losing. Someone's fist whizzed by, uncomfortably close to my face. Someone else elbowed me in the side. Yet another someone tried to grope me. I blocked his grabby hands with an uppercut that sent him reeling—and knocked my stinger from my grip.

Shit.

The weapon clattered to the ground. Frantic, I bent to scoop it up before someone could grab it, when a muddy shoe kicked it across the sidewalk. I kept my eyes on it as I chased after it, booted from foot to foot like a soccer ball whizzing toward the goal. Then, a hand reached down and plucked the zapper off the pavement. I lifted my gaze to see Rasmussen flash an evil grin and slip my weapon into his coat's breast pocket.

Shit, shit, *shit.*

Let's see what you can do, Devon had said. How about screw up completely five minutes into the mission?

Anger and adrenaline pumped through me in equal doses, and I lunged for Rasmussen. Suddenly, a pair of muscular arms locked around my waist. Ugh, another groper. I smashed my foot down on his instep. He grunted but didn't loosen his grip. In fact, he tightened his hold and yanked me out of the middle of the mob as if I weighed no more than a feather.

I squirmed in my captor's hold. "Let me go."

Police sirens wailed in the distance. The brawlers scuttled off like cockroaches fleeing the scene when the exterminator showed up. Rasmussen and his bulldog friend melted into the darkness.

"Let go!" I cried. "He's getting away—"

I cut off with a gasp. I looked down at the arms that held me pinned. I knew the feel of those arms, though it had been two years since they'd embraced me. I recognized those strong hands. I knew that scent, Lifebuoy soap and all man.

I twisted in his grip and turned to face a tall, broad-shouldered man with thick, copper-red hair peeking out from under the most ridiculous straw boater hat I'd ever seen. He looked strange in that hat, and in the civilian clothes he wore, a tan suit coat, trousers with wide legs and a high waistband, and a crisp, white shirt open at the neck.

But the rest of him was the same. The scar that slashed across his nose. Those wise sapphire-blue eyes with the smile lines crinkling at the edges. His strong, determined jaw, dotted with whiskers, and, oh, that deep Cary Grant dimple in his chin.

Of all the brawls in all the seaside villages in all the world, he had to bust into mine.

The man I desperately yearned to be with. The man I couldn't forget and hadn't been able to put behind me, no matter how hard I'd tried. The man whose life I put in danger just by being here.

Tom Sullivan.

Sully.

My Sully. The man I loved.

Damn you fate, you ironic bitch.

***

"BERYL."

My name, a single syllable, or maybe two, I could never figure that out. All I knew, all I heard was my name on Sully's lips after all this time, his deep voice filled with surprise, longing, and despair. Even a little anger.

I gazed into his eyes. I should've been all, *go away you big ox, before someone drops a house on you,* but I didn't say a thing. Mostly because the shock of seeing him had robbed me of speech. If I could speak, only two words would come out. Words that thumped in my heart and danced on my tongue.

Kiss me.

I ached for him to take me into his arms and kiss me, thoroughly, completely, and for a long, long time.

Much to my disappointment, he didn't comply. Just stood there, staring, taking me in. His gaze skated along my body, then back up to my face, his expression as turbulent and unsettled as the sky before a storm. He'd shifted his hold on me and now gripped my upper arms, his fingers squeezing as if he feared I would fly away.

I flushed from head to toe, suddenly wanting nothing more than to fly away, or more accurately, temporal skip back to the future, or back in time to the dinosaur days, *anywhere* but here. Alarm bells clanged in my ears. If the predictions from Jake and Glo and Alice's ten thousand temporal search engines were true, Sully was fated to die, protecting me. Somehow, some way, some when.

I needed to leave. I might not be able to prevent that somehow or some way, but I *could* prevent the some when. The TDC junior tingled on my wrist, ready to go. All I had to do was power it up and tornado the hell out of here.

But I couldn't budge. I'd fallen into Sully's gaze and his seen-it-all eyes. Been snared by the feel of his hands holding me. Caught by the allure of those lips I wanted kissing me more than anything else in the world.

"Beryl," he said again.

"Sully." A smile trembled on my lips. "It's really me, Sully."

"Tom?"

Sully released me and jerked back as if I were a star suddenly gone nova. He glanced behind him, and I followed his gaze to see a tall woman with an athletic build and hair as silky yellow as a newly blossomed buttercup. She wore a candy cane striped sundress, a golden suntan, and an exceedingly curious look, all wrapped in a cloud of powdery perfume and cigarette smoke.

She stepped forward and slipped her left hand into the crook of Sully's arm like it lived there full time. Light winked off the thin gold band that circled her third finger.

Her *put a ring on it* finger.

A rock the size of an asteroid settled in my stomach. The police sirens and the few men lingering after the brawl faded away as I pinned my gaze to that band of gold. My stomach sank down to my toes and kept going, all the way to the bottom of the Atlantic Ocean.

Now I knew why Sully hadn't kissed me.

He'd moved on. With a vengeance.

5

"What is it, Tom?" the gorgeous creature hanging on Sully's arm asked. "What's going on here?" She spoke to him but her sugary brown eyes lasered in on me.

Stunned, I looked from her to him. I'd expected him to move on. Hoped for it even, deep down. We could never be together. He needed to live his life. He had every right to find someone new. I could tell myself that over and over, but the honest truth, I was hurt. Sledgehammer to the heart hurt.

It didn't help that Sully had gone out of his way to find such a perfect specimen of womanhood to move on with. About Sully's age, twenty-seven, leggy and slender, she wore a silk daisy nestled over her ear and she rocked that sundress and wide red belt around her waist like a runway model. Her features were as symmetrical and country-club perfect as Jake's, as if crafted in a laboratory. Even her shoulder-length hair and pin curl bangs defined perfection, though I suspected she shellacked her hairdo into such magnificence with enough hairspray to paint a house.

Okay, getting catty now. That so wasn't me. I wasn't the type to snipe or compare myself unfavorably to other women. I am who I am and happy to be that way. But I would admit to the teeniest sting of jealousy. Well, more than a sting. As if the whole beehive attacked me all at once.

"There's nothing going on, Millie," Sully said, finally answering her question. He flashed me a hot glance. "Whatever happened is over. Nothing to worry about now."

Correct, and absolutely devastating.

Millie turned a frown on her husband. "Tom, aren't you going to introduce me to your friend?"

He stiffened at her arch tone. "Oh, sorry. This is Beryl. Beryl Blue."

"Beryl... Blue?" she repeated, sounding bewildered.

Yeah, my name. Beryl was unusual, an old-school grandma name if I ever heard one, though not as odd as my last name, which usually raised eyebrows. Blue wasn't exactly a common surname, but I didn't care to explain to Millie or anyone else the name had probably been very different and comprised of many more syllables when the Blue family had escaped persecution in eastern Europe a century ago. So, I simply nodded.

An awkward silence fell. Millie examined her perfectly manicured fingernails. I shifted nervously. Sully chewed on his bottom lip as if it were the roast beef special.

"We can't stay," Millie said, as the screaming police

sirens drew closer. She plucked at Sully's coat sleeve. "Let's depart and let the police take care of this matter."

I raised my eyebrows, all the way up. She'd rolled that *cahn't* and purred her Rs in an upper-crust, boarding-school-educated, cultured Boston accent like Katharine Hepburn or JFK. Nothing like Grandma Blue or Sully's working-class Massachusetts accent, a nails-on-a-chalkboard, dropped R squawk that sounded like a *cah* crashing into *Hahvid Yahd* at wicked high speed.

I eyed Sully. "Yeah, you should listen to your w—" *Gah.* I couldn't say it. I could barely think it, but speaking the word *wife* aloud? No. Could not do it. That would make it real, put the final nail in the coffin and bury any hope I'd once had that Sully and I could be together again someday. "The two of you should leave," I choked out instead.

He scowled at me. "Why? What are you doing here? Besides getting into a fight. What are you up to, Beryl?"

I winced. The longing and tenderness when he'd said my name before had vanished from his voice, leaving only anger. As if the brawl had been my fault. Which, technically it was, and I did not relish explaining *that* paradox to Devon when I got back. I mean, the crowd had been primed for a fight. Who knew *I* would light the fuse? But seriously, I found Sully's anger a little over the top.

And that got my back up.

"I'm up to nothing. At least, nothing *you* need to worry about, Sergeant Grumpy. Why don't you and the little woman go on your way? I can manage on my own." I winced again. That came out as bitter as a cup of cold triple synth with no sugar.

"You'll manage? You'll manage to start World War Three if I leave you here alone."

Really? Sully knew the bare minimum about time travel and my job as a time cop, what I'd let slip in our conversations before we'd parted in 1943. He knew enough to suspect I wasn't here to sightsee, but that didn't justify his sarcasm and frosty tone.

More police sirens joined the din, distracting me from a scathing retort. I suspected every squad car from every precinct in town headed our way. Millie tugged Sully's arm this time, as anxious as a criminal fearing the police were coming for her.

"Tom, we *really* should go."

He didn't budge. "We'll go in a minute, Mill," he said, tightening his jaw.

She bristled. She'd probably never been called *Mill* before in her life. Until *Tom* came along, anyway. Sighing, she withdrew her hand and stepped away. She snatched a cigarette out of what looked like a genuine alligator purse and thumbed her lighter's spark wheel with frantic clicks.

Sully didn't seem to notice her agitation, being fully occupied with glaring at me. "Out with it, Miss Blue, what brings you here?"

Oof. He'd resorted to the *Miss Blue* portion of the argument pretty early. "That's classified," I said, glaring back.

"Booshwa!"

A groan nearby interrupted our glare-off. We both swung toward the sound. The stringy-haired man Rasmussen had viciously backhanded sat on the pavement, slumped against the Slipknot's gray and gritty clapboard wall.

I flushed. I'd forgotten about him. Forgotten about Rasmussen, the loss of my stinger, and everyone and everything here in 1946, while focused entirely on my own reality show drama. Had Rasmussen inflicted further punishment on the man before he'd bolted?

Sully scowled, maybe thinking the same thing. He rushed over to check on him. I followed. Millie dragged along behind us. She pulled on her cigarette and exhaled smoke, looking down at the man, studying him with vague curiosity.

I squatted beside Sully and gave the man a more concerned once-over. He smelled like he'd poured half of Milwaukee's breweries down his gullet. Blood speckled his chin and suit coat from his split lip, his hands trembled, and he drooped against the wall, tossing his head side to side in agitation.

"What's eating you, fella? Are you hurt?" Sully ran his hands lightly along the man's arms and legs and checked the back of his head.

"No!" The man grabbed Sully by the lapels and held on tight, his watery, bloodshot eyes wide and pleading. "They're after me. Don't let them get me."

"Settle down, soldier," Sully said, both gentle and gruff, his forehead creased with concern. "No one's after you. Not anymore. The war's over. It's behind you."

Oh. Sully thought PTSD had caused the guy's freak-out, or battle fatigue as they'd called it in World War II. *If* any of them talked about it at all. History books told us Johnny came marching home, swiped Rosie the Riveter's job out from under her nose, got hitched and started making babies at a booming clip, and rarely, if ever, talked about the horrors of war. The Greatest Generation were expected to suck it up and get on with their lives.

I gazed at the man trembling on the ground and my belly squeezed. Except some of them couldn't.

Although... After what I'd seen before the brawl, I wondered if more than PTSD fueled the man's fear. A real and present danger named Niels Rasmussen.

I leaned in close. "Mister, I saw a man hit you before the fight. Why did he do that? Do you know where he went?"

Sully looked at me and his left eyebrow shot up. I might have grinned if the situation allowed for it. How I missed him and his skeptical, judgmental, sarcastic eyebrow of doom. Though tempted to tell him that, I didn't, not with his wife hovering over us like a chaperone at a high school dance.

Several police cars screeched up to the curb, sirens wailing. The quivering man on the ground shrunk into himself and covered his ears with shaking hands. A dozen cops spilled out of their vehicles, wielding nightsticks, eager to bust up a fight that had already broken up. The cops looked us over, lingering too long on Millie and me, until Sully stood, unfolding to his full six foot two, and commanding their attention. He offered a few reassuring words, one cop to many others, hands were shaken, backs were clapped, and they finally left us alone.

After their squad cars had muttered away, Sully once again hunkered down beside the trembling man. "What's your name, fella?" he asked.

The man swallowed several times before he could speak. "Brian Murphy. You can call me Murph."

"Okay, Murph. I'm Sully. Come on, let's get you up." He gripped the smaller man by the arm and hauled him to his feet, then glanced at me. "This is my... friend, Beryl."

I caught that hesitation, and also noted he did not introduce Millie.

"Hellooo, Berle," Murphy slurred. He tried to look at me, but his head lolled too much for eye contact.

"Whoa. I think I better take you home." Sully reached to steady him as he wobbled violently, as if buffeted by a stiff wind.

"Oh no you don't, Sergeant." I looped Murph's arm over my shoulders to hold him up before Sully could. Though only slightly taller than me, about five foot eight, the guy was all muscle and kind of heavy. With his weight all on my right side, I tipped dangerously to starboard. "*I* can handle things from here. I'll take the gentleman home."

And grill him about why Rasmussen had smacked him and where he'd gone. My interrogation on that score had been interrupted before it could even begin. Though with Murph's agitated state, I wondered if I could get a single coherent word out of him.

"You go on with your..." I flicked a glance to Millie, who stood nearby, drawing slowly on her cigarette, her shrewd gaze hopping back and forth between us. "You just get back to whatever it was you were doing before you stuck your nose into my business."

"Your business is brawling on a street corner? Did you get a promotion since I saw you last?"

Ouch. "I see your diplomatic skills haven't improved one bit."

"You're avoiding the answer. Be straight with me, Beryl. What are you really doing here?"

"I can't tell you," I said.

His left eyebrow shot sky high. "You can't tell me? You can't *ever* tell me. Not a damned thing." Harsh words, delivered with a rasp of resentment in his voice.

"Well, I'm sorry," I said, poked by hurt again. He'd been snapping at my heels like a rabid dog since he pulled me out of the fray. "I can't tell you, and you know I can't. It's for your own good. Please go. I can manage to get Mr. Murphy home on my own—"

Murph's knees buckled, and we both nearly toppled. I struggled to hold him up. Really, karma? Did you have to prove me wrong so quickly?

Sully turned to look at Millie. "Go back to the hotel, Mill. I'll be there in a few minutes."

Oh, she did *not* like that. Not one bit. I could tell by the calm, deliberate way she smoothed her hair.

Sergeant Oblivious missed that clue. "Go on," he repeated.

She clutched the thick strap of her alligator bag and pursed her lips like she'd eaten the sourest lemon in the batch. "If you think that's best, Tom."

She dropped her cigarette to the pavement, ground it out with her heel, and left. I watched her glide away. Sully didn't. He focused all his attention on our droopy friend. He slung his arm around Murph and subtly shifted the man's weight, managing to bear most of the burden.

"All right, fella, where do you live?" Sully asked.

Murphy didn't answer, just jerked his chin in a westerly direction and we set out down the main drag.

Sully didn't speak and neither did I. Murph muttered

and mumbled in fearful tones as we carry-dragged him down the sidewalk. We moved unsteadily until we got into a groove. I channeled my experience transporting temporal perps stunned by the cack or a stinger. I knew Sully had dragged his share of wounded men to safety during the war. I also knew if I told him that made him a hero, he'd reward me with one of his famous scowls.

Heat lightning flashed only occasionally now. The air wrapped around us like a heating pad cranked up to maximum. Sweat slicked my back, mingling with prickles of fear that danced down my spine.

Sully might dispute the whole *hero* thing, but his need to jump into the fray and help anyone in trouble tempted fate. Every step, every moment we were together could put him at risk. Would something intentional, like a bullet, take him down? Or would bad luck, like an out-of-control car jumping the curb be the culprit? Would Sully push me out of the way to safety, getting himself killed in the process? Or was there a chance the prediction could be wrong, and Sully's destiny wasn't set in stone?

I'd hung onto that last question as if clinging to a life-line on the side of a cliff since Jake had first broken the news about Sully's fate. I hoped against hope the answer would be yes. But until Alice could pinpoint how and when Sully would die and I knew the truth, my goal had to be to get Murph home and ditch Big Red as soon as I could.

People snickered and laughed as we stumbled past. Couldn't blame them. We were quite a sight, a cockeyed trio staggering down the sidewalk, like a sideshow act that had busted free of the circus. We passed bars, dance halls, and still crowded arcades. Music blared and voices roared.

The scent of fried dough and freshly popped popcorn carried on the humid air. The streetlights blazed as bright as daytime, so different from the wartime blackout restrictions when I'd first met Sully and we walked together down the darkened streets of Ballard Springs.

I stole a glance at him over Murphy's head. Back then, the attraction between us had been electric, searing, and hot enough to melt the metal garters holding up my silk stockings. Now, the heat still sizzled. On my end, at least. But Sully? He stared straight ahead, his expression unreadable. The man had an excellent poker face. He could teach Jake a master class in hiding one's thoughts and emotions.

And what did it matter how he felt about me? He was *married*. A cold, hard fact that got those jealous bees stinging me again. And got my mouth moving when it shouldn't have.

"So, Millie," I said. "She seems nice."

Sully adjusted his burden and gave a non-committal grunt.

"Quiet. Sweet. Beautiful."

Another grunt. The man's small talk skills hadn't improved a bit since the last time I'd seen him.

"I see why you like her." I couldn't bring myself to use the other *L* word. "I mean, she does what you tell her to with no argument. What man wouldn't want to be with a woman like that?" I meant to tease, but the words came out dripping with hurt, and a little venom.

"Knock it off, Beryl. I thought I'd never see you again. You went poof, into thin air, and that was that. What was I supposed to do?"

Wait for me, my heart cried, but my head told it to shut up. Sully was right. "I'm sorry. I didn't mean to be mean. Millie seems like a real peach, plus she's smoking hot and can probably bake a cherry pie with one hand tied behind her back. Probably why you married her."

He scowled at me. "Married? Me and Millie aren't married."

"Oh." Somehow that didn't make me feel better. Or soften the sting. "So, she wears that ring just for show? Or to fool the hotel detectives? I know how prudish things were, I mean are, in this time period." More hurt, more venom. "Are you pretending to be married so you can rent a room and fool around without the morality police stepping in?"

"Beryl, you don't—"

"Or is it... Sully, *no*." My hurt and anger washed away, replaced by shock as an awful thought invaded my brain, threatening to knock him off the sky-high pedestal I'd put him on. "Don't tell me there's a Mr. Millie waiting blissfully unaware at home."

He heaved a frustrated sigh. "It's complicated."

Ugh. That phrase. *Et tu, Sully?* I'd expected more of him. I'd expected perfection. "Swell. I'll stop by for tea tomorrow, and you can tell me all about it."

"Beryl."

He'd activated his serious voice. I met his gaze and shrunk down to about two inches tall, feeling like a fool. I never did know when to stop my mouth. "What happened to him?"

No hesitation. "Killed in action. At Anzio."

"I'm sorry."

"So is she." A long pause, then his voice turned gruff. "What about you? You got a fella?"

A simple question, with the most *it's complicated* answer of them all. I didn't want to go there, so I simply shook my head. Sully's eyebrow lifted a fraction. Whatever that meant. Surprise that I had yet to move on? Or did I detect a bit of hope in that slight movement?

Murph entered the chat. "I got a wife. She's a *bee-ooty*." He sighed mournfully. "She's mad at me, may never speak to me again. I did it for her, you know, but she don't understand why I took them. That's why they're after me. They want it all and I ain't handing anything over 'til I get my fair share. Not after what I done to get them."

"Handing what over?" Sully asked, snapping into cop mode.

I put my self-pity away and went on alert too. This was the most non-mumbled string of words Murphy had put together since we'd left the Slipknot. Maybe now I could get the intel I needed to snag Rasmussen and get out of here.

Imagine my surprise when Murphy went in a different direction.

"The jewels," he said. "A fortune in gems, worth thousands. Maybe a *million*." He let out a cackling laugh, full of bitterness and beer fumes. "And I stole them all."

Okay, what? Jewels? Stolen jewels, at that. A figment of Murph's alcohol-soaked imagination, or had I stumbled into a real-life version of an *Ocean's 11* heist movie?

"What are you talking about?" Sully asked, equally confused.

"The jewels. We snatched them from a German castle, right under the MP's nose. I brung the loot home and now I got them, the whole kit and caboodle. I hid 'em where they'll never find them." He cackled again. "I told them I won't turn 'em over. They can threaten me all they want. I ain't given them up until I get my due."

"Who's they?" I asked, knowing the answer. Rasmussen and the man with the scarred face who'd confronted Murph at the Slipknot. "Is it the man who hit you before the fight?"

"He's the kingpin, girlie," Murph said, as if everyone knew that and I should totally get up to speed. "Pattinson's the big boss. A greedy son of a bitch who thought up the whole plan."

"Pattinson? Fred Pattinson?" A chill ran down my back. The name on the dog tags found in my suitcase. Not a coincidence. Rasmussen had adopted an alias when he'd fled to the past and the person who'd planted the suitcase at the library wanted me to find that out. Why? To warn me he might be dangerous? No need. That vicious slap he'd given Murphy had already clued me in.

"Yeah, Freddy Pattinson. Excuse me, *Captain* Pattinson." Murph sneered. "He's a real bastard, like all the Army brass. He thinks he can order me around. Not anymore. I changed my Army greens for civvies." He swiveled in Sully's direction. "We don't have to take orders from anyone now, right, pal?"

Big Red refused to commit. "What kind of jewels are we talking about?" He shifted so Murphy's arm fell away from me, and Sully bore all his weight.

"Ah, they're something." Murph grinned. "Shiny earbobs, bracelets. Rings and pearls, some rubies too. And so many diamonds you could pave a path to Kansas with 'em. Freddy was gonna cut me out of the deal, but I outflanked him and hid—" He shushed himself, hissing like a tipsy snake. "Aw, hell. I said too much. The wife always nags me about flapping my gums. She says it's gonna get me in trouble. Best keep the rest under my hat. Mum's the word."

Unfortunately, mum was the word for the rest of the conversation too, and though I tried to bring up the subject of Rasmussen, Murphy clammed up. He didn't speak for the rest of the way, except to give us directions.

We turned a corner a few moments later into a dusty

neighborhood of narrow streets filled with shabby houses shoved up against one another. Cracks and weather-eroded holes in the sidewalk made walking for our awkward trio even more difficult. We reached Murph's place, a scrappy four-room, two-story house with a peaked roof, and sided with red asphalt shingles, half of which the wind had blown off, the other half clinging by a thread. A single light shone through one of the front windows and a small metal garbage pail stood beside the front door, gleaming in the moonlight like a silver sentry.

We stepped up onto a low porch. Sully unwound Murph's arm from his shoulder and set him on his feet. The man teetered as he reached for the doorknob then stumbled when the door swung open. Sully caught him before he could fall then guided him through a small entryway and into a stiflingly hot front room with a sagging sofa, a spindly coffee table, and a broken-down easy chair.

I closed the door softly behind me and joined them inside the stuffy room. The smell of cabbage and cigarettes whisked me to the past and those awful days after my parents were killed, when Grandma Blue and I moved into a dingy little house like this, and I was sad all the time.

Footsteps sounded from above. A woman about my height and with a similar curvy build sailed down a narrow flight of stairs, tying the belt on a pink, quilted bathrobe that brushed her ankles. Soft, silky gold hair touched her shoulders and curled under in a pageboy style, and she had a long nose sharp enough to cut glass. Murphy's *bee-ooty* of a wife, I presumed.

"Where have you been?" she cried, eyeing Murph with distaste. "Don't you know I've been sitting home all night, worried sick about you?"

She might have been worried sick, but the jury was out on the *sitting home all night* part. The stylish pumps, silk stockings, and plaid skirt I noticed peeping out from under her bathrobe suggested a different location for her worrying. I doubted she'd been home more than five minutes before we arrived.

"I'm here now, safe and sound." Murph plopped into the easy chair, hopefully avoiding the springs poking through the seat. "I wish you'd quit nagging, Dorella."

Dorella? Speaking of grandma names that would be right at home in the twenty-second century.

Her suspicious gaze lit on Sully, who sank deep into the cushions as he settled on the sofa next to Murph. He removed his hideous hat and rested it on his knee, giving me my first good look at his gorgeous red hair. He'd grown it a bit longer than the regulation short Army haircut I remembered, but he still combed it tidily, like carefully furrowed rows in a field. I longed to run my fingers through every strand and mess it all up.

Ahem. Not the time, or the place for that kind of thinking. Especially not now, as Dorella shifted her wary attention from Sully to me.

"Who are you people?" she demanded. "What are you doing in my house?"

A fair question, delivered in a sniffy, somewhat defensive voice. "I'm Beryl. This is Sully. We gave your husband an assist getting home. There was a little trouble at the Slipknot."

Her eyes narrowed. "Trouble? What happened?"

Murph settled his glassy-eyed gaze on his wife. "There was a fight, but that's not important." He touched his puffy, bruised lip. "I ran into our old friend. He's here for the jewels, but I told him no. No one gets their mitts on them until I say so."

"What does he mean?" I asked Dorella.

The color had drained from her already pale cheeks, but she waved dismissively and bluffed through an airy, "He means nothing. A pile of nonsense."

"Ha!" Murph barked. "Wasn't nonsense when you rolled up in your jeep with all those pretties tucked under the seats, expecting me to haul them home. Expecting *me* to take the risk. *I* woulda gone to the stockade if I got caught, not you."

She shushed him with a hiss that turned into a sigh. "He's mixed up. He's thinking of the jeep I drove as a WAC. I was assigned to the motor pool. I know every part of an engine like the back of my hand and can change a tire in ten seconds flat, but do you think any auto shop will give me a job?" She gave a delicate snort. "Anyway, every GI at the front bought what they thought were the crown jewels from a street corner conman." She held up her left hand, showing a gold band even thinner than the one Millie wore. "Think I'd be wearing this cheap thing or living in this dump if Brian had come home with diamonds in his kit bag? No, I would not. Believe me, these jewels don't exist, except in my husband's mind."

A fine, if lengthy, rebuttal to Murph's claim, but entirely truthful? I had my doubts. So did Sully. He ran a finger around the brim of his hat balanced on his knee, looking thoughtful.

"I'm not batty, Dorella," Murph said. "I'm as sane as you are. You know exactly what I'm talking about."

Dorella's gaze shot daggers at her husband but when she turned to me, she went all concerned and caring spouse. "Please ignore him." She tapped her temple with her forefinger. "He's not well. He's been this way since he was demobbed."

I squinted. Uh, de-whatted? Sully got my attention by clearing his throat. "Demobilized," he said. "Released from the Army."

"Sure took long enough," Murph said. "I thought I'd never get home. But the brass, they got sent home quick as a wink." He fumbled a cigarette from a pack of Pall Malls he plucked from the side table and steered it to his mouth with a trembling hand. "You served, Sully, you know those men. Makes no difference if they're Army or Navy, the brass are all goldbricking turds who sat on their fannies, while we got shot at." His voice hiked up in agitation. "I was at Malmedy. Was one of the few prisoners who escaped that massacre, but not before seeing fellas cut down by the enemy. I got out by the skin of my teeth and the grace of god, while the bastards in the rear echelon drank cognac and diddled the French girls then got to take the first boat home."

"I hear you, brother," Sully said, his tone calming. And calm, despite the horrified grimace that flashed over his face when Murph had mentioned Malmedy. "We're home now. We made it through."

"Yeah. We made it through." He gusted a bitter sigh then lit his cigarette. He held out the package, offering one to Sully. "Want a smoke?"

Sully gave the Pall Malls a longing look but shook his head. "No, thanks. I quit about a year ago."

His gaze flicked toward me, and I stiffened in surprise. *Hm.* Usually observant Beryl had completely missed the absence of cigarettes in his life. Wartime Sully had been a borderline chain smoker. In the brief time we'd been together, I'd lectured him repeatedly about the dangers. Had my encouragement had some influence in getting him to kick the habit? The thought got me all warm and squishy inside. Almost made up for his caustic attitude and simmering anger.

Murph took a deep drag and blew out a cloud of smoke. "You see why I won't give Freddy what he wants? He'll cheat me like the brass always do. As long as I've got the loot, *I'm* in charge." He clapped a palm to his chest, sending cigarette ash tumbling down the front of his shirt. "*I'm* the one who gives the orders. I hid the jewels and I ain't telling anyone where they are." He flashed to Dorella. "Not even you."

"Brian." Dorella's voice went brittle. "It's late. I've got work in the morning and need to get to bed. Why don't you stop flapping your gums and let this nice couple go home."

Murph gave a grin that held no humor. "What did I tell you? The old ball and chain, right?"

WE SAID good night and left Murphy making his way up the stairs to the second floor, slow and unsteady, even with Dorella assisting him. And whispering angrily in his ear.

We stepped outside. I nearly groaned in disappointment as Sully's put his that egregious straw boater back on, hiding his hair.

"Nice hat," I said.

He touched the brim and shot me a pained look. "You don't like it? Millie says it's a fine quality Stetson, whatever that means. She says it's smart and I should wear it."

If Millie told him to jump off a bridge, would he do that too? I *so* wanted to say that but held my tongue. What good would that do besides telegraph my jealousy over someone I had no right to be jealous about?

"Something smells about this whole thing," Sully said as we left the Murphy's house behind and strolled back toward downtown.

"Oh, yeah, *totally* hinky."

"No argument?" His eyebrow rose in surprise.

"Nope. I know you're shocked but I agree with you. I mean, Murphy claims to have hidden a fortune in jewels. Wifey dear denies it, though Murph says she's totally clued into whatever's going on. She couldn't wait to get rid of us, too. That's a *lot* of drama for some supposedly fictional gems. Plus, Dorella might've claimed she'd been hanging around all night waiting for Murph, but she'd just gotten home. She was still wearing her dancing slippers and stockings under that bathrobe."

Sully tugged on his ear. "Okay, I'll buy that. She's seeing someone?"

"Maybe. Or maybe she just took out the garbage. Or was out looking for the jewels." I bumped my shoulder against his. Well, bumped against his upper arm, what with him being taller than me and all. "In any case, I've got to find the kingpin, Rasmussen. Murph may have talked tough, but he's scared spitless of the guy."

"Don't you mean Pattinson?" Sully's eyebrow hiked upward again.

Okay, starting to *not* miss that teasing, doubtful, and somewhat condescending eyebrow as much as I thought. "Yeah, him."

"He's why you're here, isn't it?"

I nodded. "I came for Rasmussen, not to get involved in a jewelry heist, but here we are." And I had to get back on mission. After I said goodbye to *him*.

I stopped walking and turned to him. He stopped too and gazed down at me expectantly. My breath hitched and my head spun, suddenly dizzy from his closeness and the way he looked at me, and his familiar, tantalizing scent that invaded my senses. Those two words that had blazed in my brain since he'd dragged me out of the brawl almost spilled out.

Kiss me.

I schooled my features to solemn and severe, instead of dopey and lovesick. "On that note, former Sergeant now demobbed Mr. Sullivan, it's time for you to leave and…" I took a breath and forced the words out. "And go back to your girlfriend. I've got a job to do."

"Is there anything I can do to help?"

That. That right there. The reason I'd fallen in love with this man. Always there to lend a hand. To stick by me and see the problem through. I'd spent so many of my younger years adrift, without anyone to help me or anything to hang onto. Until I met Sully and found my anchor. I wanted his help. Could use his help. But that would throw us together, and no matter how much I wanted to be near him, we needed to part. Before Sully's fate could catch up to both of us.

"No, thanks," I said, reluctantly, but with finality. "This mission I'm on is too dangerous."

His expression went cold and grim. "Don't do that, Beryl. I walked through Belgium in the dead of winter with the Germans taking potshots at me. Tree trunks exploded over my head from shellfire. I saw limbs blown off. Kids cut down. I saw bodies, too many bodies, and people who looked like walking skeletons—" A hard shudder shook him from head to toe. "I think I can face whatever you're mixed up in without pissing myself."

My heart wrenched. For him, for Murphy and his narrow escape from the butchery of Malmedy, for everyone who'd suffered through what some people ironically called the Good War. There had been nothing good about it. Nothing good about any war. People died, and men like Sully and Murph were left mortally wounded, trying to put the pieces of their lives back together as best they could.

Sully gazed at me for several tense moments then took me by the shoulders, his touch gentle but firm. "Why didn't you tell me? Why didn't you tell me what my men would go through? What would happen. You could've warned me. Warned all of us about... Hell, warned us about everything." His voice deepened to a whisper of disbelief. "Why Beryl? If I could've saved just one person..."

Sadness pushed through me. This was what his anger since he'd first seen me had been about. Anger with me for not telling him, anger with himself. He hadn't been able to stop the carnage and it had broken him.

"Sully, I know this is weak, and not an excuse, but I couldn't tell you about any of it. Not a word. It's as simple and horrible and as final as that. I'm sorry, but the past is fixed. History can't be changed. It's the number one rule of time travel."

He released a frustrated sigh. "That's a shitty rule. Didn't you ever think about breaking that rule?"

I didn't ask if *he* had ever broken the rules because I knew the answer would be yes. If it would save somebody. If it would make a difference in someone's life. I wished I could be half as noble. I wished I could chuck all the rules into a garbage disposal and chop them up forever and find some way to save Sully. To save my parents and Grandma Blue and everyone. To fix the world.

But the past was the past, and Mother Fate and Father Time did not take kindly to anyone messing with that. If I changed Sully's future, I could create a timeline far, far worse.

"No, I haven't," I said, as bleak as midwinter. I reached up and touched his face. Felt the heat of his skin and rough whiskers as I traced my fingers along his jaw. "And I'm so, so sorry."

He leaned into my touch. "Beryl," he murmured, a gentle rumble filled with longing that made me ache all over. He took my hand from his cheek and entwined his fingers through mine. "I missed you."

That went straight to my heart. I missed him too. Terribly. I missed him. I loved him. Was *in* love with him and always would be. All the doubts about moving on that had tortured me for so long flew out the window. I tossed Jake right along with them. Because, standing here gazing at Sully on a humid summer night, lost in his gaze, while all of 1946 trundled by unnoticed, I knew without a doubt I would *never* be over him.

How was that for fate's irony? Jake had sent me back in time to test me, forced me and my sergeant together, hoping I'd come to care for Sully enough to kill for him, to prove my worth to Time Scope. Jake's cockeyed plan had succeeded, but he'd gotten one thing he hadn't bargained for.

Me, hopelessly devoted to this big redhead.

But I had a mission to complete. And though I wanted nothing more than for Sully to fold me in his arms and kiss me for the rest of my life, I had to end this now. I worked my hand free of his grip and placed my palm on his solid chest. I felt the racing beat of his heart. I gathered my strength—and pushed him away.

The hurt that flickered across his face nearly did me in.

"Sully... I wish things were different. I wish I could stay with you. We fit. Oh, man, do we fit. Like two peas in a pod, as Grandma Blue used to say. If I'd been born in the here and now, in this time, I would happily tie on an apron and be your baby boomer bride. I would, in a fast minute. But that can't be. I've got a job to do, a job you can't help me with. In fact, I don't want you to help me."

He shifted that beautiful, beat-up kisser into obstinate mode. "What if you need me to—"

"I swear, if you say I need you to protect me, I'll time skip you back to the stone age." I wouldn't. And he knew I wouldn't. "After all we've been through, you should know I'm perfectly capable of taking care of myself."

He sighed, echoing all of my own frustrations. "All

right, capable Miss Beryl Blue, tell me what you're going to do about *him*." He tipped his head in the direction we'd just come from. "Haven't you noticed? Someone's following us and has been since we left Murphy's place."

I stiffened and flashed a glance behind us, seeing no one, but that didn't mean there wasn't anyone there. I hadn't noticed. Hadn't noticed anything, what with all the internal and external Sully drama monopolizing my bandwidth.

"All the more reason for you to go," I said. What if the guy on our tail was The One, the person who would kill him? "You should go back to Millie. Better yet, leave town. Go home."

"Go home?" He snorted. "I'm not giving up my weekend away because a bossy dame from the future tells me to."

"It's for your own good."

"Who are you to decide what's good for me?"

I ground my teeth. "Please, Sully, get it through your head. I don't need you." Harsh, but something he had to hear. "Millie does. Go back to her. She needs you and she wants you."

He grunted, finally capitulating. "You're a real piece of work, you know that?"

My annoyance faded and tears misted my eyes at those words. *A real piece of work.* A phrase sometimes used as an insult, but he meant only with affection. "And so are you," I murmured. "Now go. Go and forget about me."

He held my gaze for a long time before he spoke again. "I may leave you, Beryl, but forget you?" His voice dipped low, and a sweet smile curved his lips. "I never will."

He turned to leave. I could almost hear my heart shredding as I watched him walk away into the night—and out of my life.

Seeing Sully and losing him again in such a short period of time had nearly broken me. But I still had a mission to finish, so I did the one thing I was good at—pushing my emotions away. I shoved the pain and regrets into a deep, dark closet in my brain and returned to work.

I headed back toward the main drag, to see if I could locate Rasmussen. Or Fred Pattinson as he was known to the contemporary crowd. Captain Pattinson, US Army, in fact. Why he'd choose to skip to this time period and throw himself into the middle of a war when he could've traveled to any era, I couldn't fathom. Well, maybe I had a glimmer of an idea. According to Murph, my target was a greedy S.O.B. who'd spearheaded a jewel theft while others were fighting and putting their lives at risk.

Without Sully to distract me, I easily spotted the man following me. He kept a discreet distance behind, a shadowy figure who matched my pace, turned when I turned, slowed when I slowed, and generally behaving as obvious as hell.

Who was he? Someone uninterested in Sully, or he would've chased after Big Red when I'd sent him back to Millie. The guy followed *me*. I glanced back and the figure half a block away melded with the shadows. Definitely a man. But who?

Rasmussen? He'd recognized me as a time cop earlier, and he'd snagged my stinger when butterfingers me had dropped it. No way could he be chasing me like a benevolent Boy Scout eager to return a lost object. I shuddered. He could be after me for a more nefarious reason, to get me off his trail by turning the deadly weapon on me. Well, deadly-ish. The stinger didn't have half the zap as the cack, but it got the job done.

I hurried my pace, hoping to shake my pursuer, whoever he was, with little luck. He dogged my steps all the way to Main Boulevard.

Time to find out what the guy wanted. I reached an intersection clogged with traffic. The light changed and cars screeched to a halt. Pedestrians moved. Instead of crossing the street, I hung a hard right and stepped into the wide opening of the first business I passed, the Land of Enchantment Arcade.

The joint was jumping, even close to midnight. Clouds of cigarette smoke hung over a brightly lit room packed with people laughing, babbling, and shouting to be heard over the dings, bells, and whistles of the pinball and Skee-Ball machines. A man dressed like a Las Vegas croupier in a vest and bowtie called for players to test their skills at Fascination, an odd game played by rolling small rubber balls across a table with two dozen round holes.

I hovered near the entrance, by the cigarette machine, waiting for the man tailing me to catch up. Didn't have to wait long. He popped around the corner a few seconds later and skidded to a stop when he realized he'd lost me. He gazed around, his narrow face squinched in frustration.

Well, well. My pursuer wasn't Rasmussen, but someone else I recognized—the man who'd pushed me at the Slipknot and kicked off the brawl. Tall and beanpole thin, with an earnest face and a healthy, corn-fed complexion, the guy could beat Jimmy Stewart in a Jimmy Stewart lookalike contest hands down. He looked to be in his late forties, and wore a loose-fitting gray suit, a short, wide tie, and no hat, giving his dark wavy hair threaded with silver ample opportunity to ruffle in the evening breeze.

He turned and doubled back toward the intersection, squinting ahead at the pedestrians waiting at the light, looking for me. I stepped out onto the sidewalk and let him find me. He nearly slammed into me. Startled, he jerked back then tried to two-step around me with an anemic, "I beg your pardon."

I jumped to the left and blocked him again. He stepped to right, and we did a modified version of the "Time Warp" dance from *Rocky Horror* until he gave up.

"All right, young lady, what do you want? Why are you bothering me?" he said, his hands spread wide and his eyes even wider.

"That innocent act's not going to cut it, fella. What do *you* want? Why are you following me?"

He hesitated long enough for me to know he scrambled to cook up a lie. Then he sighed and reached inside his jacket. I shoved a hand into my pocket for the weapon that wasn't there. With an aggravated sigh, I shifted gears and braced for a fight, but relaxed my fists when he slid a thin leather wallet out of his coat's inner pocket instead of the revolver I'd expected.

He flipped the wallet open to reveal a 1940s version of an ID, a square of paper with his picture and a few pertinent details identifying him as Aloysius Knight, US Army Criminal Investigation Division.

"Congratulations, you're a G-Man," I said. Rude, I knew, but he'd not only interrupted me in my search for Rasmussen, he'd also most likely eavesdropped on my painful parting with Sully, so I was in no mood to be nice. "That still doesn't explain why you're tailing me."

"Mind telling me your name?"

Ignoring my question to toss out a question of his own. Classic power play. "Sure. It's Beryl Blue."

"Beryl... Blue? Is that your real name?"

This again. Though, to be fair, Sully had severely eyebrowed me when he'd heard my name for the first time, so I should probably cut Agent Knight a little slack for his skepticism. "Yup, that's my name. As far as you know."

He chewed that over for a few seconds. "What brings you to town this weekend, Miss Blue?"

"I'm visiting my sick auntie."

A smile flickered on his lips. "They grow them tough where you're from, don't they?"

"A woman has to be tough wherever she's from."

Whatever time period, too. "Now it's your turn. Why are you following me?"

He tucked his ID away and tipped his head toward the intersection. "Walk with me?"

"Oh-kay," I said warily. We headed up the street. I had no reason to doubt Knight's identity, but naturally cynical and suspicious, I insisted he walk curbside, on my right, in case he got the sudden urge to push me into traffic. "Time to start talking."

He laughed. "I like how direct you are."

A compliment, or an insult? I couldn't tell. "And I find your evasiveness annoying. Are you going to fill me in or not?"

He cleared his throat. "I'll be blunt, Beryl, I'm on the hunt for some stolen jewels."

That got my attention. Confirmation Murphy had been telling the truth—and Dorella had not. "Go on."

"Here's what I know. At the end of the war, a clever gang of servicemen stationed in Frankfurt managed to, uh, *liberate* a wealth of jewels that had been hidden in Schloss Mombert. The castle was used as a recreation center after Germany's surrender, so men came and went. Anyone could've stolen the gems. In fact, we didn't know anything had been stolen until Princess Irmgard alerted us to the fact. She came to the castle looking for suitable adornments for her upcoming wedding. She knew her family had hidden a cache of valuables in the castle before they fled the approaching troops. When she showed up, her treasure was gone."

He paused to take a well-earned breath. He'd dropped a lot of information in a short time, as if reciting the details of a newspaper article or a case report from memory.

"Poor Irmgard must have gone ballistic when she discovered that," I said. "What kind of bling are we talking about?"

He frowned. "Bling?"

Erp. I really had to be more careful with my slang. "I mean, what kind of valuables?"

"Oh. A number of loose gems, diamonds, emeralds and the like. Family heirlooms, worth a fortune." We reached the intersection and Knight shepherded me across the street like a duck steering a wayward chick toward the watering hole. "Plus, jewelry. You know, the type of decoration you young ladies like to wear."

His expression encouraged me to agree with that, but I answered with a noncommittal shrug. I didn't like to be lumped into a list of what men assumed young ladies would like.

"And you drew the short straw and got sent out to look for all those shiny things," I said. "I assume this is where Point Bailey comes into the story?"

He nodded. We'd reached the other side of the street and he gestured for us to turn to the left. "I've been tracking down the men who'd been at the castle during the time in question and finally got a good lead. A former corporal named Brian Murphy."

"Are you going to arrest him?"

"Not yet. He didn't act alone. He had help. I need to identify his associates, get the goods on them, and most important, find the gems. Then I can sweep them all into my net."

Goodness, he was dramatic for a civil servant. "A fine

plan." Except for the sweep them *all* up part. Rasmussen was mine.

"And then there's you," he said.

"Wait, what? You don't think I had something to do with the robbery?" I cringed. Did I really just blurt out one of the most cliché lines in law enforcement history, the one line guaranteed to convince Agent Knight I had *everything* to do with it?

He lifted a thin shoulder in a fatalistic shrug. "You went to Murphy's house. You met up with him at the Slip-knot. That puts you on my radar."

"I was just passing by, and saw he needed help. Believe me, I would've kept going if you hadn't pushed me into the middle of a brawl."

"Pushed you?" he said, all innocent like. "You must be mistaken."

I could still feel him grabbing my arm and giving me a hard shove, so, no, not mistaken. He'd pushed me, which started the fight and kept me from getting to my target. If he hadn't interfered, I would've nabbed Rasmussen and time skipped back home long ago, with my stinger firmly in my possession.

And I wouldn't have run into Sully and had my heart ripped to shreds.

I stiffened. Maybe he'd *meant* to start the fight. I shot him a cold stare. Was this guy even who he claimed to be? Just because he had a slim piece of paper that looked all official, didn't mean it was. For all I knew, he could be another one of the jewel thieves, determined to keep me from getting to the plot's mastermind.

I stopped walking and rounded on him. "What's your deal, Agent Knight? If that is your real name. And where are we going? I hope you're not planning to arrest me or take me in for questioning or whatever it is you government men get your kicks doing."

Devon would just love that. Beryl Blue, DNA ghost, Special-with-a-capital-*S*, arrested on my most important mission. Losing my stinger was bad enough, but a mugshot and fingerprints entered into the public record for all the world to see and Alice's multitude of search engines to easily find? That would royally violate Time Scope's temporal travel rule number three—don't call attention to yourself.

The man who may or may not be Agent Knight released a heavy sigh, like a frustrated father who just didn't know *what* he was going to do with his rebellious child. "I'm not going to arrest you."

He looked over my shoulder. I swung around to see a tall signpost by the curb with a sign reading "Trolley Stop" at the top. At that moment, a trolley car rumbled up tracks that ran down the middle of the street. Its bell *ding-dinged* like something from a Judy Garland movie as it rolled to a stop.

"Here's my advice, Beryl. Don't get mixed up in this. Go home. Go back to where you're staying, gather up your things and leave. Go far away from Murphy and especially his associates. They're a rough crowd and you could get hurt. I wouldn't want that on my conscience."

I bristled. First, now I knew how Sully felt when I'd told him to go home. Frustrated and dismissed. Useless. Second, I'd never liked being told what to do. Jake and Glo had found that out fast, and Sully just had the golden opportunity to remember. And I *liked* those people. This guy? *Meh.*

I gazed at him with narrowed eyes. "I'd say your concern for my safety is touching if you hadn't shoved me into the middle of a fistfight, like, three seconds ago."

He laughed. With me or at me, I couldn't be sure. "Go home, Beryl. Do it for me."

Discussion apparently at an end, he turned on his heel and disappeared around the corner.

DESPITE AGENT KNIGHT'S ADVICE, I didn't go home, but I did go back to the inn. I realized the futility of my hunt-and-seek strategy. I could spend all night searching for Rasmussen in dive bars and arcades, only to emerge empty handed, smelling like an overfull ashtray, and with a burning urge to play some pinball. Nothing would change the fact that I'd lost my chance with my target earlier tonight.

I hopped onto the trolley. After the awkward first-timers experience of slipping a nickel into the coin slot for my fare, I sank into a forward facing and uncomfortable slatted wooden seat. The streetcar shook and shimmied as it *clack-clacked* along the tracks. I leaned back and ran over my slim range of options.

The most logical strategy would be to go visit the hopefully sober Brian Murphy in the morning and try to shake Rasmussen's whereabouts out of him. Finding that time skipper took on new urgency with the Army's CID on the trail of the jewel thieves. I had to get to the guy before the law did.

Speaking of Agent Knight... *Go home. Do it for me*, he'd said. Not an order, not a command. A simple request. An odd request. I mean, why would I? Being in the same town as Sully gave me a hell of an incentive to activate my temporal oscillator and tornado back to the future, and yet, I was still here, determined to stay on mission. How could Agent Aloysius Knight, a stranger I'd just met, convince me to go?

I jumped off the trolley two stops early and consulted the GPS function on my TDC junior to find a circuitous route back to my lodgings just in case nosy Knight had decided to follow me again. I cupped my free hand over the device to hide the light as the holographic map shot up from the watch like a mini geyser, pointing me toward the inn.

In my room, I washed up in the teeny bathroom with a sink nearly as small as my toothbrush then I changed into cotton pajamas, lavender in color, with baggy trousers and a blouse smothered in ruffles that looked like a maternity top. Somewhat fitting for 1946, the kickoff year for the baby boom.

I crawled into bed and nestled against a thin pillow. I wished I'd thought to bring a book or had searched the parlor downstairs for something to read. I needed a few moments of escape. Anything but my current read, *Party Girl*, the romance I'd started before the staff meeting this morning. That story involved a romantic triangle, and I sure wasn't in the mood for that plotline, seeing as how I'd just stepped into one of my own. Not that the outcome of our triangle was in doubt. Millie was from Sully's time. I was not. They belonged together, and no time traveler could put that asunder.

With a self-pitying sigh, I rolled onto my side and turned out the light. I'd kept the windows open, letting the warm, salty air drift in. The gentle, steady crash of the waves in the distance lulled me and though I was exhausted, it took a long time before I drifted off to sleep.

I WOKE with a start and a bit of drool. I picked up my junior from the bedside table where I'd placed it last night and groaned when I saw the time.

Damn. I'd slept in. Way in—it was after nine. I blamed the temporal skip. Time travel always took a lot out of me, not to mention the emotional gymnastics of the last twenty-four hours. I wouldn't have been surprised if I'd slept for days.

A tiny greenish-yellow light pulsed at the bottom left of the junior's small screen, indicating a number of temporal texts waiting for me to answer. Probably all from Jake, and all with the subject line, *Are you okay?* To which I could only answer *no*. I should've leaped home with Rasmussen in tow by now. I'd run into the one man I shouldn't have within two minutes of touching down in this century. I'd lost my weapon just as fast, and Jimmy Stewart's clone had basically told me to keep my nose out of his G-Man business and sent me on my way.

I scrambled out of bed and headed for the bathroom, ignoring the messages. The last thing I needed was Jake hearing about the unmitigated disaster this mission had become. He already worried about me way too much.

I got ready to go. I hadn't expected to be here long, so I didn't have much of a wardrobe—one dress, two skirts, two blouses, and one sweater I absolutely did not need on a hot day like today. After a quick shower in a space no larger than an old-fashioned phone booth, I put on a pale-yellow dirndl skirt dotted with blue flowers, pairing it with a white Peter Pan collar blouse with short sleeves. Stylish and lightweight, an outfit Grandma Blue would've deemed quite gay back in her younger days.

I pulled on my sandals and went down to the lobby. The old wooden stairs creaked all the way. A gangly white girl of about fifteen led me into the small dining room, where scrambled eggs, fresh fruit, and hot coffee awaited me.

"Morning paper, miss?" the girl asked, thrusting a thick newspaper that weighed about ten pounds into my hands.

I removed the stack of ad inserts and spread the paper across the table—it nearly filled the small space—and skimmed the headlines, unsurprised to find the story and picture of the brawl on the front page. I could just make out the back of my head in the photograph, which appeared no less grainy in this first edition than nearly two hundred years from now. Looking at the picture back in the library I'd thought Rasmussen had been staring at the camera. Now I knew he gaped at *me*, with a look of stunned surprise to see a time cop zeroing in on him.

After breakfast, where I reluctantly stopped at two cups of coffee, I returned to my room and put the newspaper into my suitcase. Just in case I was supposed to. I mean, maybe that suitcase full of seemingly random items in 2132 had sent me on a treasure hunt through time to collect those very same items. Items that would hopefully make sense to future me but confused the hell out of current me and threatened to split my head wide open with a temporal migraine of epic proportions if I thought too much about it.

So... I didn't.

Focusing on the here and now, I hit the bathroom, splashed on a bit of makeup, and left. The screen door squeaked as I opened it and stepped out onto the porch. The white-haired gentleman I'd seen yesterday had taken up residence in another rocking chair today.

"You look as pretty as a picture," he said. "Going to meet your sweetheart?"

I sure wished I was. "Not today. Going shopping." I waved goodbye and descended the steep steps, holding the rail.

The humidity had dissipated somewhat, but the heat had not and the few clouds that dotted the sky gave only occasional shade, promising a scorcher of a day. Too hot to walk, so I got on the streetcar at the end of the road.

The trolley jerked to a start and moved at a steady, if *s-l-o-o-w*, pace toward the center of town. Last night it had been too dark to see anything, but this morning, I busily peered out both windows, on the off-chance I'd spot Rasmussen, and also to see the sights. One of the perks of the time cop job, I got to sightsee in all kinds of time periods while on the company's expense account.

The streetcar's windows were lowered. A breeze drifted in, along with the bang of hammers hitting nails and the smell of fresh cut wood and sawdust. I imagined all of postwar America sounded and smelled like this, with a nationwide building boom to accommodate the baby boom.

"Enjoy the ride while you can, young lady," a slim, elderly white man in casual clothes and a creased fedora said. He leaned forward over his seat across the aisle and raised his voice to be heard over the trolley's clacking and pinging. "They're taking the streetcars away after the summer tourists are gone. Don't need 'em anymore. Everyone's got cars now that Detroit is pumping them out again." He let out a wistful sigh. "Me, I'm sure going to miss the trolleys. Where else can you ride across town for a nickel? And you never know who you're gonna meet," he added with a wink.

I returned a smile. Given the lack of passengers—we were the only two riders—and the number of cars clogging the street, putting an end to the trolleys seemed inevitable, but it made me sad such a quaint and environmentally friendly form of transportation would be going away forever.

My chatty friend tipped his hat as he got off at the next stop. Then it was only me and the conductor until I hopped off the streetcar close to Murph's street. I hoped he was awake and sober enough to answer my questions. I kept a lookout for both Rasmussen and Agent Knight as I walked, but no sign of either man. Maybe Knight thought his warning last night had been enough to scare me off.

Sweat slicked my forehead and dripped under my armpits by the time I knocked on Murphy's door. No answer. I pressed my ear to the rough wood and listened, hearing the soft strains of the Andrew Sisters warbling the romantic "In Apple Blossom Time" on the radio within. *Someone* was home. I knocked again.

Inside, a woman swore a blue streak, followed by the door creaking open to reveal an extremely displeased Mrs. Murphy. She wore a thick layer of pancake makeup and a short, leg-baring, birthday-cake-pink playsuit with a winged collar, a wide belt, and silver buttons down the front. She'd tied a matching pink scarf around her neck. Her hair, like mine, seemed to have a mind of its own.

"What do you want?" she demanded.

Well good morning to you too. "Just stopped by to see how Murph is feeling today. Is he around?" I craned my neck to peek inside. No Murphy, just Dorella and an open trunk on the entryway floor behind her. Clothes spilled out, as if she'd been frantically digging inside, looking for something.

The door creaked again as she closed it a bit, cutting off my view. And drawing my attention to the scratches on her neck, not quite hidden by her scarf. Had those gashes been there last night?

"Brian's not here," she said.

"Do you know where I can find him?"

She tapped her foot, encased in a pink, wedged-heel sandal with a delicate ankle strap. "He slipped out at dawn. He does that most days. Goes down to Cobble Cove to fish." She hesitated, crinkling her forehead. Her pasty makeup caked in the furrows of her brow. "Funny, he should've been back long ago. He usually comes home before ten."

"Maybe the fishing is good today and he's still there, reeling them in."

She let out the most scornful *humph* ever humphed. "Brian? Sister, take my word for it, he's a lousy fisherman. Never catches a thing. Just fiddles about at the shore when he should be looking for a job. Leaves me to support us both with tips from my job at Manny's Fish Shack." She stiffened and glanced behind her again.

"Look, I don't know where that fool's got himself off to, and I don't have time to look for him. I've got to get to work, and I don't want to be late, so if you'll excuse me..."

She slammed the door in my face. Though every suspicious part of me wanted to un-slam that door and bust into the house and see what—or who—she was hiding, I restrained myself. I had to focus on finding Murph. I'd start with Cobble Cove.

I retreated down the rickety front steps and consulted my junior for directions, ignoring the ten more temporal texts added to the count. I set out, heading east up the street toward the ocean.

GPS tech had improved some since I'd left 2015, but not by much. After walking for half an hour and getting turned around and around down crooked, dead-end lanes that would make even the heartiest Boston driver weep, I reached my destination, a dirt parking lot stuffed with cars.

I steered toward a sign reading, *To Hovey Beach, The Prow, & Cobble Cove*. I followed a large family group carrying coolers and umbrellas through a gulley between two sand dunes. We emerged on a flat beach area that curved in a crescent a couple miles long, with the neighborhood of older homes where my inn was located on one end, and at the other, a tall, rocky cliff that jut out into the Atlantic like a majestic ship setting out to sea. If my GPS was to be believed, I'd find Cobble Cove down that way, just before the cliff.

I set out, weaving around a sea of almost exclusively white bodies, people laughing, sunbathing, building sandcastles, and generally baking in the midday sun. The men wore high-waist swim trunks cut really, really short and terrycloth shirts decorated with sailboats. Women were more fashionable in clingy one-piece swimsuits with flared skirts or the daring midriff-baring two-piece, popularized during the war when fabric was rationed.

Gulls swooped overhead and fought over any scrap of food they could scrounge. I stopped several times to shake sand out of my sandals. *Hot* sand, heated to broiling by the blazing sun. What I wouldn't have given for a pair of army boots and a tube of SPF 1000 sunscreen at the moment.

I kept moving. The sun beat down on me and my neck kinked from swiveling left to right looking for Murph.

Suddenly, I jerked to a halt. My pulse danced to a disco beat. There he was. Not Murphy or Rasmussen. *Him*. The man I didn't want to see, but fate had decreed I bump into with malicious frequency.

Sully.

8

—————

One glimpse of Sully lounging on a towel in the sand and my temperature skyrocketed to a dangerous degree.

He sat with one long, muscular leg stretched out, the other drawn up, his elbow resting on his knee. He wore one of those short-shorts bathing suits, his powerful thighs exposed. He'd just been in for a swim and beads of water dribbled down his back. The soft hairs on his broad chest were matted to his skin, his thick hair spiked up where he'd run a hand through it. A button-shaped scar—where a bullet had grazed him, I suspected—marred his solid upper arm, an inch below his tattoo.

The tattoo.

The one Sully had gotten drilled into his arm some-time after he'd met me, somewhere in his travels during the war. An image of an impossibly curvaceous woman with flowing dark hair, lounging in a come-hither pose and winking. A red, white, and blue ribbon curled around the busty babe's legs, with the words *A real piece of work* written in bold cursive.

The woman was me. Or a reasonable facsimile.

Sully stared out at the ocean, looking bored. Why shouldn't he be? He was out of place here with these newly minted suburbanites enjoying a fine Saturday at the shore. He was an action guy, not a lay in the sun and get his skin roasted to a fiery red guy. A jump off a South Boston pier into the oil-slicked Atlantic kind of guy. Then wrestle a couple of sharks into submission.

But *she* looked completely at home, sitting in a striped canvas beach chair sunk into the sand. Millie wore cat's eye sunglasses, and her legs went on for a hundred miles. Though dressed for swimming in a cute blue polka-dot one-piece with thin straps and a bra shaped like pointy rocket cones, she hadn't set foot in the water. Her dry swimsuit and blonde hair swept back in a regal knot told the tale.

She dabbed a finger to her tongue and turned the page of her book, graceful and fluid. Okay, she couldn't be all bad, or even half bad if she liked to read. And she had decent taste in reading material, *Brideshead Revisited*. In fact, Millie was a star in all ways, and if Sully didn't nail that down quick, there were plenty of fish on the beach who would be happy to step up.

He spotted me before I could discreetly back away and out of his life. He caught my gaze and held it for several seconds. Long enough to weaken my knees and rush heat to every pore in my body. Clearly, I hadn't forgotten what a simple look from him could do to me. Not for one second.

I'd lost the power of speech, but he hadn't. "Beryl," he

said, his voice lighting up before he caught himself and continued with a mildly interested, "What are you doing here?"

Millie shifted, looking at me over the rims of her sunglasses. If my sudden appearance here on the beach surprised her, she gave no clue. She had as impressive a poker face as my sergeant. No, not *my* sergeant. Her man. The sooner I got that through my thick head… Well, it wasn't my thick head I needed to worry about. My brain seemed to be catching on, but the rest of me lagged behind in the *don't you get it?* department. Sully wouldn't be lounging on the beach under a broiling sun if he didn't *want* to be here with her.

"Good morning, Miss Blue." Millie slipped a bookmark between the pages of her book and closed it. Her cool gaze skimmed me up and down. "Are you here to swim?"

I knew I should've asked her to call me Beryl, instead of that schoolmarmish Miss Blue. But I did not want to be Millie's friend. Not at all. I wished she wasn't here. I wished for a rogue wave to crash in and sweep her and her long, long legs out to sea.

Well, no I didn't, but I couldn't help the jealous pang that stung my heart.

"I left my bathing suit at home," I said, as sweetly as I could manage. "Much to my regret." I fanned my face with my hand. "It's wicked hot out here. Almost too hot."

"After the cold of the Bulge, I like the heat of the sun just fine," Sully said. He leaned back on his elbows, as if auditioning for Mr. July in a "hot guys on the beach" calendar and, *gah*, I wanted to jump him there and then.

"What trouble are you looking to get yourself into today, Beryl?"

I dragged my mind out of the bedroom and put it firmly on my task. "I'm looking for our friend Brian Murphy," I said, all businesslike. "Have you seen him?"

He sat up straight and fixed a keen gaze on me. "No. Is something wrong?"

Ever the cop, always on the job. "I don't think so," I said uncertainly, then spilled the rest in a rush. "His wife says he comes fishing down here at Cobble Cove every morning, but he's usually home by ten."

"Should we be worried?" he asked.

We. I heard it, and so did Millie. She stiffened, ever so slightly.

"Maybe," I said. "He's way overdue. After what he was talking about last night...?"

Our gazes locked for a hot moment. My every worry seemed to be reflected in Sully's eyes. Maybe Murph had been having so much fun fishing he'd lost track of the time. Maybe he'd gone for an unscheduled stroll. Or maybe Rasmussen and his temper had caught up to the guy somewhere between his house and Cobble Cove.

"Do you need my help?" Sully plucked a snowy white tee shirt off the towel and yanked it over his head before the question was out of his mouth. His tattoo disappeared under the sleeve.

I frowned. Seriously? He expected me to say yes, with her sitting there? Millie looked at me, her expression more than slightly put out. Hers eyes were a lot like mine, brown, soft, and soulful. The color of the root beer barrels Grandma Blue used to keep in bowls scattered about the house. Depression era candies I never saw my grandmother eat. Not once.

I doubted Sully had told Millie about me. Anything about me. But I knew she'd guessed. Probably the second she'd laid eyes on me. Well, she had no clue about the time-traveling stuff, but if Millie had taken more than a passing glance at that brown-eyed babe carved into Sully's arm, she must've put two and tattoo together.

"I certainly do *not* need your help," I said. With conviction. "You just relax. You two go ahead and enjoy your beach day."

He huffed out his cheeks, the man of action totally frustrated in his attempt to get in on the action. "Suit yourself," he said petulantly.

Millie made a little sound, almost inaudible with the noise of people talking, waves crashing, and seagulls squawking. "If it's important to find your friend, Tom, don't stay here on *my* account. I've got my book to keep me company."

And a dozen swimsuit clad wolves on the beach, eyeing her like she was lunch.

"Are you sure you don't mind, Mill? You know I want to help a fellow soldier in trouble."

First, please, Big Red, stop calling her Mill. She clearly hated it. Second, Millie minded. *Really* minded. Her body language said it all. Her mouth tightened and her body went as rigid as an old-fashioned straight razor.

"No, I don't mind," she said, a lie everyone on the beach except my big, clueless sergeant could hear. "You go ahead. Do you think you'll be gone long?"

Sully shook his head. "An hour, tops."

"Oh," she said in a small voice. "I suppose I shall

manage… this." She waved, indicating their gear, her chair and a couple of canvas bags. "You will be back to the hotel for lunch, won't you?"

I heard the chainsaw being revved up in that question, ready to let loose at his answer.

"Course I will." He stood and shook himself head to toe like a large English Mastiff, spraying water and sand in all directions and splattering a copy of Bill Mauldin's *At the Front* sitting on his towel. He snatched up his tan trousers and pulled them up over his bathing suit, then slipped his feet into a pair of comfy-looking brown loafers Mr. Rogers would envy.

I watched him get dressed, couldn't help it. With those steely thighs, muscular butt, and broad, rippling chest, he was built like a Mack Truck and as fluid as a panther. Excuse me a moment for objectifying him, but he really was the most beautiful of men. Even in that awful hat he scooped up and plunked onto his head.

He stepped toward me, buttoning what I guessed passed for a casual short-sleeve shirt in 1946, but he still looked like he was heading for the office.

"Did you forget something, Tom?" Millie's voice went brittle. She lightly tapped her cheek with her forefinger.

"See you at the hotel," he said, and bent to give her a quick peck, studiously avoiding looking my way.

"What part of I don't need your help didn't you get?" I said as we headed toward Cobble Cove, leaving Millie looking as woeful as a waif abandoned by her family.

"I'm not helping you." His gaze strafed the beach, searching for Murph. "I'm helping a fellow vet. And until I know what's what, I'll do anything I damn well please."

"Even if Millie doesn't want you to?"

His head snapped toward me. "What?" His left eyebrow shot up. "She told me to go with you."

"Oh, Sully, you just don't get it, do you? She wanted you to say no, Mill, I'll stay here and worship at your feet until my tender Irish skin turns as red as a cooked lobster and peels off and flies away. That's what she wanted you to say, you dunce. Not run off as fast as you could with another woman."

He growled in annoyance, sounding like bear with a thorn in its paw. Ten thorns, actually. How I missed that growl. And that wiggling eyebrow, so obnoxiously judgmental and sexy at the same time.

"I will never understand you dames if I live to be a hundred." He flashed me his patented scowl, tempered by a hint of affection. "Least of all *you*."

WE WALKED in silence for a short while, scouring the area for our missing friend. I put myself on double watch duty. In addition to looking for Murphy, I kept alert for threats to Sully. I mean, those sunbathers we passed could be packing heat. Or the leather-skinned man tossing a ball to his Jack Russell terrier could have stashed a knife in his swim trunks. Or a meteor could fall out of the sky and drop on Sully's head. Well, maybe not, but I feared fate had all kinds of fatal schemes up its bitchy sleeve, and I needed to be prepared.

"So... apparently you quit smoking?" I said to help me focus and dial down my panic.

"I guess I did." One side of his mouth quirked up. He didn't smile much, scowls were his go-to, and this wry tug of his lips was a new-to-me kind of grin. A sexy grin. "Some bossy girl encouraged me to quit. Hard to do, though. We got cigarettes in our rations, and there was nothing to do at the front but smoke and lose money playing cards." His expression darkened. "When we weren't getting shelled or shot at."

"I'm sorry," I murmured.

He met my eyes, his gaze probing and slightly amused. "Why are you sorry?"

"It's what people say, Sully." Actually, it was what *I* said. One of my many weaknesses. Shouldering the blame. For everything. Deep down, I even thought my parents' deaths were somehow my fault.

"Well, stop. I never met a girl who sorried as much as you."

"Well... I'm sorry." He laughed for the first time since I'd seen him again, a deep, rich, welcome sound. I wondered if Millie ever made him laugh. Then I thought of all kinds of other things Millie probably made him do and ran from the subject as fast as I could. "You quit smoking, and then you moved to Ballard Springs when you got home."

His eyebrow slid upward. "How'd you know that?" He lifted a hand. "Never mind. You future people probably have all my details in a file."

"Most of them. Why Ballard Springs? Of all the places in the world, why choose to settle down there? I mean, why not go back to South Boston, where you grew up?"

"Nothing to go home to. Pop passed in '43 right after I shipped out. Didn't hear for a couple months, not 'til I got my uncle's V-Mail saying the booze finally got the old bastard. Ma went before I got home." Pain and regret flashed across his face. "While I was *waiting* to come home."

Grief rose up and nearly swallowed me. "I'm so sor—" I bit back the word. "I mean, that's a tough break."

He shrugged, brushing it off. "There's no going back, so I looked forward. I demobbed at Camp Davis. Took off my uniform and put on my civvy duds. Caught a bus, hopped off for a hot pastrami when it stopped at Ballard Springs, and I never left." He glanced at me. "I had a good reason to stay. Pat, my brother, goes to school at Camp Davis, so we got a place in town. He's on the GI Bill. The state college set up a couple classrooms at the camp for the guys who didn't want to go to school at the main campus. Guess they'd feel like old men in the middle of all those college kids. We rent a three decker on Franklin Street."

My lips twitched. A three decker wasn't a sandwich, as any New Englander would know. Three decker, or triple decker, was a local term for a three-story building, with an apartment on each floor, built to house immigrants pouring into industrial cities at the turn of the century. Grandma Blue and I had lived in a three decker after my parents died, before she bought our little house, but I didn't remember much about the place, except the long, long climb up to the third floor.

"While Pat goes to school, you work as a cop," I said. "A fitting job for a guy who cares so much about people."

"You mean a guy who likes to tell folks what to do." He aimed another of those wry smiles my way and goose bumps rocketed down my spine. "Truth? I like my job. I like living in Ballard Springs. It's a fine city."

I couldn't help what I said next. Well, I *could* have

helped it, but for some reason I just loved to torture myself. "And that's where you met Millie."

He hesitated, an uncomfortable pause. "Yeah. She works as a secretary in an insurance company near the stationhouse. We met at a diner."

"Ooh, a meet cute." *Really, Beryl?* "Is it serious?" *Please shut up.* "Do I hear wedding bells in your future?" *Just. Stop. Talking.* "Do tell, Sully."

He very much did *not* want to tell. He grunted a grunt that begged me to drop it. I dropped it. I mean, why did I pick up the subject in the first place?

He pointed ahead, saying, "We're almost there." He increased his pace and I hurried to keep up with his long-legged strides.

The terrain sloped downward and sunbathers and people playing in the surf became sparser the further we walked. The waves pushed all kinds of debris up onto the sand. Seaweed littered the beach, along with driftwood, shells, and the beachcomber's treasure, sea glass, pieces of glass caught in the tide and worn smooth over time by the water. The dunes to our right grew steeper, freckled by rose bushes and clumps of tall, spiky grass with sharp looking blades.

We paused for breath. Sully surveyed the area like a general mapping out a battle plan. Intense and focused. Ahead, the land arced around a bend. We'd reached Cobble Cove, where a spurt of ocean formed a tidal estuary roughly forty feet wide. The rushing stream bisected the beach area and funneled toward the mouth of the river beyond.

Sully directed my gaze to the cliff I'd seen earlier,

further down, across the estuary. "The locals call that rise over there the Prow."

"Well, for obvious reasons." The rock face looked like the prow of a ship. A really, really tall ship, creeping up to the water's edge, about to be launched on its first ocean voyage. A winding path cut upward to the clifftop through the scrubby bushes and other vegetation that had managed to grow on the hill's rocky surface, an incline so steep my breath caught. An understandable reaction for a woman with a lifelong fear of heights.

"What's wrong?" Sully asked, studying me with a scowl.

I held back a sigh. I shouldn't be surprised Mr. Oblivious, who'd completely missed Millie's chainsaw glares and frosty side eyes, had suddenly become Joe Observant, able to pick up on my slightest change in moods. We'd always been in sync. One of the reasons Jake and Glo said they'd chosen to use Sully for my test. The main reason. We were compatible in all ways—rough childhoods, cynical humor, combative temperament, and chemistry. Lots and lots of chemistry of the explosive kind.

"Nothing's wrong," I said. He might be able to read me like a well-loved book, but I wasn't in the mood to talk about the plot right now. I cleverly redirected his scrutiny with, "What's that up there, in the trees?" I pointed to a concrete structure at the top of the cliff, a squat and square building with slits for windows just visible through the greenery.

"That's a lookout post. A coastal defense bunker. Some guys spent the whole war hunkered down in one of those. Keeping their eyes peeled, watching the coast for

U-Boats and other threats, while the rest of us were knee-deep in shit and bullets." His voice had dipped into bitter territory. "Nice work, if you can get it."

Our gazes connected and my belly flipped. I wished I could reach out and soothe that bitterness, to ease the pain and anger that still gripped him. I looked away. I could wish all I wanted, but I couldn't act. Once, I could have. But not now. He had Millie for that.

I focused on the strip of beach across the estuary at the bottom of the cliff. "Do you think Murph could've gone over there?"

"Could be a tough haul to get there. The water's not deep, but the tide's going out and the current is strong." He glanced up at the lookout post again then swung to the right, his gaze following the estuary's path toward the river bend in the near distance. "Let's go that way, maybe he's down there. If not, we'll double back to see if he's made his way home."

There was that *we* again. "If it comes to that, I can do it on my own," I said, hurrying to keep up with him. "You should probably get back to Millie."

That hurt look from last night flashed across his face. "Yeah. Probably should. I suspect she's gone back to the hotel by now and is waiting—"

He froze, staring straight ahead. His expression chilled me to the bone, despite the heat. I followed his gaze to the area just before the bend, bordered by a tall row of dunes. Sully had lasered in on something floating in the channel close to the water's edge. With a strangled curse, he took off down the beach at a speedy clip. I flew behind him as fast as my sand-filled shoes would allow.

Barely slowing when he got there, he whipped off his

hat and flung it down then splashed into the water. He moved at top speed over to a small figure floating face down. The pull of the tide was swift and would've dragged the body out to sea if not for the cluster of slick, coral-speckled rocks close to the water's edge that corralled the man like a fish in a net.

Gritting his teeth, Sully bent down and took the dead man by the shoulders. Bile rose in my throat as he carefully rolled the body over. I slapped my hand over my mouth to stifle a scream.

I stared into the lifeless face of Brian Murphy.

9

"Beryl, help me," Sully called, trying to drag Murphy's waterlogged body to the shore.

I kicked off my sandals and waded into chilly water up to my knees, soaking the bottom of my skirt. I fought the tide and the grasping current that threatened to knock me down as I moved toward Sully. I wrapped my hands around one of Murphy's sodden arms, Sully took the other and together we steered the body around the rocks to the shore, fighting the rushing tide all the way.

We both breathed heavily by the time we dragged the dead man up from the water and onto the beach, his small, fragile form soaking wet and laid out on the sand as if asleep.

"Son of a bitch," Sully bit off. A tic twitched in his cheek. The only signs of the turbulence I knew roiled within him. How many times during the war had he looked down like this at the body of a man he knew? With the same grief-stricken expression?

I moved in close beside him and touched his arm, the only comfort I could offer at the moment, seeing as how I engaged in copious trembling myself. Horror and shock had taken hold and I shivered uncontrollably.

"What do you think happened?" I asked, my teeth chattering. "Someone must have... I mean, Murph was a troubled man, but no way did he drown himself. Or just happen to fall in the water. Someone hurt him."

Sully squatted to examine the body. He carefully pulled down Murph's shirt collar, revealing purplish bruises around his neck. "Someone hurt him all right." He sat down on the sand, his eyes narrowed. "He's been strangled."

Strangled. A blunt word, stark and bleak. Utterly devastating.

I struggled to hold onto my breakfast. A clutching sense of unreality shot through me. My knees weakened and I dropped down on the ground next to Sully. Had Rasmussen brutally murdered Murphy? The man had a vicious temper, he seemed capable. Though, Agent Knight had mentioned he was hunting more than one jewel thief. Rasmussen could be the culprit, or the man with the scar on his face, or some others unknown, even Dorella.

"Jesus, is there no end to the killing?" Sully's voice deepened with rage and bitterness. "The poor sap made it through hell. He got back safe, only to be murdered at home. And for what? For some stinking gems?" He sucked in a breath and swung his gaze toward me. "Did you know this was gonna happen?"

"*No.* God no." I shrunk back, cut to the core at the accusing look in his eyes. "Look, I didn't come to this time to get mixed up in a murder or to play Nancy Drew, I came here to…" I hesitated. I'd already spilled Rasmussen's name. What would it hurt to give Sully some other details about my mission? Glo would be pissed, Devon would be double pissed, but it wasn't like the space-time continuum would implode. "I came here to find a guy going by the alias Fred Pattinson. He's a wanted man in my time period." Sort of. I wanted him to help me catch that other most wanted man, Bishop. "Did he have anything to do with…?" I flicked a glance at the dead man. "I don't know. If he did, I'll catch him and make sure he faces justice."

Sully weighed that a moment. "Faces justice? How? Kill him like that criminal you shot in Belgium?"

He meant when I'd blasted Jake with a cack, in December 1944, just before the Battle of the Bulge broke out. Moments before Sully had gone off to face the most horrendous battle of his life. He didn't know shooting Jake had been part of my live-action time cop test. He thought I'd really killed Jake.

"No," I muttered, burning with shame for deceiving him, for letting him believe that lie, and for the gazillion other lies I'd told him. "I'll bring him in. He'll get his day in court. Only, not in 1946."

"The local boys won't be happy if you collar their man, but I can accept that. As long as the killer is caught." A steely eyed determination settled over him. "To make sure he *is* caught, I'll help you find him."

I choked. *That* wasn't going to happen. No way would we team up like a buddy cop movie.

Sully stood and gazed down at the body. "Right now, we've got to call this into the local police. I saw a couple cottages close to the parking lot. One of them is sure to have a phone."

He shook sand off the legs of his wet pants, then reached down and helped me up. He did a quick scan of the area. The sun beat down on a small wooden building that looked like an outhouse without a door standing at the foot of the dunes. Nearby, a gang of very vocal seagulls had adopted an overturned rowboat.

Sully's gaze came back to Murphy's body, then to me. "I don't want to leave him here alone. One of us should stay."

I didn't hesitate. "You go make the call. I'll stay with him."

He gazed at me a moment and I thought he might argue, but he took my hand instead and squeezed gently. "You gonna be okay?"

I gave a weak smile. "I will. At least, I will once my teeth have stopped chattering. How about you?"

"I'll live." He ran his thumb over my knuckles, his skin warm and comforting against mine. His hair had dried from his earlier swim and the sun beamed down, turning the copper tangles to fire. Which he promptly doused by covering it with his hat he scooped up from the sand. "I'm glad you didn't know about Murph. It'd kill me to find out you knew and did nothing to stop it."

My belly went as hollow as an empty well. Could I have stopped it even if I'd known?

He released my hand then turned and strode up the beach. The seagulls gathered on the overturned rowboat squawked and flapped away as he closed in on their territory. He steered toward the narrow path and nimbly climbed up and over the dune. The battle-tested military man turned cop, on task and focused.

I wished I could be as cool and steady. Fear still pushed the blood through my veins at a furious pace. I stood there a few moments, trying to pull myself together, gazing out at the estuary. The pulsing stream rushed toward the ocean as the tide went out. A hot, humid wind had blown in, and dark clouds began to push across the sky, casting ominous shadows over the rocky surface of the cliff in the distance.

A long time later, I finally got up the courage to look at Murphy. *Really* look at him. Sand matted his hair, scrapes and small cuts marred his face. Abrasions from the rocks he'd bumped against in the water, or injuries inflicted before his murder? He wore fisherman's gear, beat-up rubber boots and a pair of thigh-high rubber waders covering dark green trousers underneath. His long-sleeve green shirt had come untucked, and the collar sagged open, revealing the bruises around his neck.

Cold unreality clutched me again. "I'm so sorry, Murph," I murmured, thinking of Sully's blistering words moments ago. Murphy had made it through a brutal war, only to be cruelly murdered in peacetime.

The question singed my mind again. Could I have stopped his murder if I'd known? Could I have used my resources and all of Alice's gazillion gigabytes of data to find out about his death? Shouldn't I have done everything in my power to prevent it?

Jake's voice murmured in my ear, echoed by Glo, cooling down my angry fire to a smoldering frustration. *Time doesn't work that way. The man's fate was fixed, his destiny set.* One of the finite rules of time. *The* rule. The one that Jake lived by and insisted I live by too. Brian Murphy would've died whether or not Beryl Blue stuck her nose into time's business and tried to stop it.

I brushed sticky, wet sand off my skirt, put on my sandals, and scanned the beach, wondering if I could find something that could give a clue or a hint to who had killed Murph. If I couldn't change his fate, perhaps I could give the man some closure. And assuage my own guilt. If only a little.

Taking note of the numerous indistinct footprints in the sand, I moved away from the water, up toward the dunes. I picked my way over beach litter, small rocks, broken shells, seaweed. I skirted regular litter, too, crumpled pages from a newspaper, cigarette butts, and the stubby end of a cigar. I poked my head inside the tiny house, saw nothing more than a sandy floor and a rough wooden bench for a fisherman to take a lunch break in a shady spot or shelter from a sudden storm.

My gaze fell on what had to be Murph's fishing gear, a metal tackle box and a fishing pole with a wooden reel and a tangled ball of line resting in the sand near the rowboat. Could that be the murder weapon? Fishing line was strong, hard to snap, and could do a lot of damage in a strangler's hands. Hopefully the local cops Sully had gone to alert could find out. I was clueless as to law enforcement's forensics capability in this time period. Did they even have a 1940s version of CSI?

The tackle box sat open. I peered inside at a cluttered pile of metal fishhooks, some netting, and dozens of greenish-gold lures shaped like fish, with creepy glass eyes. The sun came out from behind a cloud, warming

my back. A sunbeam flashed off the silver fishhooks—
and winked off something small and gold.

I bent down and slid the bit of gold out from under
one of the lures. A key. Not just any key. *The* key. The one
from the suitcase, with the engraved number sixty-three.
I picked it up and studied it. Too small to be a house key.
Perhaps it fit a safe deposit box or a mailbox.

I straightened. Could the answer be as simple as that?
Murph hadn't hidden the jewels under the mattress or in
some secret corner of his attic. He'd put them in a safe
deposit box in a bank. Clearly his killer didn't know that,
or they wouldn't have shut him up for good and left the
key behind.

Voices from beyond the dunes announced Sully's
return, with the police in tow. I closed my fist over the key.
I should put it back where I found it. Or... I shouldn't?
Whatever time and fate and the future wanted me to do
about the suitcase items, I guessed I'd figure that out
later.

For now, I slipped the key into my skirt pocket.

THINGS HAPPENED FAST AFTER THAT. So fast I barely had
time to watch for threats to Sully's safety. Though, who
would dare attack either of us, with so many policemen on
the scene? A bunch of cops swarmed the beach. Even
more surrounded the body. One man carried a collapsible
stretcher, another covered the corpse with a dark blanket.
I shuddered as Murph's ashen face disappeared from view.

One of the detectives, Lieutenant Gunderson, noticed

my distress and hustled Sully and me over the dunes to the parking area, where more cops wrangled the small crowd that had gathered, drawn by the sirens. Men smoking cigarettes, families who'd left the beach, some teenage boys, and mothers and their children with eyes as round as Frisbees gawked at the police vehicles and the hearse clustered in the lot.

I spotted a skinny Jimmy Stewart lookalike in the mob—Agent Knight. He signaled for me to come over with a jerk of his head.

"Beryl?" Sully said, nudging me.

"Hm? What? Oh."

I turned back to Sully and Lieutenant Gunderson, who was interviewing us about how and when we'd found the body. The lieutenant looked like he'd just stepped out of an old black-and-white movie in his pinstriped suit and fedora covering hair the color of straw. He repeated his question, asking what brought Sully and me down to Cobble Cove today.

"I was taking a stroll on the beach and ran into an old friend, Mr. Sullivan," I said, leaving out *why* I'd been taking a stroll to avoid further questions. "Sully decided to join me on my walk. We saw something in the water and went over to investigate."

I nailed Sully with a *back me up on this* look. His left eyebrow did all kinds of *are you kidding me?* gymnastics, but he confirmed my falsehood with a curt nod.

The lieutenant nodded too, asked us both where we were staying, then tucked his notebook and pencil into his breast pocket, signaling the end of the interview. Sully begged to differ. He peppered Gunderson with a dozen questions, most revolving around Murph's murder and the weapon used to strangle him.

Agent Knight waved to me again. I dropped a hasty "excuse me" Sully seemed too occupied with his interrogation to hear, then went to see what my G-Man friend wanted.

He'd moved to the edge of the crowd of onlookers. In his sunflower-yellow shirt and short yellow bathing suit that revealed every inch of his long, white legs, he looked like Sesame Street's Big Bird on summer vacation. He smelled like pepperoni pizza and another scent, faint and fleeting, but familiar. A smell I couldn't quite place.

"I thought I told you to leave town. I thought I told you to stay away from Murphy," he said, like an irate and extremely disappointed dad.

"You can't tell me what to do," was my petulant teenager's response.

He huffed impatiently, stopping short of telling me to go to my room *this instant.* "You're the most headstrong woman."

Was that supposed to be an insult? "Looks like you'll have to scratch Murphy off your list of jewel thieves. He's dead. Strangled."

He adopted a mournful expression. "I'm sorry. Truly."

I met his eyes with a challenging stare, wondering if he was as sorry as he claimed.

He shifted uncomfortably and looked away, sweeping his gaze over the row of police cars, coming to a stop on the hearse. "Do you know what happened?"

"I was hoping you would know. Or have some idea which of your suspects in the heist could've done it. Are you any closer to locating them?" I scanned his beach attire. "Or are you taking a vacation day?"

"I'm trying to blend in and not look like a policeman," he said quickly. "I heard Murphy was down at the cove and thought we could talk. Or some of his associates might show up." He cleared his throat. "Seems like one of them did."

"And...? Which one—?"

"Beryl?" Sully had finished grilling Gunderson and ambled up to us. "The lieutenant offered to give us a lift downtown when things wrap up here. We'll pick up some sandwiches and go back to my hotel. I bet Millie's hungry too."

The word *sandwich* ignited an uproar in my empty belly. The name *Millie* set off a different reaction in my heart. I'd nearly forgotten about her. Okay, I hadn't forgotten about her for a second, but with everything else going on, she'd slipped way, *way* down on my list of things to worry about. Top of the list should be ensuring Sully's safety. I'd tempted fate long enough.

I had to push him away. Had to remind him there was no *we*. Couldn't *be* a we. "I'm sorry, I can't join you. Agent Knight already offered to bring me back to my hotel."

To his credit, Knight barely blinked at my lie. Sully was equally stoic, but I caught his slight wince of disappointment.

"Agent Knight?" He studied the man intently, as if he planned to pick him out of a police lineup later.

Knight returned the favor, sizing Sully up with a cool gaze. Then he stuck out his hand. "Aloysius Knight, Army Criminal Investigations."

"Tom Sullivan, sergeant, Ballard Springs police." The

two men shook hands like opponents marking the end of a long feud. Frosty, stiff, but willing to let bygones be bygones. "Army CID? I read about you fellas in *Stars & Stripes*. You're a new division, the Army's very own detective bureau. Are you tracking the jewels?"

"He is," I said. "He was following us last night."

Sully's left eyebrow popped up. "Did you think Beryl stashed the loot in her pocketbook?"

Knight offered a scowl that could've prompted Sully to sue for copyright infringement. "I didn't know *what* to think," he said. "You were seen with my chief suspect in the robbery, and I've been out hunting for his accomplices." He glanced my way with a smirk. "Now that I've met Beryl, I know better. She's no lying thief."

Sully bristled. And though he had just cause to debate the lying part of that statement, he didn't argue the point. Instead, he tossed out a blunt, "Did you serve, Agent Knight?"

"Yes. I was in the MPs. How do you like living in Ballard Springs?"

Sully's eyes narrowed. Mine did too. Knight had done that answering a question with a question thing again, flipping the conversation away from himself.

"It's okay for a small town. Got a nice library."

A blush heated my cheeks and rushed all the way down to my toes at the affectionate note in Sully's voice. The library. My library that had become *our* library in 1943. The place where we'd fallen in love. Not that I'd known that at the time. The moment when my wild attraction for Sergeant Gruff and Sexy Sullivan had shifted to something more, something deeper, I'd fought it. Tooth and nail. Up until then, I'd run from that four-letter *L* word as if an army of angry ghosts chased me and I was determined not to be caught.

Until I was.

A mournful murmur passed over the crowd as several figures appeared in the distance at the top of the dunes. They made their way carefully down the steep, sandy hill, carrying the stretcher holding Murph's body, shrouded in a dark blanket. The somber procession quickly reached the parking lot, and the policemen steered their gruesome burden toward the hearse.

The crowd watched them pass in mournful silence, riveted to the horrific scene. Though my stomach twisted into knots, I couldn't look away either. Sully edged in next to me and took my hand.

The policemen gently slid the stretcher inside the hearse. As one of the men closed the door, another squad car rolled up. Dorella Murphy scrambled from the passenger seat. She'd draped a white cardigan over her shoulders but still wore her revealing clothes. They must have brought her here straight from work.

"Where is he?" she demanded of no one in particular, her frantic voice ringing out across the pavement. Her gaze lit on the hearse as it slowly rolled away, its tires crunching over sand and small stones. "What happened?"

A moment of indecision ended when Lieutenant Gunderson took her aside. He spoke softly, gesturing toward the dunes and Cobble Cove beyond. She shook her head in disbelief as he murmured his condolences.

"I want to see him," she wailed. "Take me to him."

Gunderson escorted her back to the squad car that had brought her here and tucked her inside like a breakable egg. A moment later, the young policeman behind the wheel steered across the lot, following the hearse. Dorella pressed her face to the window and aimed a steely look at Sully and me as the car puttered by. Sully and I exchanged glances. She seemed not quite as grief-stricken as she had just seconds earlier.

The crowd broke up after that, returning to the beach or heading to their own cars or on foot toward the nearest trolley stop.

"About that ride to your hotel?" Agent Knight said to me. "Are you ready to leave?"

I looked down at Sully's hand, still entwined with mine. "Give me a minute," I said, my voice shaky.

Knight nodded. "Of course."

Sully turned to me as Knight stepped away. He squeezed my hand. "Are you sure you can trust that guy? I heard CID recruits from the MPs, but he sure doesn't look like any military police I ever tangled with."

"Oh? You tangled with them a lot, did you?"

"On occasion. But don't change the subject. Something seems off about him." He watched Knight climb into a sleek, cherry-red car with lots of chrome and a large and slightly phallic hood ornament. "That's a Buick Roadmaster. Pretty fancy car for a government man. Mighty suspicious."

"Sully, would you quit worrying about me?"

"Why, is it a crime?"

"No. But you should know by now I can take care—"

"You can take care of yourself. I know. And if I ever forget, you remind me of it every second." His lips curved in a rueful smile before his usual scowl returned. "If ever there was a time to be on your guard, this is it. There's a murderer out there. He probably knows we were with Murph last night. He could be gunning for us. Until he's caught, it's not safe for you or me or any of us."

I shivered. I hadn't thought of that. Could Sully's fate be connected to Murph's murder? I didn't want to stick around and find out. "I'll be careful, I promise. Now…"

"Now it's goodbye."

He held my gaze and the world fell away. His fiery expression, full of need and a dose of heartbreak, matched my own aching emotions. We still held hands, neither of us willing to let go. Neither of us ready. A mob of butterflies danced in my stomach. I wanted so, so desperately to kiss him. One last kiss before we parted forever. I was all but certain he wanted the same thing.

"Beryl," he said, a pleading murmur. "Will you tell me why you keep—"

Honk. Knight's car horn bleated, the sound blasting across the lot. We both jumped. The electric moment fizzled. Whatever Sully had been about to say died on his lips, cut off by a frustrated curse. I silently thanked that G-Man for breaking us apart. I mean, what was I thinking? Lingering here, willing Sully to kiss me. Tempting fate. Delaying my parting from him and putting him at risk.

Though it took all I had, I unlaced my hand from his. "I've got to go," I said, no more than a whisper.

He straightened and took a step back. With a smile that held little warmth, he said, "Goodbye, Beryl Blue."

Blinking back tears, I turned away and didn't look back.

10

———

My chauffeur drove as slow as Grandma Blue had at night, after her eyes began to fail. Except, my grandmother's car wasn't nearly as nice as this one. She'd spent every dime of her meager nurse's pay to keep me clothed and fed when I was a kid and could only afford to drive a beat-up old Ford Taurus that groaned when it sped up and griped when it slowed down. It also belched smoke like a dragon with an upset tummy. It had sold for parts after Grandma died, along with our little bungalow she'd managed to scrape up a down payment for.

This car neither groaned nor griped. It purred like a well-fed cat. A brand-new cat, complete with new car smell and immaculately clean interior. No seatbelts, which kind of freaked me out, but lots of other comforts. Cushy seats, lots of leg room, and a round analog clock installed in the dashboard next to the radio, which played "I'll Walk Alone" at a low volume. A melancholy song from the war years about separated lovers pining for one another but knowing fate and circumstance would keep them apart, probably forever.

Just the song I did *not* want to hear at the moment.

"What's on your mind, Beryl?"

I glanced at Agent Knight, hunched over the steering wheel, gripping it tightly. In his cheesy beach attire, he didn't quite fit in this car's classy interior. He didn't seem to fit anywhere, to be honest.

"I'm thinking this is a pretty sweet ride for a government man," I said, echoing Sully's words, and his suspicions.

Knight chuckled. "Rein in your taxpayer's outrage. It's a rental. I'll turn it in when my work here is done."

"Yeah, about that work." I shifted, facing him. "With Brian Murphy gone, how will you find your other jewel thieves now?" And more important, how would *I* find Rasmussen. Agent Knight was my only connection now.

"I don't know. I'm making it up as I go along."

"Join the club. That's pretty much been the story of my life."

He chuckled again, followed by a frustrated sigh. "I've been on this case for a long time. A *long* time. It's worn me down. There's a lot of pressure from above to nab my target. I've gotten bullseye close to him too many times to count, but he always slips away."

"Him? You're talking about Ras—" I caught myself, hoping Knight hadn't picked up on my bobble. "I mean Pattinson. Fred Pattinson. The head jewel thief. The ringleader. Tell me what you know about him, maybe I can help you find him."

He shot down that suggestion with an alarmed snort. "You know, for a girl visiting her sick auntie at the shore, you sure are anxious to get yourself mixed up with a gang of thieves."

Was he serious? "Well, this *girl* might not be so curious if a sad little guy with wicked PTSD she met yesterday didn't get strangled while he was out fishing a day later. So, please, if you don't mind, be a little honest with me instead of dancing around like a G-Man Fred Astaire."

A wistful smile softened his features. "Beryl, you've got a lot of ginger, and twice as much courage, but I can't involve you. You said it yourself. A man is dead. I'm convinced Mr. Pattinson is responsible, though I have no proof. Nonetheless, it's *my* responsibility to find him, not yours. I can't let you put yourself in danger. I'd never forgive myself if you got hurt. My superiors at the division would never forgive me, either. I don't care if it upsets you, but I will *not* let you get mixed up in this case."

Upset? Upset was too mild a word for the feelings boiling within me. My mission had gone to hell. The memory of Murphy's lifeless body stretched out on the sand had been seared into my brain. I'd just said goodbye to the man I loved for the second time in the last twenty-four hours without a single kiss to send me on my way. And now, Agent Knight-not-in-shining-armor, my only lead to Rasmussen, had basically just patted me on the head and told me to keep my nose out of important men's business.

I folded my arms across my chest. "I'm very disappointed in you."

"Disappointed is better than dead, young lady. Which is what could happen if I let you get within fifty feet of a killer." He took his eyes off the road to look at me, his expression curious, and a little sad. His gaze dipped to my wrist. "That's an interesting watch you're wearing. An unusual style."

I tensed, though really, how could he have the slightest inkling what the junior really was? I said the first thing that popped into my head. "It's a family heirloom. It was my mother's."

Something unsettled flashed in his eyes. "Your mother's," he echoed, turning his attention back to the road. "From the sound of your voice, I take it she's gone?"

I nodded. "Long ago." Grief bubbled up and joined the rest of the emotions having a pity party in my brain.

He stared straight ahead, something tormented and ashamed in his expression, before offering a mournful, "I'm sorry."

Unexpected tears gathered in my eyes. Well, maybe expected, after everything that had happened since opening that suitcase only a day and a half ago. I thought of what Sully had said about the words, *I'm sorry*. Two words people say to get through a moment, sometimes sincere and welcome, sometimes not, but always there. Whatever Knight's intention, his sorrowful sentiment threatened to break the somewhat fragile dam holding back the emotions I fought so hard to keep in check.

"Stop," I suddenly cried, startling him—and myself. "Here's my hotel."

He pulled up to an open spot at the curb in front of a svelte and elegant brick building called City Hotel.

"Thanks for the lift," I choked out. No thanks for the trip down memory lane.

"Wait." He stopped me with a touch on my arm as I opened the door and tried to slide out of the seat. "Stay away from Pattinson. I don't need your help. I can catch him, and I *will* catch him. I'll catch all of them. Go home and let me do my job."

Fear invaded his expression and strained his voice. It touched me that this odd little man I barely knew would worry so much about my safety.

I murmured something placating but vague—I could hardly promise to stay away from Rasmussen when he was the very reason for my visit to this decade—then slipped out of the car.

The door closed with a soft click as only an expensive car could. I stepped toward the hotel's revolving door entrance, watching over my shoulder until the Roadmaster glided away. I hoped this would be my last encounter with Agent Aloysius Knight. I hoped I could find Rasmussen before he did.

And most of all, I hoped I could put the memories and emotions and Sully behind me and get the hell out of this town, this year, and this century as soon as possible. If not sooner.

I STOOD a moment outside the City Hotel, trying to decide my next move. The door to the *Howard Johnson's* restaurant next door opened and the smell of French fries and fresh coffee wafted out. My stomach rioted, adding physical distress to my mental chaos, and though I wanted to answer hunger's call, I figured I'd better return to the inn instead. I needed a quiet space to regroup and make a plan of action. And grab a bite to eat.

I started down the sidewalk toward a trolley stop a

couple of blocks away. I glanced at my junior. The pulsing green light at the bottom of the tiny screen announced a million more messages needing my attention. Maybe I'd finally check in with Jake, and ask for help with my Rasmussen problem, which I hated to do. The *last* thing I wanted to do.

The hazy sun had lowered in the sky and the air had grown oppressively humid and much stickier here in the center of town, away from the ocean's somewhat cooling breeze. The buildings I passed were a mix of old and new, some tall, some not. Cars jammed the street, but foot traffic was light, with only a fraction of the pedestrians who'd packed the sidewalk last night. People had most likely been driven indoors or to the beaches by the heat.

Half a block ahead, the jingle of bells cut through the traffic noise as a deli door popped open. A man wearing an ugly hat and clutching a bag of what I guessed were sandwiches stepped out. My stomach both clenched and pirouetted. Then sank all the way to my feet.

Sully.

He turned and strode in my direction. Because of course. Fate wouldn't have it any other way but to throw us together, time and time again.

Hoping he hadn't seen me, I made to dart to the other side of the street before our paths crossed, when a pair of steely arms suddenly clamped around me. A brawny man who smelled of onions and cheap cigars pulled me into an iron grip, crushing my ribs and pinning my arms to my sides. I struggled as he dragged me sideways into a cool, shadowy alley between two brick buildings.

My desperate hope that Sully hadn't spotted me was dashed a nanosecond later, as his broad-shouldered silhouette filled the alley opening. With a growl of rage, he flung his sandwich bag to the ground and his hat flew off as he bombed into the passageway—and into the waiting arms of two thick-necked brutes with beefy biceps that practically split the seams of their suitcoats.

The next moments raced by in a terrifying blur. I fought my captor, stomping down on his foot with as much force as I could muster then kicking back, bashing his shins. He groused in pain but did not loosen his firm hold. Sully had better luck than me. He shook free of the men who'd grabbed him and went on the attack. The sound of fists crunching against bone filled the alley, along with vile curses that would make every sailor in the US Navy blush.

I finally got enough leverage against my opponent to jerk back in a reverse head butt and smack the guy in the chin. He shrieked and loosened his grip. I whirled and delivered a knuckle pop to his throat. He gagged and choked but before I could get away, he slammed me against the wall. My face scraped against the bricks, and I yelped in pain.

"Beryl!" Sully cried.

The other men took advantage of the distraction and pounced. Weak and dizzy from kissing the wall, I watched helplessly as one of the goons pinned Sully's arms behind him while the other beat him mercilessly with rapid blows to the gut and face, as if he brutalized a punching bag at the gym. Sully's head snapped from left to right and he coughed and wheezed, the wind knocked out of him.

"That's enough!" a man cried, his voice echoing off the alley walls.

The goons instantly ceased their pummeling. They held Sully in place as the man who'd ordered them to stop strolled toward us. I recognized him right away—the guy who'd been with Rasmussen and Murphy outside the Slipknot. Not nearly as large and brawny as the other men, he had a bulldog build, ears like jug handles, and a deep scar that sliced his face from ear to chin.

He closed in on Sully and examined him from head to toe.

Sully studied him right back. "Whoever you are, you sure picked a hell of a way to say hello," he said, panting and winded, but calm, his voice edged with danger. He jerked his head toward the goon holding me. "That's no way to treat a lady."

Scarface gave a grim smile. "She's fine, and she'll stay that way. *If* you tell me what I want to know." He spoke in a gravelly growl, like Edward G. Robinson or one of those tough guys who menace the hero in all those old Hollywood gangster films. "I understand you been spending time with Murphy." He looked to me then back to Sully. "What did he say to you?"

Sully's expression flashed disdain. "He can't say anything now. He's at the morgue. He was murdered."

The man barely blinked at this breaking news. "Too bad. Where's the jewels?" he demanded. Sully shrugged. Scarface frowned. "So, it's gonna be that way, huh, pal?"

He snatched a switchblade right out of *West Side Story* out of his coat pocket. A flick of his wrist and the knife snapped open, pointed at Sully's jugular.

I nearly peed my pants, but Big Red didn't flinch. He looked the man in the eye. "Get that thing the hell out of my face."

Scarface let loose a stream of spit that splashed between Sully's feet. "Brave fella." He glared my way. "Let's see if your girlfriend will be more chatty."

Sully's posture went as hard as steel, and he seemed to grow muscles on his muscles. He shook off the men holding him as if they were puny flies and charged at Scarface.

And the switchblade.

11

---

hit. This was it. The warnings and vague predictions come true. Sully would be cut to pieces, protecting me. Fate's ironic bitchiness on full display.

Not on my watch.

Fueled by anger and desperation, I ripped out of my captor's hold and threw myself between Sully and the knife.

"Wait," I cried and flung out my arms like a traffic cop trying to halt a head-on collision. "Wait, wait, *wait*! I know where the jewels are."

Sully jerked to a halt and glared at me. I glared back. A lie. Another lie, but a tiny one compared to some of the whoppers I'd told in my time cop career. Most of them to him. But to save his life, I'd say anything.

Scarface's grip on the knife tightened. "Why should I believe you, girly?"

"Why shouldn't you believe me?" Fake confidence. False courage. Inside I trembled and shook and seriously considered throwing up. "Murph told me where to find them before he died."

"She's telling the truth," Sully put in. His voice held conviction, but his eyebrow expressed his displeasure. In fact, it had gone into convulsions the second I'd claimed to have the jewels. "*We* know where to find them."

Scarface's skeptical gaze jumped between us. "I think you and your boyfriend are bluffing."

"First of all, his name is Sully. Secondly, he's not my boyfriend."

"Could've fooled me."

Did that guy just smirk at me? And then wink? *Ugh.* "And thirdly, I *never* bluff." Except for right now, and every minute of the day.

He eyeballed me for several tense seconds before he lowered the knife. Much to my relief. "Okay, you got the loot. Where is it?" he demanded.

"In a safe place. I'll hand everything over to you, but I want to speak to Fred Pattinson first."

He narrowed one eye. "What for?"

Fear shut down my brain and I couldn't come up with a plausible answer, so I settled for something evasive but kind of the truth. "It's personal, between Mr. Pattinson and me."

Scarface's gaze practically painted the Sistine Chapel on my body as it brushed over me, taking in every curve and curl of my hair. His puffy lips spread in a lewd grin. "Personal? I *bet* it is."

His minions chortled and elbowed each other in the ribs. Sully growled and threatened to Hulk out again. I kept my cool and kept my eyes on the man with the scar.

"What does it matter why I want to see him? That's *my* business, not yours."

"Suppose I agree, what's to keep you from blowing town the second I let you and your boyfriend go?"

"I'm not going anywhere. Not until I see Pattinson." I let that sink in before adding, "Do we have a deal? The location of the jewels for a meeting with your boss. Take it or leave it."

He smiled. Not a nice smile. More like calculating exactly how he was going to screw me over. "Yeah, you got a deal." He tucked the knife away then dug a matchbook out of his breast pocket. "Here. My cousin has a beer hall over on Fourth Street, a place called Chaisson's. Be there by nine tonight. Bring the jewels."

He thrust the matchbook into my hand. I didn't even have to look at it to know it was the same one from the suitcase. I was beginning to think a *ding!* should sound, like when you get a correct answer in a game show, each time another item from the suitcase made its 1946 debut.

"I'm warning you, lady, no cops, nothing shady." He nodded to the goon who'd been using Sully as a punching bag. "Tony, show them I mean business."

Grinning, Tony sucker punched Sully in the gut. He gurgled in pain and doubled over. One of the other men kicked him and knocked him to the ground with a thud.

Scarface snickered. "Pull a fast one, and your boyfriend gets more of the same." He pinched my cheek like a creepy uncle and lumbered away. The rest of the cast of the *Sopranos* trailed behind him.

I shoved the matchbook into my pocket with the key and crouched beside Sully as soon as they were gone. "Are you okay?"

He sat up, rubbing his chin, his eyes blazing. "Why did you do that? Jesus, Beryl, you could've been killed. Jesus."

"That's a fine way to show your gratitude for saving your life."

He hauled himself to his feet, somewhat unsteadily. I didn't offer to help. He-man Sullivan would only shrug me off. "I had the situation in hand."

"Oh yes, a knife in your face and a couple brutes beating you senseless."

"What? I could take them. Two against one's my favorite odds." He grinned. "You did pretty good yourself." His smile faded, turning to concern in an instant. "Hey, you're trembling."

Noticed that, had he? "Well, I just had a switchblade stuck in my face." In Sully's face, actually. Wicked close. The thought made me tremble more. "That doesn't happen every day, you know."

Usually, *I* was the one shoving a weapon into someone's face. Pulling the trigger too. I'd fired my zapper at a dozen time runners and temporal troublemakers with barely a blip to my emotional equilibrium. But this? A real and present danger to Sully's life had left me with a serious bout of post-trauma tremors.

He took my arm and guided me the few short steps to the wall. He settled me gently against the cool bricks like a delicate teacup. "There. Catch your breath," he said, his voice a tender rumble.

I gave him a rueful smile. "Some time cop I am. I guess I'm not as tough as I thought." Or pretended to be. "But you, you were as solid as the Rock of Gibraltar."

"Not true. I was scared. Still scared. The jitters will

catch up to me, tonight or tomorrow. In the quiet time." He leaned his shoulder against the wall and faced me, his expression careworn. "I'd rather that than be like some of the guys I served with. They faced the enemy without a blink. They were as cold and hard as Plymouth Rock. Dead inside. No hope, nothing left of what they used to be. I prayed I wouldn't end up like that." He expelled a heavy breath. "I prefer sometimes getting the shakes to being like them."

My heart wrenched. I knew even just admitting that had cost him a lot. "Sully, I..." He met my gaze, both eyebrows rising expectantly. "I-I've got to go."

"No. This battle just escalated to full-out war. We need to stay together. There's safety in numbers."

"Not in this case."

He frowned. "What does that mean?"

"It means..." My belly twisted. I swallowed, terrified of what I was about to do. Jake would pop a blood vessel. Steam would shoot out of Glo's ears. But I had to tell him. *Needed* to. Of all the shitty rules Time Scope had set in place, not being able to tell Sully about the threat to his future was the shittiest. But his dogged determination to play my bodyguard frightened me even more. Enough to say to hell with the rules and Jake's lectures and the risk of creating a paradox and everything else.

He needed to know. He *deserved* to know.

"Okay, this is important and really big." I turned to face him. "Something that terrifies me more than anything in the world. It's something about the future. *Your* future, I mean. And it's pretty bad."

He plastered on his poker face and stood at full attention. "Go on."

I tamped down my nerves. "Sometime in the near future, I don't know when, it could be soon or not so soon, though soon is a relative term and—"

"Spit it out, Beryl."

I took a deep breath and looked him straight in those wise and beautiful blue eyes. "You're going to die, Sully. Protecting me. We don't know how or when. Sometime in the post-war years. The information's fuzzy, but something's going to happen when we're together and you're going to save me. When you do that, you'll die." I said that last part in a whisper, as if lowering my voice would make the fact less real.

His gaze on me softened. "Is that why you've been giving me the bum's rush since we met up again? I thought you didn't want me around anymore."

"Oh no. No, no, no. I lov— I mean, I just don't want to be the cause of your death. Could be a few years from now. Could be tonight." My voice hitched up to a squeak of panic. "As long as I'm with you, you're in danger."

"Don't." He put a finger to my lips. "I'm scared to die. Any sane man would be. But if I learned anything over these last years, it's if your number's up, your number's up. Can't change that." One side of his mouth tugged upward. "And if I gotta go, saving you isn't the worst way to do it."

My belly flip-flopped. That didn't go at all as I had planned. "Oh, Sully. *What* am I going to do with you?"

He reached out and tucked a wayward lock of my hair behind my ear then smoothed a finger over the scrapes on my cheek, a light touch I barely felt yet seared me down to my core.

"What am I gonna do about *you*?" he said, his voice a hoarse whisper.

I shivered, and it wasn't from the adrenaline of fear. Well, maybe a little of that still lingered, but mostly from Sully, his closeness, his warmth hugging me, the intensity in his voice and the deep, consuming way his gaze held mine. Intense emotions galloped across his face. Frustration, longing, need, desire. Everything I felt too. My pulse raced and my blood rushed through my veins like a thoroughbred sprinting toward the finish in the Kentucky Derby.

The natural thing happened next. He bent his head, I tipped mine back, and we joined together in a kiss.

His warm lips claimed mine. Familiar yet different. More hungry, more desperate, a heat matched by my own lips as I gave my all to him. This was the kiss I'd wanted since the moment I'd seen him and with every heartbeat since. The kiss he'd wanted too. I knew that. I'd felt it simmering between us every second we'd been together. The kiss we'd been avoiding but was as inevitable and as glorious and beautiful as a summer sunrise.

He pulled me fully into his embrace and everything fled my mind. Millie, Scarface and his gangsters, Murph, and the jewels. Rasmussen and 1946 winked from existence. Jake too. Nothing and no one mattered except *us*. Here, now. Embracing each other, embracing the moment in a blistering, all-consuming, toe-curling kiss.

We parted for a brief moment and smiled into each other's eyes, then I cupped his chin and steered his lips to mine once more. He pulled me close and pressed me against the wall, kissing me with ferocious abandon. I returned fire with equal need. His tongue staked a claim on my mouth that ignited a blaze in every nook and cranny of my body. My skin tingled and sparks flew through my veins like shooting stars.

I kissed him with all the conviction in my heart, propelled by that four-letter word I'd once run away from as if all the beasts of the underworld chased after me. *Love.* I loved this man. Hard. I loved him so hard it stole my breath. It made me dizzy and giddy and angry and heartbroken all at the same time. I loved him and always would.

The *bang* of a passing car backfiring echoed off the alley walls and we broke apart. I came back down to earth with a crash. Sully released me from his embrace. His hands settled on my waist, and he moved me away from him as if tucking away a precious memory.

"Beryl," he said, with finality, but no regret.

"I know," I said with finality, too, and a whole truck full of regret. If only love was enough. The other *if onlys* that had haunted me since I'd fallen for Sully back in 1943 got in the way. If only things were different. If only we could be together. If only we could be happy.

I shoved every emotion and thought deep into a mental suitcase and closed the lid. I'd unpack all of that later. When the mission was done. When I was back in my time and Sully was safe in his. With Millie.

Where he belonged.

12

———

We made our way back down the alley, finding a somewhat mangled bag of sandwiches near the opening, along with Sully's Stetson. I considered kicking the thing into the gutter where it belonged but bent to scoop it up instead, handing it to him along with the bag.

"C'mon," he said, putting the hat on then tipping his head in a westerly direction. "We have a lot to talk about."

"Talk about what?" Not the kiss. I had a feeling talking about the kiss might lead to more kissing, so a good idea to avoid the subject.

"Talk about who killed Murph, and our plan is for tonight. Come with me to the hotel."

He was serious. And completely loopy if he thought Millie would be hunky dory if he brought an unexpected guest home for lunch. Not just any guest. The woman he'd abandoned her on the beach to run off with. The woman he planned to run off with again, to confront a gang of jewel thieves.

"Uh, no, Sully, you're not going with me tonight."

"The hell I am. I'm a cop. A man's been murdered. I am not passing up the chance to look his killer in the eye."

"Didn't you hear what I said earlier? It's too dangerous for us to be together." In more ways than one, as I'd just learned from that heated clinch.

"I heard. A vague warning of an uncertain doom." He scowled. "How do you know you didn't just stop that prediction cold by stepping in front of the knife?"

He had a point. Had my rash action changed his fate? Could it be as simple as that? "I don't know. Fate's a demanding beast. It will find some way to get what it wants."

"Not if we know to be on the lookout for it."

"Sully, please—"

"Beryl, do you remember back in Ballard Springs when you told me that Jake fella was after me? You wanted me to run and hide."

"I remember." I flushed with warmth as the moment came back to me. Sully's fire, his bullish protectiveness that had kindled a fire in me that had never really gone out. Never would go out. "I also remember you strutting out into the street, daring the boogeyman to come and get you."

His eyebrow danced in amusement. "The plan worked, didn't it? We got him in the end."

He'd conveniently forgotten the long, treacherous road we'd taken to get to the end of that drama. And, though we didn't know it at the time, Sully had never really been in danger. This time was different.

"Beryl..." His voice shifted into his specialty whipped

butter persuasive mode. "You know me. You know I don't hide from trouble or run away from what scares me. I face it, and I know you have the strength to face it too. There's a killer out there and the way I see it, we're both at risk. I learned something besides how to kill and never volunteer for anything in the Army. I also learned you have to watch each other's backs. You need me and I need you. We'll work together, find your man and Murph's killer too. And kick fate in the teeth should it drop by to visit."

I searched his face. His cheeks had reddened during his little speech, his breath puffed like a steam engine, and his sapphire eyes sparkled with an eager gleam. An entire flock of butterflies roared into my belly, flapping in excitement and desire, each of them begging for a repeat of that kiss. I squashed every last one of them.

"I suppose you'd just tag along behind me if I put my foot down and say no?"

His eyes crinkled in a smile. "Why should you get to have all the fun?"

Oh, Thomas Sullivan, thy middle name should be Mule, as in as stubborn as one of those ornery creatures.

"All right. I know when the battle is lost." I'd seen it in his eyes, heard it in the grit of determination in his voice. Whether it was facing down an alleged time-traveling assassin in the dimpled form of Jake Tyson or leading his men into battle, Sully was up to the challenge, and the risk, of taking on the danger head-on. "I might need your muscles anyway."

A wolfish gleam of satisfaction lit his face, his *I won* expression I both loved and loathed. He shifted the sandwich bag from one arm to the other and we set off toward his hotel.

And Millie. A different kind of challenge.

———

"Tell me more about this fella you're after," Sully said, after we walked in silence a few moments. "Did he kill someone in your time, and they sent you here to get him?"

The usual *it's classified* response popped into my mind, but I pushed it aside. I'd already violated company rules in a million ways, already lost my shot at time cop of the year, might as well go all the way. "He's important. To me in particular. He might know how to find the man who killed my parents."

"Killed your folks? I thought you said they died in a car accident."

"I thought so too, until I learned the truth." Hopefully the truth. Not that I thought Jake and Glo were lying to me, but both were quite skilled in avoiding the facts. Especially Jake. "A man named Oliver Bishop killed them. Niels Rasmussen, the guy calling himself Pattinson here, might have a clue how I can find him."

I told him what little I knew about both Bishop and Rasmussen, including a brief recap of my time skipper's vicious attack on Murphy at the Slipknot last night.

Sully grunted. "Sounds like a damned bully. Like that murderous gink you took down in Belgium." His expression turned confused. "What gives? I thought you said when you shot that man all that was done. I thought killers from the future would stay put."

We'd come full circle, back to my alleged shooting of Jake. I hated that Sully thought I'd killed Jake but didn't see any way out of that bit of confusion without a long explanation that would probably make his head explode. And itch to get his hands on Jake, Glo, and anyone else involved in the plan to trick me like that.

"Well, this is one killer I didn't know about," I said quickly. "Plus, we can't be sure Rasmussen *is* a killer, despite Agent Knight's suspicion. For all we know, Mr. Scarface did the deed. He didn't bat an eye when you said Murphy was dead."

"Could've been one of his bully friends." He touched a reddish spot on his chin then leveled a glare at me. "That fella who banged up your face better hope I never see him again."

Hyperbole, I hoped. For my attacker's sake. "We can't leave Mrs. Murphy off our suspect list."

Sully tugged his ear. "I don't know. Murph was a bantamweight, but it takes a lot of strength to strangle a fella, no matter what the weapon."

"Don't be getting sexist on me. Dorella could've done it. Of all people, Murph would probably let her get close enough that she could. She was acting weird when I saw her at her house earlier, and she had some scratches on her neck, like she'd been in a fight." Scratches she'd tried to hide with a scarf. "You heard her last night. Each time Murph brought up the jewels, she changed the subject. Plus, there wasn't much love lost between the couple."

Sully kicked that around a moment. "She could've been in on the heist, but to kill him? I don't know. She seemed awful wrecked to find out her husband bought the farm."

"Or she's a good actress." I gave him a curious side glance. "What about Lieutenant Gunderson? You were grilling him pretty hard. Did you find out anything from him?"

"A few things, not much else. He's damned untalkative."

"Even to a man as gentle and persuasive as you? I'm shocked." Sully responded with a profoundly put out expression. "Well, he probably doesn't want a bossy sergeant out of his jurisdiction muscling his way into his investigation."

His eyebrow expressed his dissent, but he said no more as we'd reached his hotel, a sprawling, four-story wood structure with a peaked roof and green awnings over each window that flapped in the humid breeze. A vintage and possibly haunted place, with *Point Bailey Inn* painted in gold leaf over the front entrance.

The revolving door spun us both out into a lobby as homey and comfortable as the inn where I was staying, with one important difference. Air conditioning. Cool air enveloped me like a blanket, raising goose bumps on my arms.

"Good afternoon," the bellman on duty said, rushing over. His eyes popped when he took in our disheveled appearance, especially Sully. With that Stetson pulled low on his brow, he looked as bruised and battered as an old west bandit after the posse had caught up with him. "Is everything all right, Mr. Sullivan?"

"We're fine," Sully said, a peppy declaration that did a lot of work, considering my current state of mind. Still jumpy after our switchblade close encounter, still reeling from that kiss, still frustrated at Sully's determination to stick to me like a burr. A tall, sexy burr, but a nuisance, nonetheless. Topping it all was the tension building as we left the bellman behind and made our way up a wide flight of stairs to the second floor.

And closer to Millie.

We walked down a cool and carpeted hallway to room 203, followed by Frank Sinatra crooning the romantic tune, "Sunday, Monday, or Always" from a radio in a nearby room. Sully shifted the sandwich bag and dug through his pockets with his free hand until he found an old-fashioned skeleton key.

My knees knocked in anticipation as he opened the door and we entered a spacious room with an air conditioner madly clanking out cool air in one window and a view of the city's main boulevard out the other. Sparsely furnished, with a small, round table and two chairs in front of one of the windows, a tallboy bureau against the wall between a closet and the open bathroom door, and against the other wall...

Well, something surprising. I'd expected, no dreaded, to walk into Sully and Millie's love nest and see a heart shaped bed with oh-so-sexy satin sheets and rose petals strewn about. Imagine my surprise to find a pair of ordinary twin beds separated by a stout nightstand, and each covered with an embroidered quilt as sexy as Grandma Blue's old housecoat.

Sully followed my gaze. "I asked for separate beds." He took off his hat and tossed it onto the bureau. "To protect her. I sleep a little rough sometimes."

Meaning, he thrashed about at night, reliving the war in his dreams. A bleak statement that cut me to the core. "I'm sorry," I murmured, longing to take his hand.

To tug him into my arms and hold him and never let go.

"It's about time, Tom," came from inside the bathroom and we jumped apart. Millie emerged, showered, fresh, smelling of perfume and a hint of gin. She'd traded in her bathing suit for a baby blue dress with a below-the-knee A-line skirt and a narrow belt cinched around her slim waist. Her golden hair shone from a recent brushing. "I was beginning to think I'd been abandoned—"

She stopped short, seeing me. Seeing us. Her bewildered gaze popped back and forth between us. "My gosh, what on earth happened to you?"

Sully's gaze flicked toward me. I shuffled my feet. Couldn't she tell what had happened? I mean, the kiss hung over us, and between us, and all around. Surely she could feel it.

He cleared his throat. "Yeah, sorry, Mill. We ran into some... trouble on the beach and lost track of time. I asked Beryl to join us for lunch."

Her lips drew down, and with slow, deliberate calmness, she slid a cigarette from a package resting on the table by the window and placed it between her red-painted lips. Sully watched her light it with a yearning expression, though frankly I thought he coveted the cigarette more than the woman holding it.

"I brought sandwiches," he said, holding out the bag to her like a peace offering.

"How kind." Millie exhaled smoke out of the corner of her mouth, a fierce burst from an irritated chimney.

Sully practically hurled the sandwich bag onto the little table then darted into the bathroom. To wash the dirt and sand off his face and clothes or to avoid the icicle missiles shooting out of Millie's eyes, I couldn't be sure. Or quite possibly to escape the guilt of his momentary fall off the fidelity wagon.

My own guilt heated my face as Millie turned to me and looked me over critically, from my sand-dusted shoes to my wrinkled skirt, to the scratches on my cheek, and finally reaching my hair, which the humidity had puffed up like a dust mop on steroids. Though, to be fair, my hair always looked that way.

"Your face looks a fright," she said, taking another deep drag. "Would you like me to try and locate a bottle of mercurochrome to put on those scrapes? They look awfully nasty."

Mercurochrome? I had a vague recollection of Grandma Blue slathering that 1950s version of antiseptic all over my cuts and boo-boos when I was a tot. It stung worse than my injury and stained my skin as red as blood for days afterward. Plus, pretty sure the stuff was made with mercury, so... nope.

"Oh, no thanks, I'm good," I said, touching my cheek. "Sully got the worst of it, I'm afraid."

Her eyes narrowed, expressing a hint of jealousy before the ice queen snapped back into place. "Oh? You must tell me all about this adventure. Were you able to locate your lost friend?"

Sully came out of the bathroom, drying his hands on a white towel. "We found him." He tossed the towel onto the bureau next to his hat. "He's dead."

Millie's expression turned baffled. "Dead? What do you mean?"

"He was strangled, Mill, and left alone on the beach." Had to hand it to him, he didn't sugarcoat the bad news.

Millie's cool façade cracked. Her lips pulled into a surprised *O,* and she sank into a chair at the table. Her gaze bounced between me and Sully. "W-what happened?"

We told her. Sully did most of the talking. I sat across from her at the table. He stood beside her and held her hand as he explained in a terse and succinct manner, leaving out the more gruesome details.

Millie shook her head in disbelief. Her delicate chin quivered, and her eyes glistened with tears. "That poor man," she said in a small voice. "Who could've done such an awful thing?"

Sully squeezed her hand then let go, flashing me a glance. "I don't know, but I aim to find out."

Millie stiffened. "Yes. Yes, of course you will." She crushed out her cigarette in the nearly full ashtray and reached for the bag of sandwiches. "I suppose we should eat. It's been a long time since breakfast. Though I confess, my appetite has all but run away."

Sully had bought four sandwiches, two roast beef, two ham and cheese, so there were enough for each of us to have one, and one left over. Waxed paper crinkled as we opened each individually wrapped sandwich. Millie picked daintily at hers, as she had predicted. I ate with more zeal, too hungry not to. Sully dropped onto the end of the closest bed and tore into a roast beef on rye like a lion deprived of sustenance for a week. Or a soldier fortifying himself for the battle ahead.

"What brings you to Point Bailey this weekend, Miss Blue?" Millie asked after a while, switching to a more benign topic. She dabbed at the corners of her mouth with a napkin, despite not a drop of anything to dab that I could see.

"Please call me Beryl, Millie." Because the stiff, formal way she said my name made me feel like old maid Mary Bailey about to close up the library in the movie *It's A Wonderful Life*. "I'm here to find an old friend."

She eyed Sully and forced a laugh. "Looks like you found him."

"Well, actually, I was on the lookout for someone else. Running into Sully is just a happy accident." I shifted my gaze to Big Red. "I'm just sorry bumping into you dragged you into a murder."

"Glad I could be there to help."

I gave him a grateful smile then turned back to my ham and cheese, more than glad he'd been there. He'd kept me grounded in a horrific situation. I'd seen my share of zonked-out time runners zapped by the cack or a stinger and I'd witnessed a lot of bloody fights between my foster brothers and the bully of the moment when I was a teenager. I'd steeled myself against that kind of brutality. But I'd never seen anything as grisly as Murphy's ashen face, the bruises ringing his neck, and his limp, waterlogged body on the beach.

"Murder," Millie repeated in a strained voice. "I still can hardly believe it. Point Bailey seems like such a safe place. How could a murder happen here?" She gazed at Sully as if he had the answer.

"Murders happen everywhere, for all kinds of reasons," he said, looking thoughtful and a trace frustrated. "In this case, Mr. Murphy got himself mixed up with a gang of thieves."

She gasped. "Thieves?" She aimed a confused look at me. "Did you know anything about this? Did you know your friend was a thief?"

"Murphy wasn't the, er, friend I came here looking for." I took another bite of my sandwich. "The guy I'm after might've killed him, though."

"We'll know more after tonight," Sully put in.

"Tonight?" Millie's puzzled expression deepened.

I frowned at Sully. "I still don't think you should come with me. Too dangerous."

He snorted. "You don't know how that gangster's going to react when he finds out you don't have the jewels."

"Jewels?" Millie's befuddled gaze bopped back and forth between us. "What jewels?"

"With any luck I'll have my man and be gone before Scarface figures that out," I said. "I don't need you."

His expression went as sullen as a kid who'd been told he couldn't go to the fireworks display. "And what if he figures it out *before* you disappear?"

"Sully, what part of it's too dangerous don't you get?"

"If that's supposed to put me off, you don't know me like I thought you did."

"Tom!" Millie cried, startling us both. We shut up and snapped toward her. "Will you *puh-lease* tell me what all this nonsense is about?"

When this mission was done and I uploaded my final report to the Interface, that was how I'd always remember Millie. Bewildered. Confused and mystified. Though, to be fair, I'd be perpetually puzzled too if I went away for the weekend with my main squeeze and his kind of, sort of ex-girlfriend popped out of nowhere to crash the party.

And dragged him into the middle of a crime spree. And started kissing him the minute her back was turned.

"It's a long story, Mill."

"Which I have *every* right to hear," she retorted, her voice climbing to a pitch high enough to alert dogs from four towns away. I'd say she'd gone shrill, but people used that word to diminish women, so I'd banished it from my vocabulary. Plus, her anger was justified. We both needed to stop being evasive. We owed her an explanation.

Sully and I exchanged glances and I nodded. "Tell her, Sully."

In the end, we both told her. Millie lit another cigarette and smoked while Sully and I tag-teamed to fill her in on everything that had happened, minus Scarface's knife and vile threats. The kiss, of course, remained unmentioned.

She squinched her forehead and listened without comment until the end, when she said, "Let me see if I've got this right. You're to meet with a gangster who beat you up in an alley and the mysterious leader of a gang of jewel thieves this evening, at a hole-in-the-wall nightclub, and hand over some nonexistent jewels. This is your plan?"

"Well actually," I said. "When you put it that way, it does sound kind of nutty."

"And you want Tom to be your date?"

I *well actually'ed* her again. "It's the other way around. He insists on being my muscle man. I've told him, repeatedly, I'm totally fine on my own. I can take care of myself."

Millie seemed inclined to agree, but Sully folded his

arms across his chest and scowled. "And I've told *you* there's safety in numbers. This is something too dangerous to do alone."

Millie sized him up, calculating exactly how dangerous the plan would be for their relationship, too. Then she sighed. "You're absolutely right, Tom. We can't let Beryl do this foolish thing alone."

Uh-oh, *we* again. With a plus-one.

"Absolutely not," Sully said. "It's not a good idea for you—"

She iced him with a frosty glare, and he snapped his jaw shut. "It *is* a good idea. Beryl needs our help. I know *you* won't be happy unless you're in the thick of it." She placed her cigarette in the ashtray and stood, moving to the closet. "Let me see if I have something suitable to wear."

She opened the door to reveal a wealth of 1946-style loveliness inside, summery dresses and skirts, blouses, shoes, and hats. She'd seriously overpacked for a weekend visit to the seaside, but I felt dead-on certain she could find the right ensemble for a date with a bunch of jewel thieves. And quite possibly a murderer.

My brain chugged on overdrive. How could I stop this runaway train? How could I shake both Sully and Millie and get this job done on my own, with no one getting hurt? An idea popped into my mind and latched on. A simple idea that might actually work. Get there early to snag Rasmussen and whisk him back to the future before Sully could arrive. Leaving him fuming and cursing my name no doubt, but safe and sound.

"That settles it," I said, embracing the idea before any

pitfalls and *what ifs* could present themselves. "Tonight, we'll be a threesome."

The scowl Sully aimed at me could've melted a glacier, but tough toenails, as Grandma Blue used to say. An odd and somewhat gross expression I never fully understood until now. I headed for the door, announcing I needed to go back to the inn and also dredge up something to wear, though my sparse wardrobe didn't exactly include anything suitable for a night out.

Sully reached for his hat. "I should make sure you get—"

"Nope. No way," I interrupted before Millie could explode in real time. "I got this, Sully. You stay here. You need to get ready for tonight, too. I'll meet you at Chaisson's at nine o'clock sharp. See you later, alligator."

I booked it out of there, with Millie's puzzled gaze and Sully's dour and vaguely affectionate, "be careful, for once in your life" following me out the door.

Outside, late afternoon sunlight blanketed the street and sidewalks in an ominous crimson glow. I turned to head for the trolley stop on the corner, feeling eyes on my back.

I didn't need to look behind me to know Sully watched me from his hotel room window.

13

I hopped onto a trolley at the corner and sank into one of the wooden seats. As uncomfortable as hell and probably another one of the reasons the streetcar system was about to go the way of the dinosaur. The car heaved into motion, waddling like a one-legged duck along the tracks. A hot breeze pushed through the open windows and touched my face and ruffled my hair.

I leaned my head back against the seat and closed my eyes but couldn't relax. Everything that had happened since the temporal vortex had landed me here raced through my mind.

First and foremost, Sully's absolute pigheadedness. And his courage, though I expected no less from him. It should've come as no surprise he'd brush off the *you die* finale of our star-crossed love affair and want to face the danger head-on. Heroic and brave and absolutely maddening. My stomach lurched at the memory of Scarface's knife inches from Sully's throat. Thankfully, fate had decided *not yet*. Or perhaps my rash action had something to do with it, as Big Red had suggested. What-ever, that had been one close call I didn't care to repeat.

Especially not tonight, with Millie there to get in the way.

Then there was the kiss. That exquisite kiss. I could still feel Sully's lips tasting mine, our tongues dancing, our bodies pressed together, yearning for more. The subtle pressure of his hands touching and caressing me. The most perfect kiss this side of *The Princess Bride*. A kiss that had been absolutely and completely *right*.

And totally wrong.

A momentary slip for Sully. For me, the logical but foolish conclusion to my trip down memory lane. I'd been seduced by the echoes and callbacks to our precious moments together when we'd first met, seduced by the hope that perhaps those time ripples showing him falling while saving me were *not* absolute, and that we could somehow be together.

I rubbed my tired eyes with the heels of my hands and shook off the thought. The kiss was a mistake, and so was letting Sully anywhere near me. Two of the thousand mistakes I'd made since I started this mission. The TDC strapped to my wrist shimmied as another temporal text came in, joining the mass of messages in the queue. I ignored it. Mistake one thousand and one, probably. More ammunition for Devon to use against me in my next time cop performance evaluation.

The trolley curved around a bend, people got off, others stepped on, and soon I'd reached my stop. I jumped off, leaving my woes and self-pity behind. I'd mope about Sully and everything else later. Right now, I had to get ready for my date with Rasmussen.

Back in my room, I took a shower. A *long* shower. The water was lukewarm and spit from the showerhead in no more than a trickle, but it was wet and refreshing and washed away the sweat and grime and most of the regrets I'd accumulated over this long day.

Feeling somewhat better, I put on my makeup, doing what I could to cover the scrapes on my left cheek. From my few outfits in the closet, I chose a ruby red skirt splashed with white tulips and a white peasant blouse with a boat neckline and puffy sleeves. I finished the ensemble with a pair of sensible red pumps.

Not very fancy, but it would do. Not like I was headed for a swanky night spot. Or trying to compete with Millie in any way. She'd already won by virtue of living in the same century as her Tom.

I dressed quickly, dragged a hairbrush through my untamed locks, then did a quick look-see in the oval mirror. The skirt hugged my hips, and the peasant blouse was a bit too low-cut for my taste, but I looked pretty good. Hot, even. If I were going on a date, and not chasing down a time-skipping jewel thief who may or may not have murdered someone earlier today. And stolen my stinger. I hadn't forgotten that embarrassing fact, and I planned to demand Rasmussen return my property the second I nailed his ass. No way would I return to Time Scope without the weapon and prove Devon's *Beryl is a screwup* suspicions completely true.

I still had plenty of time before I needed to leave, so I toddled downstairs to the dining room. Most people staying at the inn had headed into town to the restaurants, but I was able to score a hot meal of baked beans, hot dogs, and New England brown bread—round, thick slices of bread made with a healthy dose of molasses that came out of a can. Served warm, steamed, not baked, and moist and as squishy as hell. Grandma Blue loved brown bread and could eat a whole can of the gooey stuff in one sitting.

Still pretty hungry despite the sandwich I'd had at Sully's hotel, I devoured every scrap on my plate, my mood climbing along with my blood sugar. The coffee I had with my meal put me in an even happier frame of mind. I sure would miss that when I went back to the future. Which would be soon. *If* all went according to plan tonight.

After eating, I went back to my room, brushed my teeth, and packed my suitcase. I dropped the matchbook and the key on top of my folded clothes with the morning newspaper, touched by regret. The key could be the key to locating the jewels, and I kind of wanted to do that, to find what Murph had died for. I probably should have turned the key over to Agent Knight when we were in his car. Mistake one thousand and two of my 1946 misadventure.

I closed the suitcase and secured the snaps. Once I got home, I'd ask Alice to send the key to Knight via temporal express, with a big you're welcome from me.

Home. Funny to think of Futureworld that way. Not the home my heart wanted but my head knew it would have to do. Home with my cat Jenjen, Alice and Glo, and Jake. My *friend* Jake. I knew now I could never be with him, not with his connection to my past and to Sully. Maybe in time I could move on with someone new, someone who didn't know anything about Beryl Blue, woman out of time, or my status as Special-with-a-capital-*S*.

But I had my doubts.

———

I LEFT THE INN, running a half hour early. Dusk had fallen, the twilight time when the last wisps of daylight faded into darkness. Also, the cue for the first mosquitoes of the evening to make their appearance. They buzzed around my ears. I slapped them away, thankful I didn't have to wait long before the streetcar rumbled up.

When I'd returned to the inn earlier, the trolley had been sparsely populated with riders. Now the car was stacked to the rafters with revelers heading toward the center of town for Saturday night fun. More people squeezed into the car at every stop.

I kept an eye out for Agent Knight in case he'd decided to accidentally-on-purpose bump into me again. I did not want him to get a jump on me and grab Rasmussen before I could. I didn't see him anywhere in the streetcar's rowdy mob. I had time to spare, so to be on the safe side, I hopped off a couple stops before my destination and hoofed it the rest of the way to our nightclub rendezvous point.

The night was humid and sweat dappled my forehead by the time I reached Chaisson's Fun & Frolic, a long, flat building with few windows and a stark white exterior that made the place look like a gigantic dentist's office. I looked up eagerly at the club's neon sign that promised air conditioning inside. I made to follow the people pushing by me to the door when a cab squealed up to the curb.

With Sully and Millie inside.

I narrowed my eyes. How dare he steal my idea to get here early and save me the trouble of a face-to-face with a couple of killers alone. Despite my anger, my pulse revved up to top speed as Sully's broad shoulders and muscular form emerged from the cab. He made an imposing figure in his suit and his Stetson set squarely on his head. If he had to wear that awful thing, that was the way to do it. No rakish angles, straight-edged Captain America all the way.

He turned back and offered his hand to help Millie from the vehicle. She'd moved on to the evening wear portion of the Miss America competition. She wore a silky, summer green dress with a slim skirt and ultra-thin spaghetti straps, delicate strappy sandals, her hair swept up, and a frilly fascinator headpiece balanced precariously above her forehead.

She looked gorgeous, and completely overdressed for a night out at a beer hall.

"You're early," Sully accused.

"So are you. I guess sneaky minds think alike."

"I figured you'd try to ditch me. Ditch us both." He tossed a gloomy look at Millie. I was a hundred percent certain he'd tried to shake her too and what I wouldn't give to have been a fly on the wall for that discussion.

He surged forward to open the door, his head on the swivel and his posture alert as we stepped into a packed room half the size of a football field. I kept on guard too. After our bruising encounter with Scarface and his gang earlier, neither of us should be taking any chances.

Millie's nose crinkled in distaste as she surveyed the crowd. The air conditioning chugged at full speed, pushing around humid air smelling of beer, body odor, and cigarette butts, but doing little to cool the heat of so many people drinking and mingling. Tables circled a massive dance floor at the center of the room, where people danced to a quartet of horns playing something noisy and impossible to recognize. A dozen or more pinball machines lined the wall next to the long bar, also stuffed with people.

Sully pulled off his hat and flashed me a warm glance. I returned a heated smile, sharing his thoughts, and his memories of our adventure at the Hi-Hat Club in 1943, when we bickered and bantered, and he accused me of being a spy. And we'd danced. Well, Sully had danced. I'd mostly stepped on his toes.

He led the way into the eddying mob as if clearing a path for his troops. Some of the women we passed were dolled up, like Millie, some were dressed down, like me. A few men wore uniforms, but most of them sported civilian clothes that must've felt like a uniform in its conformity, lightweight gray or tan suits like Sully's, white shirts, and wide, stubby ties that fell far above the belt, an odd fashion fad I hoped would be short-lived.

"There they are." Sully tipped his head toward the back of the room. "Looks like they brought a guest."

I followed his gaze to see Scarface sitting with Rasmussen at a small, square table by the back wall— with Dorella beside them. She'd changed into somber mourning clothes, a black pencil skirt, a Joan Crawford-style blazer with shoulder pads and wide lapels, and black shoes. She'd topped off the outfit with a pillbox hat and a veil that brushed her nose.

"All our suspects in one place," Sully said gleefully and took off toward them in a hurry. Some men liked to shoot pool, others to trip the light fantastic. Sully's idea of a fun night out on the town was the chance to grill a trio of thieves. Come to think of it, so was mine.

Millie raced to keep up with him. I followed at a more deliberate pace, scanning the room, doing a thorough assessment of my extraction opportunities, as Jake had taught me. There were five exits, with only one near Rasmussen's table. I had to figure out how to get him out of his chair and out that door. Past his partners in crime, past Sully, and past Scarface's goons, who huddled at the next table, wearing dark suits and shifty-eyed expressions, looking like a cast reunion for the movie *The Untouchables*.

"It's about time you got here," Scarface groused when we reached him. He changed his tune when he caught sight of Millie. "Well, hello beautiful." His gaze slithered over her, and he puffed madly on the cigar tucked into the corner of his mouth. "Glad you could join our party. I'm Lester Ford, at your service, doll. This is Dorella Murphy." He nodded toward Murphy's widow, then he jerked his chin at the other man. "That's Fred Pattinson."

Pattinson, or Rasmussen as I knew him, greeted us with a courtly nod. In his early forties, with a slim, lanky build and patrician nose, he wore a tailored, cream-colored pinstripe suit. A smoky beam from an overhead light shone down, turning his brushy blond hair to gold, and glinting off his gold watch, cufflinks, and the fancy bejeweled tie clip holding down his chocolate-brown tie.

Sully looked him over and his left eyebrow did a little dance. I fully agreed with its assessment. Rasmussen seemed out of place here. One of those Gentlemen with a capital *G* kind of guys. A man who would be more at home at the opera or Millie's debutante ball than hanging out at this dump sitting beside a sinister mug like Lester Ford who would stab him in the back as easily as saying how-do-you-do.

"It's a pleasure to meet you." Rasmussen spoke in a clear, strong voice touched with a light Southern accent, Virginia, maybe. He stood and leaned over the table to shake Sully's hand.

"Likewise." Sully firmly gripped Rasmussen's hand. "I'm Tom Sullivan. Call me Sully."

The rest of the introductions were made. Lester did a double take at my last name, but Rasmussen barely blinked. Suspicious in and of itself.

Lester invited us to sit, then summoned a waitress by letting out a whistle that pierced the crowd noise like a hawk swooping in on a sparrow convention. Rasmussen's nostrils flared in disgust. A twenty-something brunette in a short skirt and tight blouse bustled over. Lester didn't let his ogling her curves get in the way of ordering beer for all of us.

"*I'll* have a gin and tonic, if you please," Millie sniffed.

The waitress toddled off and a charged silence fell. We clustered around the table as awkward and uncomfortable as strangers gathered to read a distant relative's will. Dorella ran a hand through her tangled hair. Lester chewed on his cigar. Millie lit yet another cigarette and fidgeted with the matchbook. I considered delivering a stern lecture on the dangers of smoking, but I'd already stuck my nose into her life enough for one weekend.

Only Sully seemed relaxed. Cool and in charge. "Thank you for coming," he said breezily. "You're probably wondering why I brought you here tonight."

I threw him a sardonic smile. Okay, Hercule Poirot, pretty sure *I* had instigated this little party, but do go on. I needed the delay to figure out my exit strategy, anyway.

"We're here 'cuz you have our loot," Lester said, with a *duh* smirk

"We'll get to that," Sully said. "First, I have a few questions about this robbery and how it came about."

Our table companions grumbled like he'd announced a pop quiz. "What's it to you?" Lester demanded. "You a cop?"

I tensed and Millie puffed violently on her cigarette, but Sully barely blinked.

"Me, a cop? Lord no." His chuckle landed somewhere between incredulous and disdain. A fine piece of acting, in my opinion. "I'm simply curious, and you seriously can't expect us to turn over the treasure to you without a few answers. Where'd you find the jewels?" He peered into each of our suspects' faces. "Which one of you planned the heist?"

Dorella and Lester aimed furtive looks at Rasmussen, who cleared his throat, assuring our complete attention.

"Let's just say it was a group effort," he said. "An example of cooperation across the ranks. I was stationed at Schloss Mombert. Mrs. Murphy was frequently assigned as my driver, and we became quite friendly. One day we were, *ahem*, inspecting one of the castle's many parlors and boudoirs and she looked over and discovered what turned out to be the door to a hidden room. Inside were riches you could never imagine."

"I dunno. I've got a good imagination." Sully eyed Dorella, who lifted her veil and returned a defiant glare. He turned his attention to Lester. "What was your part?"

"Mr. Ford has particular skills we put into use," Rasmussen said when Lester refused to comment. "He relocated the merchandise under cover of darkness with no one the wiser. The gems were ferried in Mrs. Murphy's jeep to her husband, who smuggled them home in his gear."

Sully let out a thoughtful grunt. "And what was your role as this all played out, Mr. Pattinson?"

He offered a superior smile. "*Someone* had to supervise the operation."

Sully nodded. "A successful operation. The plan went off without a hitch." His voice went dangerously mild. "Until you tried to double-cross Murphy, and he hid the jewels. Did you kill him?"

He stared at Rasmussen, his gaze probing. If Big Red turned those sapphire eyes on me in that soul-piercing way, I'd fold like a pile of laundry and confess to every crime under the sun, but Rasmussen was made of sterner stuff.

"Turn your suspicions elsewhere, Mr. Sullivan." He scratched his cheek and adopted a bored expression. "I didn't strangle Brian Murphy. *I* couldn't kill anyone."

"I didn't strangle him either," Dorella burst in. "I would *never* hurt Brian. I loved my husband, for all his faults." She chewed her bottom lip, transferring bits of waxy red lipstick to her front teeth. "I was at work at the clam shack when it happened. Ask my boss. Manny keeps track of my every move. He's so busy watching my bottom wiggle he forgets to take the clams out of the hot oil, and they burn to a crisp."

A bit too much information, in my opinion, and Sully offered no follow-ups. He returned his scrutiny to Lester. "What about you? I heard there were a couple of cigar butts found near the body."

Ford leveled a murderous glare at Sully. "I was nowhere near the beach today."

"I didn't say he was found on the beach."

"You smug son of a bitch," Ford snarled, like a rabid bulldog on the attack. "You're trying to railroad me. Ain't gonna happen. *Nobody* puts the finger on Lester Ford." He balled his fists. "C'mon, let's step outside and I'll show you why."

"I'm happy to." Sully pushed back his chair. "I owe you a punch in the mouth. Why don't you bring your boys along?" He flashed to Ford's gang gathered at the next table and his voice turned as sharp as broken glass. "I particularly want a crack at that gorilla who beats up on girls."

Rasmussen stepped into the fray. "Settle down, gentlemen. While it may be entertaining to see you beat each other to a pulp, that will get us nowhere closer to our goal. Let's discuss more important matters." He looked from Sully to me. "You have something I want. Are you prepared to hand them over?"

"Yeah, about that. I don't actually *have* the jewels, but I know where they are." I nodded toward the rear door. "If you'll come with me, I'll show you."

Sully spun an eyeroll that could've won awards at that bold, Hail Mary move. Millie let out a nervous, *Beryl's lying* titter. I yearned for legs ten feet long so I could reach past Sully and kick her under the table.

But Dorella bought it. "You heard her," she said, bright and excited. "She's got the goods. What're we waiting for?" She reached for her purse.

"No, not you," I said hurriedly. "Just him. I'll *only* deal with the boss. How about it, Mr. Pattinson?"

"By all means," he said. My excitement soared, then fizzled out just as quickly at his next words. "But it's *my* turn to ask questions now." He turned to Lester. "Mr. Ford, I believe Mrs. Whitmore would like to dance." He dipped his head at Millie.

Lester gurgled an objection. "Boss, you trying to get rid of me?"

Rasmussen's expression hardened. Just a bit, but enough to express his displeasure. "Mr. Ford, do I have to ask again?"

Lester glared at him for a second before he stood, shoving his seat back with a squawk of wooden legs against the floorboards. "Don't pull any funny business while I'm gone. We're partners, remember?" He turned to Millie and stuck out his hand. "Come on, sister, let's cut a rug."

Millie gaped at his hand if it were a giant slug about to attach to her face. "Tom," she cried. "Surely you don't approve of this. Do you actually want me to go dance with this... stranger?"

Sully hesitated, looking pained. The protective bear inside him surely didn't approve, but I suspected his inner cop would let Millie and Lester toddle off to Niagara Falls this very minute if it would get her out of the way so he could hear what Rasmussen had to say.

"I see." She angrily stubbed out her cigarette and dragged off beside Lester to the dance floor, where they joined the crowd doing a lindy hop or the cha-cha, or whatever dance craze got these 1946er's feet tapping.

Rasmussen watched her and Lester stroll away like an indulgent uncle, then turned to Dorella. "Would you be a dear and go to the machine and get me a pack of cigarettes?"

"But, Fred, you don't smoke."

"I'm considering taking it up. Please go, and don't be quick about it."

Scowling, she snatched up her handbag and tottered away on spiky heels.

"I'm not going anywhere," Sully said when Rasmussen eyed him. His chair creaked as he leaned back and folded his arms across his chest.

"He's okay," I said. "I trust him." With my life. And everyone else's.

Anger flared on Rasmussen's face, quickly masked as he settled his gaze on me. "Fair enough. Let's talk about why you're here, Beryl, and why you're carrying this." He patted his coat's breast pocket, bulging slightly with what I guessed was the stinger he'd stolen.

Really? The man had broken a hundred rules to disappear into the past and he didn't know why a time cop had come looking for him? "I'm here to extract you. I thought you knew that the minute you saw me." He frowned in confusion. "Last night, outside the Slipknot? Before the fight broke out?"

"Ah, yes, you're a time cop." Wariness gleamed in his eyes. "And you've been instructed to extract me because...?"

Again, he couldn't put two and two together? "Time Scope is looking for a murderous time runner named Oliver Bishop, and we think you might know where we can find him."

His posture loosened and his wariness faded. "Ollie Bishop? Now, that's a name I haven't heard in a long time."

"So, you know him."

"Oh, yes. We go way back."

"How far back?"

"Since the early days. When we were at Time Scope together."

"You worked developing the time tech. Until something drove you both into the past." I knew I should just take Rasmussen and leave, but my curiosity muscled in and overrode my need to finish this mission. Why had he run? Why had Bishop done what he'd done? Given the wall of secrecy I expected when I got back home, this could be my only chance to get some answers. "Can you tell me why you time skipped? And about Bishop?"

He thought that over a moment. "I'll make a deal with you. I'll tell you everything I know about Ollie. I'll tell you why I left. I'll even return your weapon." He shifted and leaned forward, his gaze on me cool, calculating. "For a price."

Of course, the catch. "You want the jewels."

"I do. If I were a less greedy man, I might share what I know freely. But I went to great lengths to secure those baubles, and I deserve to profit from my labors." He paused. "You do have the jewels, don't you?"

"Of course. Well, we're pretty sure we know where Murphy hid them. He told us last night." Sully's left eyebrow went wild, and I couldn't blame it. I was digging myself into a lie hole I'd never be able to get out of. "Is it a deal? I tell you where to find the loot, you tell me about... everything."

He nodded and I sat back to listen, both excited and dreading his next words. Excited someone connected with the future and Time Scope actually wanted to answer my questions, dreading what he had to say.

"Oliver Bishop," he began, a faraway look in his eyes. "We were friends, as much as anyone could be friends with such a man. We worked at Time Scope in the early days. As you pointed out, we developed the technology. That was a heady time, full of try and fail, mostly fail, but we kept plugging away. There were twenty of us in the core group, including Ollie and—"

Our waitress finally returned. She placed five pilsner glasses full of foamy beer and one watery-looking gin and tonic onto our table then left. Rasmussen lifted his glass and tipped his head back to drink. I caught a glimpse of a silver chain around his neck that appeared to be dog tags. Fred Pattinson's tags.

"Time Scope funded our research," he said, putting the glass down and picking up the tale again. "A necessary evil, I'm afraid. They saw profits, we saw a means to an end. They proposed a use for the technology that intrigued our team. A venture for temporal excursions. Vacations in time, allowing travelers to learn about history, with minimal impact on the past, like in that old Ray Bradbury story."

"'A Sound of Thunder?'" I asked. "We all know how *that* turned out." Well, most of the *we* gathered at the table knew. Sully didn't know and wouldn't for a while—

that time-traveler-steps-on-butterfly story wouldn't be published until the 1950s. But Sully nodded anyway.

"Yes, and like in the story, we didn't think about repercussions," Rasmussen said. "Didn't think beyond the science. We were young, idealistic, and broke. We needed the funding." He shrugged. "We agreed to Time Scope's terms and signed the contracts. The company was very generous. The team would all share equally, with payouts on profits for the rest of our lives."

Massive profits, I knew. Time Scope had an unbreakable monopoly on the time travel tech and an aggressive team of litigators that terrified anyone tempted to question that monopoly. They'd even been able to keep the defense department's eager paws off the technology, but for how long, nobody knew.

"Then there was an accident in the lab. A woman on our team was killed." Rasmussen's voice lowered to a hush. "Her name was Lexie."

"I'm so sorry," I murmured. Seemed I'd jumped to conclusions and Alice's theory had been correct. The pain and sorrow in his voice suggested he'd been so wounded by Lexie's death he'd fled into the past to escape his grief. "That must have been a blow to everyone. Was Bishop involved in any way?"

His gaze caught mine and his anguish intensified, coupled with anger. "Beryl, Lexie's death was Ollie's fault." He dug at his cheek, scratching hard. "He should've been made to pay, but Time Scope called it an accident and made it go away. He was fired and lost all his benefits."

Sully let out a low whistle. "He walked free, but he lost out on a million bucks, I bet."

I touched his forearm. "More like millions, thanks to inflation. Probably even a billion."

He grabbed his drink and took a noisy gulp, looking stunned.

Rasmussen drank too, his expression thoughtful. "Soon after that, members of our team began to die. Car crashes, accidental drowning, electrocution. One team member fell into a volcano while on vacation in New Hawaii."

"They weren't accidents," Sully said. "That was revenge."

Rasmussen nodded. "We'd been whittled down to a dozen before that became clear. Bishop was systematically murdering every one of us." He scratched his cheek again, like he had the world's itchiest mosquito bite. "Killing us out of resentment, and greed. Ollie figured with us gone, he'd have all the coin. And that, my dear Beryl Blue, is where Time Scope comes in. They didn't take the threat seriously, or maybe didn't want to. What better way to keep it all in the corporate family than by letting a serial killer get rid of anyone else leeching off the profits? I wouldn't be surprised if they set Ollie onto us."

Both of Sully's eyebrows rose. I blinked several times, equally shocked. I mean, no corporation does anything unselfish and noble without expecting something in return. Like plucking me out of time to be their go-to DNA ghost. But this accusation seemed far-fetched. At least, I hoped it was.

"Time Scope did nothing to protect us, so we chose to protect ourselves." Rasmussen's gaze flicked from Sully to me. "We fled into the past."

"You became the ultimate time runners," I said. That explained why there was so little information on the scientists who'd developed the tech, why everyone went all hush-hush when the subject came up. The wall of secrecy around the team protected not their privacy, but the true story of what had happened to them.

"We had to run," he said. "Fortunately, we had the means. We knew the technology backward and forward." He looked pointedly at the junior on my wrist. "That's a portable oscillator. I didn't recognize it at first. The design's changed a lot from the wristband model I invented." He pulled up his jacket sleeve, revealing the wide leather band anchoring a clunky version of a TDC, with red and blue pulsing lights chasing each other inside a bulbous globe. "I built this one. It's not pretty, but it skips me from time to time without much fuss."

Sully's eyes widened and I had to admit to gaping a bit, impressed by the homemade, do-it-yourself-ness of the whole thing.

Rasmussen pulled his sleeve down, covering the device once more, and he took another swig of beer. "Most of the others cobbled something together too and skipped as soon as they could. We chose different time periods and locations to minimize the risk of Ollie catching up to us."

He paused, as if marshaling his strength, then pinned me in his gaze. A sudden sense of déjà vu coiled in my belly, squeezing hard. I had an inkling where this story would lead, and it would not be to a good place.

"I went to war," he said. "Which kept me off Ollie's radar, but he found where some of the others were hiding." His voice dropped down low. "He found them, and he killed them."

Fingers of ice clawed my veins. What was he saying? A thousand puzzle pieces seemed to shower down on me all at once and I couldn't grab a single one to put the puzzle together. Maybe I didn't want to.

Sully shifted closer, eyeing me intently. Rasmussen watched me too, an odd smile curving his lips. "You look just like her," he said.

The icicles in my blood turned to glaciers, freezing me from head to toe. "Just like who?" My voice dropped to no more than a whisper.

"Your mother, Beryl."

14

My mother.

The words rang in my ears. My mother. A woman I barely remembered. Barely remembered my father, either. They were fuzzy faces drifting in the back of my mind, fleeting images of people I never really knew. A tall, slender man who read to me at night, a woman whose high heels ticked across the floor when she took me to the library. A beautiful woman with dark, flyaway hair like mine. People who hugged me tight and sometimes talked in urgent whispers.

Now I knew what those whispers were about—my parents were time travelers on the run.

The world flipped upside down and inside out. Stars burst in front of my eyes. My brain clogged like a stopped-up drain. I couldn't think, couldn't hear, could barely breathe as the truth punched me as hard and sudden as a fist to the mouth.

Now I knew what Jake had been hiding. What he and Glo had avoided telling me and lied about and had buried in a lockbox so deep I'd have to dig through the earth to find it. And why they'd never told Devon the truth about my identity.

I was the child of time travelers. Time travelers who'd fled into the past to escape a vengeful killer.

Sully leaned closer to me and took my hand, providing the anchor I so desperately needed at the moment. Tethering me to him, to this time, and to a reality turned completely on its head. He held on tight and gazed at me with the compassion and understanding of a man who'd been gut-punched more than a few times of his own.

Rasmussen's gaze stayed on me, too, but without a whiff of Sully's sympathy. "I knew you were Mabel's daughter the second I saw you last night."

Last night? I blinked, trying to focus. Oh. When he'd seen me at the Slipknot. That explained his confusion earlier, and my confusion too. I'd thought he'd pegged me as a time cop. He'd recognized me. Sort of. "You worked with my parents?"

"I did, for many years. Your mother was beautiful, smart. The brains of the whole bunch, actually. Felix, your father, was the luckiest man on the whole team." His gaze held me again. "I knew they had a daughter, born soon after they time skipped to the past." His voice dipped, filling with anger and a hitch of disbelief. "I was sure you died in the attack. You know, when..."

"When Bishop murdered my parents," I said bleakly.

I tightened my grip on Sully's hand. Hatred boiled through me, directed at one man. *Oliver Bishop*. My anger and loathing for him burned brighter than the fires of Pompeii. I'd wondered many times if I had what it took to kill him if we ever met. Now I knew beyond a shadow of a doubt. I would hit the kill button or pull the trigger or bash him over the head with whatever weapon I could grab. I would kill him in a heartbeat if—no, *when*—I finally caught up to him.

"Now it's time for your part of the bargain," Rasmussen said, his eyes glimmering. He patted his breast pocket with my stinger inside. "Take me to the jewels and I'll give you this." He jerked his chin toward the exit I'd singled out earlier. "We'll go right now." He flicked a glance at Sully. "Just the two of us."

Big Red's snort announced how he felt about that, but that was how it had to be. Just the two of us, alone. I'd lead Rasmussen to a secluded spot where we would temporal skip. No muss, no fuss, no witnesses. Except for poor Niels, who'd be mighty pissed to discover I'd lied about taking him to the jewels.

If I could even do it. If I could move at all. Rasmussen's info dump had floored me. His claims about my parents had left me breathless. His scathing indictment of Time Scope's negligence unnerved me. He'd basically accused the company—the company I now worked for—of ignoring Bishop's murder spree for the sake of profits.

What was the truth? Would I even get close to it if I brought Rasmussen home and let him be swallowed up into an *it's classified* black hole, never to be seen again?

I had to decide fast. Applause sounded as the music ended and Millie and Lester made their way back to the table. Sully released my hand and leapt up to hold Millie's chair. She sat down daintily, her cheeks red from dancing, her questioning gaze on me.

"Well?" Lester demanded as he flopped into his own chair. "Do we have a deal? Where are the jewels?"

"Patience, Mr. Ford. Miss Blue is considering her options. I expect to have this matter resolved momentarily. Beryl?"

I nodded. I had my doubts about skipping him back to 2132, but I didn't have a lot of options. And neither did Sully. I'd more than overstayed my welcome in this time period and I didn't need Millie's hostile stare to remind me.

Rasmussen stood, a giddy grin spreading across his face. His expression curdled a second later as his gaze caught on something behind me. I glanced back to see what had agitated him. Aloysius Knight wended through the tables toward us, looming head and shoulders above the crowd like a giraffe in a tweed suit.

I groaned. Leave it to my G-Man friend to barge in and try to steal my time perp, just when I finally had him.

"*You* led him to me," Rasmussen spat, hitting me with a fiery glare.

He took off before I could bleat a denial. The exit door banged open, and he disappeared into the darkness beyond. Knight bolted after him. I followed, with Sully close on my heels and Millie's befuddled, "Tom!" trailing after us.

We burst out into a narrow, dimly lit passageway. Cold, too, despite the humidity, and stinking of stale beer, potato peels, and other rotting food drifting from the trashcans ranged along the walls. Sully charged ahead, in the lead as always, as we tore down the alley and veered around the corner.

He suddenly rocked to a stop. "Son of a bitch." He

grabbed me and yanked me back before I could trip over the body on the sidewalk.

Agent Knight.

MY STOMACH CHURNED. Knight lay on the pavement, sprawled next to a tipped-over trashcan and garbage strewn about. Pedestrians tossed curious looks as they hustled by. An acrid scent hung in the air, cutting through the other smells. A scent I recognized all too well. Like acid struck by lightning. A pungent stench that could only belong to one of Time Scope's deadly zapper weapons—a cack or a stinger. *My* stinger.

Had Rasmussen killed Knight using my weapon? The man was a nuisance, but he didn't deserve to get his insides fried to a crisp like that.

Heart in my throat, I dropped to one knee beside him. Relief flushed through me as he rolled over and groaned. Alive, thankfully. He sat up, looking dazed. The scent of a zapper clung to him, but I saw no visible burn wounds. Rasmussen had missed his target completely.

"Sorry, Beryl. I lost him," Knight muttered.

Footsteps pounded down the alley behind us and Dorella and Lester spilled out, followed by his muscled minions close on their heels.

"Where's Fred?" Dorella said.

"Does he have the jewels?" Lester demanded. He plunged his hand into his pocket, reaching for his switchblade.

Sully went into combat mode, but I didn't relish a return engagement with Lester's knife or his goons, so I pointed down the sidewalk and spilled a hurried, "He went that-a-way. *With* the jewels."

Dorella swore, Lester seconded that emotion, and the whole crowd pelted down the street.

A moment later, Millie peeped her head out of what had become the world's most heavily traveled alley. She looked around before stepping out, as if making sure the coast was clear. She held her purse in one hand and Sully's hat in the other.

"My goodness," she gasped when she spotted Agent Knight sitting in the middle of the sidewalk. "What in the world happened?"

"It's not that bad," he said with a feeble laugh. "He got me with a trash barrel. I tripped over it."

"Oldest trick in the book," I said, looking him over. Blood streamed from his nose and dripped from a cut on his head. "You're a wreck. Should I call nine-one-one?"

Sully eyebrowed that anachronistic slip of the tongue. Millie gave the most perplexed forehead squinch I'd ever seen, the furrows deep enough to hold a spring downpour.

"I'm fine," Knight bit off. "I don't need an ambulance. I just need to catch that bastard."

He pushed me away and hauled himself to his feet. Wobbling a bit, he lurched off in Rasmussen's direction, as determined to get his man as Inspector Javert chasing Jean Valjean through the streets of Paris in *Les Misérables*.

I watched him go with a sigh of resignation. I'd lost Rasmussen yet again, maybe this time for good. I supposed I couldn't have asked for a more absurd end to this absurd evening.

Then Millie upped the ante.

"Tom, I want to leave."

Sully eyed her as if he'd forgotten who she was. "Right. Let's get Beryl back to her lodgings first, then we—"

"No, Tom. I want to leave, and I want to leave *now*." She thrust his hat into his hands. "Please call a cab."

"Sure thing." No argument, no pushback this time. He knew she meant business.

He jammed the Stetson onto his head and stomped off to hail a cab. Millie sidled up to me. Time for girl talk, I gathered.

"You know, he's barely looked at me since last night," she said. "Since we ran into you." Not an accusation, a statement of fact. "I lost someone in the war. He was very dear to me, and it dashed me to pieces when he died. I doubt I'll ever get over him. He's with me still, in my memories, and everything I do." She twisted her wedding ring. "Always will be, I suppose."

I made no comment, not even an "I'm sorry." She didn't want me to editorialize or interrupt. She wanted me to listen.

"I knew Tom had lost someone too. He never talked about you, but you were always there, like Dennis is with me." A pained smile thinned her lips. "When we met, I felt we were kindred souls. Both of us hurting, in mourning. We took up together with one rule. No commitment, no attachments. We set out to have fun, and we have. Being with him has helped ease the grief and soften my loss. I began to believe I could finally move on. With Tom. I thought perhaps, in time, he could move on too. Now I meet you and I know the truth. He *never* will. Because he's still in love with you." She met my gaze. "And you're still in love with him."

"Not true. I'm not—"

"Don't lie to me. Or lie to yourself. It's obvious how you feel. It's there on your face whenever you look at him."

Served me right for not having a poker face. Not even a *Go Fish* face. Much as I claimed to hide my emotions, Grandma Blue used to say I wore my heart on my sleeve for all the world to see. Grandma was a wise old bird, and so was this young bird staring at me with teary eyes and a wounded expression.

"I know we girls tend to get our backs up when people give us advice," she said. "We want to be free to make our own mistakes. But I offer this advice, Beryl, because I care too much for Tom to keep silent. Let him go. If you can't be with him... If whatever unspoken secret that you two share is what keeps you apart, and you can't fix it, then say goodbye. Say goodbye for good."

Sully returned before I could digest any of that. "Cab's here. Ready to go?" he asked, his voice dour.

"Yes, I'm ready to go home. I mean, *home*, home, Tom. But I know you're not."

Sully's turn to look bewildered. "What're you talking about?"

"I'm going back to the hotel. I'm going to pack my bag, and I'm leaving."

To give him credit, he didn't ask why. Nor did he argue. "I guess I deserve that. I've acted like a damned heel. I've neglected you. Left you waiting when I shouldn't have. Dragged you into a den of thieves and the middle of a mess." He snatched up the trash barrel and set it upright against the wall, out of the way. "But Murphy needed me. Beryl was in trouble, and I couldn't—"

She stopped him with a lift of her slim hand. "I know. Someone needs your help. Someone somewhere needs saving. I understand. You helped me, in many ways. It's what I love best about you." She smoothed her hair, though every strand sat perfectly in place. "I know we said no ties, no strings attached. I knew this wouldn't be a long affair. But I did hope to get your attention at some point along the way. Perhaps stake a claim in a small corner of your heart." She glanced at me. "Now I know I never will."

He tugged off his hat and slapped it against his leg. "Damn it, Mill. Can we at least talk about it?"

She put her hand on his broad chest and sighed. "Let's not. I've seen that motion picture, and it doesn't end well for the third wheel. I know when I'm licked. Why you want to run all over creation with her, finding dead bodies and tangling with ruffians and thieves, I'll never understand. And don't worry about me. I'm a big girl. I can take care of myself." She hiked up onto her toes and gave him a peck on the cheek. "Goodbye, Tom. See you in the funny papers."

She sashayed to the curb and slid gracefully into the back seat of the cab. The driver closed the door and the vehicle puttered down the street a moment later. That was it, and that was class. A clean and final breakup. Her voice barely raised, no dishes thrown, no Real Housewives-style table-flipping.

I watched Sully watch the cab roll away, surprised by the lump in my throat.

15

We stood on the sidewalk for several minutes. Dark clouds had pushed in, threatening a storm. People rushed past, their voices filling the humid night air. So did music and noise from the various nightspots around us. It all faded into nothingness as Sully and I gazed at one another, not speaking, not touching. Lost in each other's eyes.

Rasmussen was gone. Scarface and Dorella and the rest of the gang had raced after him. So had Agent Knight. If he caught him, Rasmussen would be swallowed up into the 1946 justice system. Our path to Bishop had all but disappeared. My mission was shot all to hell. I'd failed a thousand times over. I'd failed in everything, except one thing. The most important thing.

I'd found Sully again.

Correction, *we* had found each other.

His gaze held mine, and everything he felt for me simmered in his eyes. Everything I felt for him flooded me from head to toe and radiated from every pore. I was sure everyone within a ten-mile radius and even Millie in her taxi tooling its way across town could see and feel how much I loved this man.

"Let me take you home," he said, his voice low and husky. I opened my mouth to protest but he put a finger to my lips. "No argument. It's been a long day. I'm sure you're tired."

I watched him step to the curb and raise his hand to signal for a cab. Tired? Minutes ago, I was exhausted. Now, after what Millie had said and what I'd seen in his gaze, that word had been deleted from my vocabulary. He was still in love with me. I felt like I could run to the moon and back again.

A shiny yellow taxi polished to a gleaming glow sailed up to the curb. Sully opened the door and helped me inside. He dropped his hat onto the seat beside him as he settled close to me. *Very* close. Like fire up the grill and set Beryl ablaze close.

"Where to?" the driver asked. A solid, broad-shouldered Black man of about thirty, he wore a blue coat and skinny bowtie over a white shirt and a chauffeur's cap perched on his head.

"The Seaside Inn," I said.

The driver banged the handle on the meter, and I jerked back against the seat as the cab rocketed into traffic.

"Pretty girl on your arm, a smile on your face," the driver said, meeting Sully's gaze in the rearview mirror. "You look like you're enjoying civilian life."

Sully chuckled. "I don't know anyone who isn't."

The driver gave a good-natured snort as he steered around a corner. "Dunno, sometimes I miss those days. Where'd you serve?"

"ETO, First Infantry."

The driver whistled. "The battling bastards of Bastogne."

"More like the freezing fannies of the First. We spent a hell of a lot of time in foxholes." Bitterness cut through the amusement in Sully's voice. "What about you?"

"Army Air Corps. I was a flight tech with the Tuskegee group. If you ain't never been to French Morocco, I'm telling you, you're missing something." He sighed. "Now I'm here, piloting this piece of junk. But it pays the bills." A car cut us off and he hit the taxi's horn. It honked like an offended goose. "Where'd you learn how to drive?" he yelled, sticking his head out the window.

The driver focused on the road after that. The meter *click-clicked*, racking up the tab as the taxi sped along.

"How're you doing, sweetheart?" Sully murmured. "Rasmussen said some pretty heavy things in there."

"Well, yeah, finding out your parents were time travelers is a real punch in the solar plexus." I laughed because I didn't want to cry. "What do you think, was he telling the truth? Was all of that on the level, to use a bit of your slang?"

He considered that a moment. "He's not as confident as he put on. I suspect he was lying about some things. He has a tell." Sully scratched his cheek. "That. No one's face is that itchy unless they have a bad case of poison ivy. My guess is, he's lying about a lot." His scowl turned tender. "But what he said about your folks... *That* felt genuine."

I nodded, appreciating his candor. So different from Jake, who spent more time thinking up a way to evade the truth than he did answering my questions.

"At least now I have some idea why Bishop came after my parents," I said. "He must've gone after Grandma Blue, too, and she temporal skipped to the past with them."

Wait. Or had she?

I gazed out the window, remembering the last time Sully and I were together, in 1943. By chance, or maybe by design, we'd been invited to Sunday dinner at a farm outside Ballard Springs. The Carter family farm, Grandma Blue's family home where she grew up. In between devouring lamb stew and fresh-baked cornbread and plotting ways to sneak out of the house with Sully for a quickie in the hayloft, I got the rare chance to chat about books and movie stars and generally get to know then ten-year-old Minerva Carter—my grandmother.

At the time I'd noticed Minerva, her brother Augustus, and everyone else in the Carter gang were blue-eyed blondes. I'd shrugged it off, crediting my brown eyes and chestnut hair to my Blue genes taking over my DNA. But there could've been a different explanation. A different and mind-bending explanation that sent a chill shuddering through me.

Maybe my grandmother wasn't a time traveler at all.

Oh, I loved Grandma Blue to pieces. Still did and always would, but maybe she hadn't come into my life at birth, but a lot later. Perhaps she'd stepped up to adopt me after my parents were killed.

If true, I knew exactly who'd made that happen. Jake. The lying liar who lied. The man who'd arranged every other part of my life, including sending me back for that Sunday dinner with Sully and the Carters.

"What's wrong?" Sully asked. "You went quiet all of a sudden."

I smiled ruefully. If *I* had a "tell," that was it. *Not* talking. I shook my head and stored the Grandma Blue questions into a file marked *things Jake needed to answer the minute I saw him again* and focused on Sully.

"What about you? Are you okay?" I slid my hand over his, resting on the seat between us. "I mean, how do you feel about what happened with Millie?"

"I dunno. I feel bad. She wanted me to put the cop in me away for the weekend and I couldn't, not even for a day. Even before you showed up, I was bored, looking for a firetruck to chase. When I saw that brawl break out last night, I ran right for it." He released a heavy sigh that rivaled a hurricane's gust. "I guess I couldn't give her what she wanted. But we said no strings and I thought she meant it. She's still grieving her husband, not ready for an attachment. Me...?" He searched my face with an intensity that stole my breath. "I've been waiting for—"

"Here we are," the cabbie said as the taxi squealed to a stop in front of the inn.

We got out, Sully paid the fare and handed our driver a couple extra dollars, saying, "Have a beer on me and the late, unlamented General Patton."

The driver gave Sully a jaunty salute and we turned toward the inn.

"Hey, buddy," the cabbie called after us. "You forgot your hat." He tipped his head toward the back seat.

Sully glanced at me then back to the driver. "You keep it. I'm done with it."

The cab rumbled off into the night. I grabbed Sully's hand, and we climbed up the steep porch steps side by side. A light burned in the parlor window, but the rest of the place was quiet. Even my rocking chair friend had toddled off to bed.

I turned to Sully at the door, right back where we we'd been when we first met in 1943. Him, awkward on the threshold, me, eager for him to step in. I wanted him now as I'd wanted him then. Even more so, because back then I'd kept my heart shuttered and firmly closed and I didn't know the joy and heartbreak of this little thing called being in love. Opening myself to another and giving my all to them. Unafraid to let them see who I was, warts and all.

Right now, gazing at Sully's beautiful, beat-up kisser, the heartbreak portion of this love condition kicked in. "It seems we're always saying goodbye."

"Do you want me to go?" he asked, his voice a gruff whisper that sent a shiver down my spine.

"No, I want you to stay." Millie's words pulsed in my brain. *Let him go.* "I mean, if you *want* to stay. I've got to go soon, and we won't be together long—"

He put a finger to my lips and stepped closer. His breath brushed my face. His body heat warmed me, though a blaze already burned within.

"You want to know the real reason I went to Ballard Springs after the war? I went there looking for *you*, Beryl. Isn't that the damnedest thing? I knew you weren't there. Knew you'd never be there again. My head told me so. I'd seen you disappear. But my heart hoped." He took my hand and pressed his warm lips to my palm then lifted his gaze to meet mine. "And I never gave up hoping you'd come back to me."

"Oh, Sully." My heart soared. He had to be the most romantic man in the world. In the universe, maybe.

He touched my face, gently caressing the fading scratches on my cheek. "I guess that's why Millie and me never clicked. I was waiting for you. Now you're here. Right in front of me." He spoke as if he still couldn't believe it. "Remember all those years ago when we first met? We knew then we had so little time. You said we should embrace the now. Felt like poetry to me then and touches me still. I love you Beryl, and I know I can't have you forever. Let's embrace the now. Take the moment. You and me, together, even if it's just tonight. We don't have much time, let's make it count."

I melted inside and out, and only one word remained to be said. *Yes.*

He smiled a smile that could've lit up the entire town and most of the Massachusetts seacoast. Then he took me in his arms and kissed me.

———

SOMEHOW, we were outside my room. I didn't know how we'd gotten there, teleportation or magic or whatever. All I knew was our lips barely parted as we kissed our way from the front porch, up the stairs, and down the hall to my door.

I fumbled with the key. We sailed inside. Sully kicked the door shut with his foot and we were alone. Finally, alone. Away from everyone and everything. The outside world melted away, leaving just us.

The kiss at the door became the kiss as we crossed the room to the bed. His lips lingered against my throat and brushed my ear. I arched my back as he caressed my breasts then trailed his hands further down, getting reacquainted with my curves, and making me gasp as he slid my skirt upwards to explore the heat between my legs. I peeled off his shirt and ran my hands over his muscled back. We kissed and tasted and stroked. Touched each other with the joy of rediscovery.

We twirled around and Sully sank onto the bed. He pulled me to him, and I stood between his knees looking down at him. I traced my fingers along his jaw, over his oh-so-pleasing lips, and playfully touched my finger to the adorable dimple in his chin. I'd been dying to do that since I first ran into him and, frankly, was amazed I'd been able to hold out this long.

His hands slid up my arms, over my peasant blouse's puffy sleeves, and across my shoulders to my neck. His warm touch lit a fire on my skin that turned to a bonfire as he slipped his fingers under my top's elastic collar and slowly dragged the fabric down.

"What do you have hiding under here?" he said.

"Why, Sergeant Sullivan." My heart thundered and my blood rushed. Moaning, I pressed closer, wanting him to uncover me and find out. To discover me, and us, once again. He met my gaze and his eyes burned with everything I felt in my own heart. Love, desire, need. My body burned for him and his touch.

I sighed, content. For two years I'd kept my heart closed to any new romance. I held off, waiting to get over him. Or so I'd thought.

I hadn't been waiting to get over him. I'd been waiting *for* him.

He drew me down onto the bed and his lips claimed mine.

16

We drifted off in a haze of satisfaction and happiness. With me curled up beside him, Sully slept like the proverbial log. Until that first flash of lightning, followed by a crack of thunder that shook the whole building.

He bolted upright. His entire body turned to iron. Rigid, unyielding. Ready to fight. Another flash of lightning brightened the room and lit his face, shining on his locked jaw, his glassy eyes, his expression hard and almost feral.

I touched his sweaty shoulder, felt the tense muscles underneath. I slowly smoothed my fingers down his back. "Hang in there, Sully. You're here, now. You're safe."

He tensed as another roll of thunder grumbled across the sky. The splash of raindrops tapped against the eaves and the porch roof, a slow patter that picked up the tempo until heavy rain pounded the ground. More thunder and the wind gusted in through the slightly open windows, bringing with it cooler air.

"I'll be okay," Sully said, his voice as strained as I'd ever heard it. He shuddered, as if shaking it off, forcing himself through the fear. "Loud noises startle me the worst. Especially thunder. Takes me back to where I don't want to be." He turned to me and took me in his arms, pulling me back against the pillows. "*This* is where I want to be."

He kissed me, soft, tender, taking my warmth and support, giving me love in return. All I'd ever wanted and more.

We held each other while the storm raged. His coiled muscles gradually relaxed and his tension eased. I stroked my hand over the soft gold-red hairs on his chest, traced the outline of that tattoo on his solid bicep, and ran my finger gently along the scar across his nose. A scar he'd earned in a different kind of war than the one troubling him now. He'd won that gash long ago, while protecting his mother from her abuser—his father. He'd been a protector, a helper, a solid, dependable man his whole life. And he never asked for anything in return.

"I love you, Sully," I murmured. "You know that, right? It's the one thing time and distance can never change. I love you."

"Really?" A devilish smile touched his lips. "How much do you love me, Beryl?"

His husky voice and the sparkle in his eyes sent my insides into a full-scale riot. "How do I love thee? Let me count the ways."

His left eyebrow rose to an impossibly playful arch. "Why waste time on that?" He shifted and pulled me on top of him. "When you can just show me."

I showed him, he showed me right back, and we

made love until the condoms ran out. After that, we improvised.

The storm subsided and moved out to sea. Sully drifted off but I lay awake, watching him in the muted light. His chest rose and fell with his steady breaths. I remembered watching him sleep back in Ballard Springs, the way his dog tags nestled on his chest. No dog tags now. I imagined he'd torn those off the moment he'd been discharged. But the war had stayed with him, and probably would for a long time. As it would for so many people who'd stepped into the face of danger, in all the wars we humans could never manage to avoid.

Let him go.

Millie's words pushed into my mind again, but I didn't want to listen. Like Sully when he'd gone back to Ballard Springs hoping to find me, my head knew I had to let go, but my heart wasn't ready. Would it ever be?

I settled down, resting my head on his shoulder. His arm snugged around me protectively, lovingly. Automatically, even as he slept. Wrapped in his warmth and care, I fell asleep.

I BLINKED awake hours later to almost blinding sunlight. Through the windows, I saw the sun sparkling on the ocean.

"Morning, sweetheart," Sully said. He turned on his side and propped his head on his fist, gazing at me.

Sweetheart. He'd called me that several times before. A Valentine candy sweet nothing that sent tingles of delight dancing over my skin. An old-fashioned endearment that fit Sully well.

I kissed him quick. "I'm going to miss this so much when I go." His face fell. Mental note—don't mention leaving. It had to happen sooner or later, but why remind him of it? I pulled back and caught the scent of coffee drifting up from the kitchen below. "Ah. Good old Folger's from a can. I'll miss that too."

He chuckled and feathered his fingers through my hair. Well, not exactly feathered, more like struggled to get through my unruly locks, like Indiana Jones chopping through vines in the jungle.

"Coffee?" he said. "What do you mean? Is coffee rationed where you're from? I thought you future people had most everything."

I smiled, warmth and affection bubbling in my breast. We future people did have most everything. Except him. "It's a long story." I ruffled his hair and kissed him again. "I'll tell you all about our coffee woes and all the rest over breakfast."

I meant the *all the rest* part. I'd broken the number one rule about time travel club by blabbing about my mission and what fate had in store for Sully. Might as well let the truth flow about my time jump from 2015, the time cop test, and especially about Jake. I didn't want any secrets from Sully, ever again.

I'd removed my TDC at some point last night and placed it on the bedstand. I picked it up and put it on. Or tried to. Having never worn a watch a single day in my life before junior came along, I always had trouble securing the fastener. Sully watched, his eyebrow rising in amusement.

"Let me help." He ably secured the strap then peered at the rectangular-shaped watch face. "Still can't believe this thing's a time machine. H.G. Wells must be kicking himself for not thinking something like this up. Tell me how it works."

I didn't hesitate. Might as well begin my true confessions with this. "It's called a temporal displacement catalyzer and it can do a ton of things. See this?" I pointed to the tiny flashing light at the bottom of the screen. "This means I have a lot of messages from my team." Thirty-seven to be exact. All from Jake, I was certain. "Tap on one of these icons scrolling across the screen and it pulls up the GPS. Uh, a 3-D map, I mean. I can also get current news from our digital database, so I'll know if there's trouble or a natural disaster that could get in the way of the mission. This tornado icon activates the temporal oscillator." Sully's eyes had started to glaze over. Mine had too, so I wrapped up the tutorial with a simple, "It's how I travel through time. It's how I can be here." And what would take me away from him.

I tapped the tiny tornado and a swirl of pixels rose from the watch face like a rainbow and settled into a 3-D screen. Sully didn't run screaming from the room, so I held out my arm and activated the oscillator function with a flick of a finger.

The watch hummed, tickling my wrist. I took a breath and braced myself as the activation sequence kicked in. The device pressed down like someone had dropped a fifty-pound weight on my arm. A flame of cerulean blue light shot out, spinning in the middle of the room like our own personal cyclone. A warm wind kicked up, followed by that delightful time travel smell, like sulfur doused in cheap perfume and rolled in lutefisk. All I needed to do was set the coordinates.

I bumped Sully's shoulder with my own. "Want to take it out for a spin? We could pop back in time wherever you want to go. None of the stores are open on Sunday. We could time skip to last Monday and get more condoms."

He didn't laugh. Not even a twitch of his lips. "No. I never want to go back."

I sobered at his grim words, the bleakness in his voice. A simple tap of my finger and the temporal tornado winked out. The vibration stilled and my time machine shut down.

"I'm sorry," I said. "Don't want to open old wounds."

He passed a hand over his face. "*I* should apologize. I don't mean to be a grouch. It's just, I don't want to think about yesterday, or tomorrow. I only want to think about now, and you."

He drew me into his arms and kissed me, long, lingering, and with a passion of a man who knew we had so little time and wanted to make each moment count.

A long time and a lot of improvising later, I kissed his forehead and reluctantly slid out of bed. Coffee and the call of nature demanded it. I headed for the bathroom, picking up my clothes on the way, scattered across the floor like a trail of breadcrumbs.

I washed and dressed quickly, taking the final outfit I'd brought along with me out of my suitcase I'd packed last night. I pulled a blue-and-white checkered jumper dress over a short-sleeved red blouse. Postwar style was all about bright color combinations, apparently. Sully met me at the bathroom door when I stepped out and kissed me deeply, as if we'd been separated for an eternity, rather than a few minutes.

"You're as pretty as a picture," he said when we parted. His eyes sparkled with all the joy that bubbled through me. "Don't wait to go to breakfast on my account. I know how desperate you are for that coffee. I'll be right down."

I slipped on the red pumps I'd worn last night and drifted down the stairs, floating in a happy, dreamy bubble, like Glinda the Good Witch of Oz. I knew this bliss wouldn't last, but right now, this moment, I had Sully and coffee and a beautiful morning at the beach. And that was all I needed.

I sailed into the dining room and over to a vintage silver coffee urn with claw feet, though I supposed the pot wasn't considered vintage at this point in time. Not many people were about. Sunday, they were off to church or sleeping in. I pressed the spigot and coffee gurgled into my cup. The smell wafted up and tickled my nose. I closed my eyes and breathed it in, letting the rich, roasted scent fuel my happiness to a dizzying height.

"Beryl."

My eyes popped open at the sound of a voice I didn't want to hear. A voice I particularly didn't want to hear *here.*

Jake.

He'd stepped in from a side entrance and strode across the room toward me with determination. His cobalt eyes seized mine, his perfect lips pulled into a frown that made him look a dozen years older, and somehow smaller.

My bliss bubble burst. Hard and fast.

"Why, Jake, what a surprise. What brings you here?" I said pleasantly.

He winced. When Beryl Blue went all *how do you do*, watch out. Anger coiled in my belly like a cobra about to strike. I'd crashed back to earth and my happiness had hotfooted out of town, leaving only fury to fill that hole. It flooded my every pore as I remembered everything Rasmussen had told me last night about Bishop and my parents.

Everything Jake had known about.

Everything he'd held back.

"I haven't heard from you for days," he said, and mighty grumpy, too. "When you activated your oscillator but didn't follow through, I thought you were in trouble."

My anger kicked up another notch. Not because he'd been tracking me, but because he'd raced across time to save me. As if Beryl Blue couldn't save herself. "Don't be silly, Jake. I'm not in any trouble. Coffee?"

I pushed my cup into his surprised hands, earning me the mother of all *WTF?* looks.

"I don't want coffee." His voice hiked up to maximum whiny and he put the cup down with a decisive *thunk*. "We need to talk."

"My, aren't you cranky for so early in the day."

"Beryl, it's almost noon."

He stiffened and glanced around the dining room. The few people gathered here had turned away from their brunch to watch us bicker. With a mighty sigh, Jake took my arm and led me to the door. Correction, I *let* him lead me.

We stepped out onto the porch and into a gorgeous day, not a smidge of humidity. A gentle sea breeze ruffled the branches of the lilac bushes, and fluffy white clouds drifted across the bright blue sky.

"What's happening?" he demanded, moving me down the porch, so the old man in his rocker couldn't overhear. "Where's Rasmussen? Why haven't you kept me updated?"

I offered him a Sully-worthy scowl. His last question was the most important. Why had I left *him* out of the loop? For the first time since I'd met him, I'd done something on my own, without telling him my every move. The truth hit me square between the eyes. Jake had been guiding me and holding my hand for so long, he didn't trust me.

Worse, I hadn't *let* him trust me.

"Yeah, I found Rasmussen," I said, my voice brittle. "Then I lost him, but not before he got *real* chatty. He told me everything. About Time Scope and Bishop, and the scientists who ran into the past. He told me about my parents. He said..." I looked Jake straight in the eye. "He said they were time travelers."

Jake stared at me, his entire body on alert, like an animal catching the scent of danger.

"Well, is it true?"

An agonized expression creased his pretty face, and after a long, maddening pause, he nodded.

"Oh." Deep down, I'd hoped Sully had been right that parts of Rasmussen's story had been a lie, but Jake's confirmation crushed that feeble hope. "Why did you keep that from me? How could you? How could Glo, or anyone else who knew my parents were time travelers not tell me?"

"Beryl—" He reached for me.

"Don't you dare." I stepped back, bumping against the porch railing. "You do that every time. Shield me, protect me. You think I'm an infant who can't take care of herself. You treat me like a child. You don't think I can handle the truth about my past."

"I had to keep it from you," Jake muttered. "To protect you."

Ugh. That line, worse than *it's complicated* and *it's classified* combined. Ten times worse. "I'm not a baby."

"Then stop acting like one. I did what I had to do to keep you safe. There were too many risks to you knowing the truth."

"Seriously?" I struggled to hold onto my temper. "What's risky about knowing that my parents were fugitives, hiding in the past to escape a killer?"

He stilled, his gaze going nuclear. "They weren't hiding to protect themselves. They were hiding to protect *you*."

I flinched as if he'd slapped me in the face. "What?"

"Bishop wasn't after just them. He wanted to kill anyone involved in the development of the tech, anyone in line to profit. *You* included. I was sent to protect your family and I blew it. I lost them. Got to the car too late, as Bishop ran from the scene. I was going to chase him but saw you in the back seat. Somehow, he missed you. The fire ate up the car like it was a free lunch. You were choking. I dragged you out. A crowd had gathered, including a nurse who lived in the neighborhood. She took you in her arms and I ran after Bishop, but too late. He was gone."

Jake spoke in a dry, *just the facts, ma'am* monotone. Emotion free. But his eyes glistened, and I knew he felt the pain as if it happened just yesterday. Tears stung my eyes too, but I choked them back. I feared if I let myself cry now, I'd never stop.

"That was the worst moment of your life," he said, clearing his throat. "Mine too. The days that followed were a blur. I couldn't eat or think or do anything for weeks after it happened. I'd failed in my mission. I failed everyone..."

His voice drifted off and so did his gaze, staring into the distance, as if seeing the past. His past, my past.

"I moved forward the best I could. I'd made a promise to your parents to protect you, should something happen to them. They didn't know who I was, that I was sent there to keep an eye on them. They thought I was a neighbor. A friend. A guy they had beers with and who rolled gutter balls when we went bowling. They trusted me. I kept my promise and volunteered to oversee your future, just to make it right."

There it was. The crux of the issue and the answer to everything. Jake's guilt. It had fueled his every waking moment since my parents' death. Guilt kept him frozen in time, unable to move on. Guilt had kindled what he thought were feelings for me. He'd fallen for the orphan waif, like the kindly guardian in a romance novel who falls for the ward he's cared for and protected her whole life.

I searched his face, guilt of my own taking hold. I'd put Jake on a pedestal almost as high as the one I'd hoisted Sully onto, and that one reached the clouds. How could I not? Jake had saved my life. I respected and admired him. Even sort of worshipped him. I'd turned to him out of gratitude and loneliness, hoping deep down he could fill the gaping hole Sully had left in my heart. That wasn't fair to either man, especially Jake.

"Jake..." I ached for him, but I held back the "I'm sorry" that sprang to my lips. I wouldn't shoulder the blame this time. This was a mess we'd both created, a mess we both had to dig ourselves out of. "Thank you for telling me. For being honest with me, like an equal, which is what I want to be. It's time for you to stop treating me like a fragile flower and see me as a real person. Time for me to stop leaning on you and depending on you the way I have. I want to stand on my own two feet and live my life. I think it's time for you to live yours, too."

A volcano of emotions went to war on his face. He gazed at me with such intensity I could feel the heat. Then the fire drained away. Cool and cool-headed Jake snapped into place. He buried his feelings once more.

"I'll do my best," he said with a terse nod. He glanced at my rocking chair buddy, who'd nodded off, then he lifted his arm and tapped on the junior hugging his wrist to activate it. "You ready to go home?"

"No," I said quickly. Too quickly. Jake's eyes narrowed in suspicion. "I mean, I still need to catch Rasmussen."

If Agent Knight hadn't caught up to him last night. If he'd been arrested, extraction would still be possible, but disappearing a rogue time traveler from a federal lockup would be tricky, not to mention violate six hundred Time Scope rules and give Devon yet another reason to call me a screwup.

I glanced over Jake's shoulder, through the window into the dining room. I stiffened. Sully prowled the small space like a panther on the hunt for its mate. And not very pleased to find her missing.

"Have faith, Jake. I'll catch the guy and bring him in. Now, you'd better go."

He followed my gaze. "Sullivan. He's here? No wonder you didn't check in with me. You've been busy." An accusation, filled with bitterness and a touch of disappointment. "You know the risk you're taking being with him."

"I do. And he knows it too." I huffed out an annoyed breath. "I told him. Just about that, not about anything else." Okay, I'd told him a few more anything elses, but Jake didn't need to know that.

"And he stayed with you? What a hero."

"Don't be petty, it doesn't suit you."

"Don't be stupid, Beryl. I've been trying to keep him alive by keeping you apart. You're tempting fate."

"You're one to talk about tempting fate. Isn't that what you do every day? Isn't that what you did with Sully in the first place? You chose him for your little test, completely messing with his timeline, and now he faces a death sentence because of it. You created a paradox within a paradox wrapped in a paradox."

"That's not the way it works, Beryl. You should know that by now. His destiny has always been to die, protecting you. That's the simplest explanation. The rest is—"

"I swear by the goddess of time travel and all that's holy, if you say it's complicated, I'll time skip you into the next millennium where you'll be eaten by Morlocks."

To my surprise, he grinned. Dimples and all. "You're so much like your mother, it's scary."

That got me all squishy inside, aching and a little

resentful. Jake had gotten to hang out with my mother, and my dad. Rasmussen had known them. Even Bishop had, before he'd hit the sociopath trail. I wished I had stronger memories of them both, wished I could tornado back in time and see them again, even once. But... what kind of a paradox would that create?

"You knew my parents. You must've known my grand-mother too. Who was she? Was she really my dad's mother and traveled back in time with them? Or was she...?" Something he'd said earlier clicked in my mind. "Wait. Was she the nurse at the scene of the car fire? The woman you handed me to when you ran after Bishop?" Well, of course she was. And wasn't that the weirdest thing? "Did you arrange for her to take care of me? To adopt me?"

Jake's face flushed an unbecoming shade of red. "That's a story for another time." He said that to his feet because he couldn't meet my eyes for some reason. "Finish your mission. We'll talk when you get back."

Without another word, he tapped on his junior and vanished in a cloud of blue fire. I had no time to weigh any of what had just been revealed as Sully stepped out onto the porch. He'd ditched his suit jacket and wore his white shirt with the collar open and the sleeves rolled up. He looked cool and casual and supremely suspicious. His nostrils twitched at the TDC's sulfur and lutefisk cocktail smell that stung the air like spoiled eggs.

"Everything copacetic out here?" he asked, his scowl telling me he doubted it.

"Mm, sort of?" I looped my arm through his. "Let's go inside and get something to eat. I have a lot to tell you."

17

———

We took a seat at a table with an ocean view in the now empty dining room and dug into our breakfast. Scrambled eggs, fruit cup, and coffee for me. Steak and eggs with a mound of buttered toast and blueberry jam for Sully. A fresh summer breeze rolled in through the open window. Outside, the sun's rays warmed the sand and the waves crashed in a steady, comforting beat.

While Sully wolfed down his massive meal as if he'd just returned from a thirty-mile march on an empty stomach, I told him everything. The whole truth and nothing but. Jake had lied to me, again and again. He'd done it for what he'd thought were the right reasons, but still. I'd trusted him, and he'd failed me.

I didn't want to be *that* person to Sully. Not anymore.

I told him about living in 2015 and the library and the plan Jake and Glo had cooked up to extract me, and even about my cat Jenjen's comical trip through the temporal oscillator. I saved the *ha-ha, I didn't really kill Jake like you*

205

thought I had reveal until the end. Sully took that news surprisingly well. But the full truth about the test I'd been put through to earn my time cop stripes? Not so much.

"Jake tricked you, damn it." He banged a fist on the table, rattling coffee cups and silverware. "He used you. Stuck you between a rock and hard place. Left you with no choice but to join them."

Outraged bluster, but still, good thing I'd sent Jake on his way well before Sully heard this news. "Well, Glo had something to do with the plan. And what part of, I was going to hit my head and die didn't you hear? I had no other options."

He bit into a slice of ham. "You sure they weren't lying about that too? People die from head wounds all the time, but in my experience, your skull is a sturdy piece of luggage, awful hard to break."

I snatched a slice of toast slathered with jam off his plate and nibbled on it while mulling that over. I'd believed Glo and Jake when they'd told me I would die from a fall and smacking my noggin. I had no reason not to. Call me gullible, I guess. But now, as I discovered new lies, half-truths, and blatant omissions every day, I had to wonder.

"Sully, how did you get so wise?"

"Practice. A lotta practice." He sawed off another piece of ham and popped it into his mouth.

Laughing, I dipped a strawberry into a bowl of whipped cream, made with fresh cream, a bit of sugar and a dash of vanilla, just like Grandma Blue or whoever she was used to make. Sully watched me take a bite, his expression affectionate, amused, and aroused. "What are you grinning at?" I asked around a mouthful of strawberry. "This is *real* whipped cream."

"Yeah, what else would it be? Don't tell me you don't have real cream in the future? No coffee, no cream. You still got sugar I hope."

"Yeah, sugar's still around in abundance." I didn't go into the restrictions on alcohol.

"Glad to hear it. I wouldn't want to live in a world without cotton candy." He polished off the rest of his breakfast then lifted his gaze to meet mine. "What do you want to do today?" He jerked his chin upward, toward my room above, and his face corkscrewed into a comical leer. "Besides the obvious."

Delight shivered over me. That would be the best, and most fun, way to keep Sully out of harm's way. I snuffed the desire out. I still had a job to do. "I have to find Rasmussen. I can't go home without him."

"Killjoy." He sat back in his chair and ran a hand through his hair. "I s'pose the fella's still out looking for his treasure."

"Unless he found it." Or Agent Knight had found him.

"I dunno about that. He doesn't know where it is. None of them do. Why else would they believe you when you said knew where Murph had stashed the loot? Now, if we really had the jewels, that could be the key to finding your man. Could use the gems as bait to lure the thieves into the open."

I went completely still as one of his words stuck in my mind. "Oh, you dunce."

"Beg your pardon?"

"Not you. Me. *I'm* the dunce. I forgot all about the key." He frowned and I hurried to explain. "After we found Murphy's body and you went to get the police, I did a little poking around and I found a key."

Ooh. His left eyebrow didn't like that. "You shouldn't have touched anything. You should've left it for the police to find."

Should I? Or did time and fate want me to take it and put it in the suitcase with the other items? As a way for me, or the me that had opened that bag in the future two days ago, to know that when I found the key on the beach that it had some significance, and I would have to... *Oof.* My temples had begun to throb and in order to avoid a full-fledged temporal migraine, I put the questions and circular explanations out of my mind.

"Don't lecture, Sully. I took the key for a reason." A reason that would make his head pound too. "I found it in Murphy's tacklebox. It could be the key to a shed or cellar door. Could also be the key to a safe deposit box. With the jewels inside."

He scowled. "And you didn't think to tell me about this minor discovery?"

"Well, I forgot. We kind of got busy with me going off with Agent Knight, and Scarface and his gargoyles cornering us in an alley and all." And by all, I meant all the kissing.

He grunted, conceding the point. "Where's this key now?"

A minute later we ended up where he'd suggested we go—in my room. I dragged the suitcase out of the closet, tossed it on the unmade bed and unsnapped the clasps. Sully's eyebrow arched as he took in the newspaper and other items on top of my clothes, but he said nothing.

I handed him the key and he held it up to the light

drifting through the window, examining it with an adorably inquisitive expression.

"Looks like a locker key to me," he said. "Probably a locker at the train station. See the number?" He leaned in close to show me. My body's inner furnace kicked in with its usual reaction to his nearness. "Locker sixty-three. Some storage lockers are dime-in-the-slot, others use a key like this one."

"The train station? Would Murphy have stored something so valuable in a locker?" I thought of my high school locker, with its flimsy hinges and easy to open combination lock.

"Maybe. I still wish you'd left it for the police to find." Excitement undercut the sternness in his voice. "Since you didn't, it couldn't hurt to go to the station and check it out."

"Great idea." I wrested the key from his grip. "I'll go look."

He scoffed in frustration. "Not just you. *We'll* take a look."

"You *know* I can handle this."

"I do, sweetheart, but you know I'm not gonna sit here twiddling my thumbs while you're out there, facing a killer."

"But the risk to you..."

"The risk is there, and always will be." He reached out and took me in his arms, gazing into my eyes. "I know it's dangerous, but I want to help you, and I also want to catch Murph's killer. I can't ignore his murder. He deserves justice. He got used by those chiselers, then brutally murdered. I *want* to take them down, and that means finding these goddamned jewels and luring them out into the open. If I get my hair mussed and a few new bruises and just happen to save your life in the process, so be it."

Oh, Sully, you heroic fool. But he was right. He knew the risks. How could I be angry with Jake for swaddling me in bubble wrap to protect me from danger, while I kept trying to do the same thing to Sully? While refusing to let him make his own decisions about his fate?

"Yeah, okay," I said, with reluctance. "*We'll* take a look. But we'll have to be *super* careful."

He grinned. "I always am. Now, when do we leave?"

WE LEFT, but not right away. Sully and I had a little more improvising to do before we set out. It was after two when we finally left the inn and hopped the trolley into town. We took a seat near the back and the streetcar herked into motion. I was going to miss this waddling beast. Nowhere near as sleek and luxurious as the transports in my future world, not even as comfortable as riding the T's Green Line in Boston, but it had a certain charm.

Sully leaned back in his seat and put his arm around my shoulders. "Tell me a little more about the future," he said. "What's the world like?"

A casual question that required a complicated answer. Several complicated answers, depending on which future he wanted to know about. The era I grew up in and left behind in 2015? Or where I lived now? Each era had their challenges, each had their pros and cons. Each had technology that would make Sully think he'd stepped into a sci-fi movie. Then there were all the social changes, most for the better. Though how could I tell him that despite the war he fought to save democracy, we still had to fight to preserve democracy every day?

I sighed, going for vague. "The future's different, and the same in a lot of ways. That's all I should probably tell you. I already broke a lot of Time Scope's rules telling you about Jake and the test and... your future."

"You sure have a lot of shitty rules in your time."

"There's a lot of shitty rules in every era."

He conceded the point with a *touché* grunt and reached up to pull the cord, signaling the conductor we wanted to get off. The streetcar rumbled to a stop a moment later. Sully offered his hand to help me down the steps, a quaint, protective, and totally unnecessary gesture that got me all warm and squishy inside.

We turned and headed toward the train station. Afternoon sunlight beamed down, igniting Sully's red hair. I celebrated his decision to abandon his hat for good. It had been a terrible crime to hide his beautiful hair from admiring eyes under that ridiculous straw bonnet.

We strolled past restaurants, arcades, and funhouses crowded with people even on a Sunday. The scents of fried dough, cotton candy, and the ever-present cigarette smoke drifted on the air. We held hands like carefree lovers. Something I desperately wished we were, instead of two people on a treasure hunt, keeping an eye out for an unknown threat.

Sully glanced over his shoulder then guided me across the street. "Let's take our picture." He gestured to a freestanding photobooth, a large, boxy cubicle with a curtained entrance, outside one of the arcades.

I raised an eyebrow at this side trip from our main

journey but didn't object. We squished inside the booth. He sank onto the small stool and steered me onto his lap, then pulled the curtain shut with an efficient swish. I bounced around as he dug into his pocket for a quarter. He didn't mind me wiggling around one bit and it took a minute before he leaned forward and dropped the quarter into the slot.

The machine whirred to life. It clinked and clanked with more conviction than a temporal oscillator. I hugged Sully's neck, he wrapped his arms around my waist, and we stared into the mirrored camera lens, grinning like demented hyenas. The machine captured our pose with a click and a blinding flash of light. We posed again, a pose that turned into a kiss.

"I think we picked up a tail," he whispered against my lips.

I pulled back, eyes going wide as the camera flashed again. "Rasmussen?"

"No. I think it's Mrs. Murphy. Not sure. You dames insist on wearing hats that shade the face like a criminal, it's hard to tell. I ducked in here to see if she's still following us when we're done."

I put on a mock pout. "Really? I thought you brought me in here for some lip lock, not to evade a shadow."

"Oh, that too. First, and always."

He demonstrated that by locking his lips on mine again and we kissed a kiss that lasted a long, long time after the final flash. His lips were hot and demanding and his tongue explored my mouth with the zeal of a mountain climber conquering a new peak. Explosions rocked my insides, and my entire body sang. I looped my arms around his neck and ran my fingers through his thick hair. He cupped my breast and rained kisses along my throat.

"Ah, Beryl," he murmured. "My beautiful girl from another time. My sweetheart. My love."

Dang, he was good. He had the magic touch and the magic voice. Rich, deep, as smooth as real whipped cream and equally tasty. How could I resist? I'd do anything for and with this man, including copious improvising, right here, right now and maybe would have if not for the male voice somewhere in the middle of puberty that squeaked, "Hurry up in there," from outside.

I giggled and Sully aimed a glare at the curtain and the two pair of legs visible below it. One pair belonged to a boy with knobby knees, the other a girl wearing saddle shoes and knee socks rolled down to her ankles, what the swing kids of the era called bobby sox.

The young man beyond the curtain piped up again. "Hey, you bums! We're waiting out here."

I tried to slide off Sully's lap, but he held me tight and kissed me once more before letting me go. I slipped out of the booth. He followed, squeezing his broad shoulders through the narrow opening. The squeaky-voiced kid gaped and looked up and up as Sully straightened to his full height. The boy gulped, grabbed his girl, and dove into the photobooth. He drew the curtain with a nervous swish and completely missed the benevolent smile Sully turned their way.

I grinned. My guy may be built like Old Ironsides, but he was a softie through and through, the teddiest of all teddy bears.

We had to wait several minutes for the machine to develop the photos, an eternity to someone raised in the digital, instant-upload age. Sully leaned against the booth, casual and relaxed, but his eyes searched. I looked around too, but couldn't spot anyone familiar, not even a thin man who looked like Jimmy Stewart.

Finally, the machine whirred and spit out a strip of black and white images. With our mementoes safely tucked in Sully's shirt pocket, we continued on our way.

"I think we lost her," he said about a block later.

"Good." Dorella we could lose. Lester too. I only wanted to find Rasmussen. And the jewels. I had to admit a growing need to finally get a look at those baubles after all the drama we'd been through. "A clever and successful diversion, sergeant." I slid my arm around his waist and hugged him. "What do you say we do it again later?"

"More pictures? Or more, what did you call it, lip lock?"

"How about both?"

That wry, sexy grin twitched his lips. "On the way back. Right now, you've got a key in your pocket in need of a lock to fit into."

Our destination came into view a moment later, the Point Bailey depot, a long, single-story building, with patterned brickwork, dormer windows, a hip roof, and a semicircle turret at one end, topped by shingles that rose to a point like a witch's hat.

We crossed the boulevard and entered the building through one of the three revolving doors. For some reason, revolving doors were quite popular in mid-twentieth century America. Maybe a clever ploy to keep the dying profession of the neighborhood shoe repairman in business, since chances of getting one's foot caught and your best Sunday pumps mangled by the spinning door's treads were exceedingly high.

Inside, several large fans suspended from the high ceiling spun madly, keeping the station's interior cool. A couple of kids darted by us, chasing each other. Their laughter and shrieks competed with the roar of other voices, the footsteps tapping across the tiles, and the rumble of a train's idling engines in the train yard beyond a row of doors. The smell of diesel fuel hung in the air.

The place was pretty busy, with the crowds headed home from a weekend away at the beach. A line of people stood at the ticket windows. Others sat on wooden benches, waiting for a southbound train to Boston or to points north. A timetable hung on the wall next to the ticket counter, showing arrivals and departures in blocky white letters.

Sully's earlier playful demeanor evaporated, replaced with a cool, calculating expression. He did a 360-degree turn, checking all our flanks before he cleared a path across the station like General Patton. He grew even more cautious when we reached a narrow hallway with a sign reading *To Storage & Lockers* under an arched entrance-way. I tensed too. Well, *more* tense. Despite the quips and kissing, fear and worry had simmered within me since we'd left the relative safety of the inn.

"Maybe you should wait here," I said. "You know, just in case. I'll recon first."

"Recon? What do you think this is, a war movie? We go together."

We went together. We moved side by side down a hallway smelling of floor wax and the stale stink of mold. Pendant lights hung overhead like upside down umbrellas, fitted with light bulbs of the five-watt variety. In short, dark and creepy. I bit my bottom lip. Sully hunched his shoulders and peered every which way as if he expected an ambush.

The corridor opened into a wide and much brighter room with four rows of lockers stacked on top of each other like in my high school's gym. We were the only ones here. Though there had to be twenty or more lockers per row, Sully found number sixty-three with minimal hunting, in the middle of the stack, near the end of the second row.

I swapped out my stress for anticipation and excitement as I stared at the locker door. Could Murph really have hidden his treasure here? Were we about to see what all the fuss was about?

I dug the key out of my skirt pocket. Sully held out his hand for me to give it to him and I laughed. "Do you even know me?"

The corner of his mouth tugged up then he stepped back with a goofy bow that would've melted me into a puddle of delighted goo right there and then if I didn't have work to do.

I took a deep breath and fit the small key into the lock. The hinges squeaked as I opened the door. Sully and I crowded together to look inside. He swore and I squinted in disappointment at the locker's empty interior. No jewels. No diamonds or rubies. Though, seriously, what had I expected?

"The key's just a ruse," I said, completely let down. "To throw his partners off the scent while he stashed the loot somewhere else."

"But where?" Sully shifted his gaze. "What's this?"

He reached into the locker, all the way to the back, and removed a postcard. A vintage postcard, in fact, a panoramic and colorized picture of Point Bailey's beachfront at sunrise, circa 1910. The cliff known as the Prow stood tall and mostly unchanged from today at one end of the long beach area. The other end, the north side, was far less developed than now, with only a smattering of houses along the shore.

I took the postcard from Sully and flipped it over. No stamp or postmark, and no address on the other side, nothing except three words scrawled in ink, *Kilroy Is Here.*

"Kilroy?" I said. "That's a World War II thing, right? Grandma Blue used to write *Kilroy Is Here* and draw the face of a guy with an egghead peeping over a wall. She did it all over the place, on steamed up mirrors and in chalk on the ground when we played hopscotch."

Sully's lips twitched. "Your grandma sounds like a pistol. But it's Kilroy *Was* Here, not *is*. Murph got it wrong." He tugged his ear. "Seems strange though. How could he foul that up when everyone knows the Kilroy slogan?" He shifted suddenly, pasting his gaze on the postcard in my hand. "Unless... Murph got it wrong on purpose."

"Meaning?"

"Meaning it could be a message. To his wife, probably. In case something happened to him. The picture is of the beach area. What if he was trying to let her know the jewels are somewhere on the beach?"

"That narrows it down. You think he buried his treasure like a pirate? That's a big stretch of sand to dig up. And the last time I checked, we suspected Dorella of killing her husband. Why would he leave her a clue to where he hid the jewels?"

"*You* suspected her, not me," he said. "Murph was in a bind. He found out Rasmussen was gonna fence the loot, then cut him out of the deal. Probably cut Dorella out too, so Murph seized his opportunity like any good infantry man would. He hid the jewels and refused to bargain until he got the surrender terms he wanted."

"Only it didn't turn out as he expected."

"No. The man miscalculated, and he's dead." Sully plucked the postcard from my hand and held it up as if it were Exhibit A in court. "But he left behind this one small clue for his wife to find. A hint that could lead her to the gems if she was smart enough." His gaze on me turned mischievous. "A clue the police would have now if some nosy girl from the future hadn't gone pawing through the crime scene like Sam Spade in a skirt."

I huffed in mock annoyance. A little real annoyance, to be honest. Before I went home from this mission, I'd have to tell Sully all about the suitcase, its odd collection of items, and the paradox that brought me here. If only to clear my name.

"Okay, Sergeant Sullivan, you've convinced me. What now? Do we go dig up every inch of the beach area looking for the gems?"

"Nope. Just one section. Cobble Cove. Did you see that fisherman's shack and overturned boat down where Murph was found? We start there."

I chewed over the pros and cons of that plan, not that there were many pros in a situation offering only cons. Cobble Cove was a smaller area to search, but that would put us into the open again.

"I'll agree," I said. "On one condition. We be extra c—"

"I know, be careful." He tucked the postcard into his shirt pocket with the photos. "You worry too much. I can take care of myself."

Irony stepped up and tapped me on the shoulder. He'd thrown my words back at me. The same words I'd repeated over and over to him, and to Jake before I'd left on this journey. Now I knew how ridiculously cocksure those words were. Especially in the face of a fate that couldn't be changed.

"I wouldn't worry, Sully, if you didn't always run head-first into trouble."

"Better than letting trouble find me." He chuckled. "Unless that trouble comes in a package named Beryl Blue." He kissed me on the tip of my nose. "Come on, sweetheart. It's time for us to go on a treasure hunt."

18

Instead of hopping the trolley, we hailed a cab. This driver was less chatty than our chauffeur last night and drove twice as fast. Maybe because Sully offered him five bucks to step on it and get us to the beach at warp speed.

The cabbie dropped us at the entrance to the parking area then squealed off, showering us with dust and pebbles. A dozen or so cars were parked here, but no one was in sight. Still, we kept alert as we steered toward the far end of the lot and the long, flat path to the dunes and Cobble Cove.

My shoes slipped on the loose sand as we climbed the dune, but Sully held my hand tight, guiding me to the top. Yesterday's humidity had been blown away by the storm. Sunlight sparkled off the water and turned the rugged stones of the Prow across the estuary to a lustrous golden brown. Voices drifted on the wind from the ocean-front, but the cove area was deserted.

After the locker disappointment, I tried not to get my

hopes up, but my blood raced all the same. Had Murphy hidden the jewels somewhere down there? Buried in the sand like the pirate booty in *Treasure Island*, only without *X* marking the spot?

We'd soon find out.

Sully started down the steep path. I followed, doing my best not to look down and activate my fear of heights. We reached the beach. The aroma of drying seaweed, beach roses, and sand baking in the sun invaded my senses, a comforting and timeless scent. No sound, except for the steady pound of the surf and the occasional cry of seagulls.

Sully's gaze drifted to the estuary and the rock cluster where we'd found Murphy's body. His jaw went rigid. Regret shaded his face. I touched his shoulder and he nodded.

"I'm going to nail the bastard who strangled him," he rumbled, then he stiffened. His left eyebrow shot sky high. "Son of a bitch."

"What? What is it?"

He shook his head. "I'm not sure. A hunch. More than a hunch. I'll figure it out later. Right now, we've got work to do. We'll take the boat first. It's the most obvious place."

I shook sand out of my shoes then we headed toward the overturned rowboat, or maybe I should have called it a dinghy, based on its size. Long and wide, made of some kind of sturdy wood, the boat had probably once hung on the side of Captain Ahab's *Pequod*. A lone seagull perched on the keel. He took off with an indignant squawk as we closed in.

I got down on the ground on hands and knees. Most

of the silver-gray paint that had at one time coated the boat's hull had peeled off. Paint chips littered the sand, sticking to my palms. Sully bent and gripped the bottom, or the top actually, near the oarlocks. With a dramatic groan, he lifted one side of the boat about a foot off the ground.

Light poured in underneath. A horde of greenhead flies poured out. A cross between a giant mosquito and a fly, greenheads were *the* pest of New England beaches, munching on whatever tender skin they could find and drawing blood. Thankfully, this bunch of greenheads objected to us disturbing their nesting area and buzzed angrily away without stopping for a snack.

"Take your time. I can do this all day," Sully said with Captain America pluck.

"Sorry." I knelt again and cautiously peered under the boat. "I can't see that well. There's not enough light. Though I doubt—"

With a magnificent grunt, he lifted the boat like Superman on a mission and flung it over, right side up, revealing a wet patch of sand that smelled like rot and what looked to be a mole or a vole skittering away.

And nothing else.

My heart sank, though, come on, under the boat had to be *the* most ludicrous hiding place in Point Bailey. Murphy was smarter than that.

Looking equally disappointed, Sully offered a hand to help me up and we searched the rest of the area, for what it was worth. With the exception of broken shells, cigarette butts, and bits of driftwood, there was nothing to find. I dumped sand out of my shoes and circled the fisherman's shelter. Sully stepped inside the little house, neatly filling the tight space with his height and broad shoulders.

While he kicked at the dirt floor for some sign of digging and peered under the bench, a rustling sound in the brush at the base of the dune caught my attention. The mole-vole that had vacated the underside of the boat now searched for a shady place to hide from the sun. I followed the critter's trail as it scampered through the tall grass and scrubby bushes. My gaze lit on a patch of blue.

"Sully, come look."

I couldn't wait for him to do so. Too excited. Anticipation built as I picked my way into the brush. Thorns caught on my skirt and scratched my legs, a greenhead fly buzz-bombed me, aiming for a juicy spot on my neck, and I was certain a thousand deer ticks attached themselves to my ankles, but I kept going until I found what I was looking for, under a tangle of beach rose bushes and half buried in the sand.

"Beryl, is it...?" Sully reached out and took my hand, helping me out of the brambles into the clear.

I held up my treasure with a triumphant smile—a heavy burlap bag about the size of a potato sack, with *Spencer R. Field Seed Company* written in faded navy-blue letters on the front. The items inside clinked together as I shook it.

Sully's eyebrow danced in excitement. "Open it—"

His jaw snapped shut as a sudden burst of light lit up the beach, followed by a swirling gust of wind that kicked up sand and filled the air with the sulfur scent of time travel. I gasped and we both flinched in alarm as Niels Rasmussen stepped from the temporal tornado. Cool, casual, and completely upright, a more adept landing than I could ever manage.

The oscillating cocoon quickly faded and that's when I spotted the weapon in his hand. Not just any weapon. *My stinger.* The breath left my body and terror moved in. Our plan to hunt for the jewels had drawn Rasmussen out, but not how we'd wanted. I could practically feel Fate circling overhead, about to sweep in on Sully with bitchy finality.

Sully reacted fast and tried to shove me behind him. I tried to jump in front of him at the same time, and we ended up smacking into each other like a couple of clowns at the circus, only not funny. Not at all.

"Will you stop dancing around?" Rasmussen said, his upper lip curled. "We have business to take care of and not a lot of time. My associates aren't far behind."

"How'd you find us?" I asked, lifting my chin to keep my teeth from chattering.

He smirked. "Dorella. She's quite the bloodhound. She thought you might try to leave town, so she suggested we keep an eye on the station. Imagine our surprise when you traded in a train for a taxi. She called a friend at the taxi company to discover your cab's destination."

Sully swore and I echoed his frustration. I guess we hadn't managed to ditch Dorella after all. "So, while she and the others are headed here using more conventional means, you got the jump on all of them with a temporal skip shortcut."

Another smirk. "All's fair in love and time travel." His gaze dipped to the bag in my hand, and he licked his lips.

"Now, if you don't mind, throw me the jewels and I might just let you live."

I lifted the bag to throw it, but Sully gripped my wrist, stopping me. "Answer my question first. You killed Murphy."

Not a question, more of a statement that caught Rasmussen off guard. "In case you haven't noticed, soldier, I'm the one with the gun. *I* give the orders. Now, toss it over."

"I'll take that as a yes. Confirming my suspicion you did it. You gave yourself away last night. You mentioned Murph had been strangled, but I never said how he died. Mrs. Murphy knew, but you didn't. Took me a while to figure that out." He gave an offhand shrug. "Guess I'm thick that way. One thing I wanna know is, why?"

"Sully, please," I begged. My knees knocked together in fear and here he was, calmly going all *Murder, She Wrote* killer reveal. Well, not calmly. Not in the least. He'd balled his fists so tightly his knuckles had whitened, and anger coiled in his voice like a cobra readying for the attack.

"No, Beryl. Murph deserves an answer," he said, aiming a death glare at Rasmussen. "Why? After all the killing over there, why murder such a harmless fella? Why take the risk?"

"I *like* taking risks." An odd, greedy kind of giggle bubbled from his mouth. "Murphy was a big risk. I knew he was unstable, and a drunk, but he was the perfect patsy in case the plan went sour. Everything worked perfectly. We all came home, and the jewels were waiting for us. Until Murphy hid them." Frustration caught his voice. "He disobeyed me. Held my treasure hostage.

When he started mouthing off about the jewels to anyone he met, he threatened the entire operation."

Sully scowled. "You followed him here and strangled him. Even though he didn't tell you where to find the loot."

"I tried. I threatened Dorella, but the fool wouldn't give up the jewels, even for her. So much for love, eh?" He giggled again. "The man needed to learn *no one* takes what's mine from me. No one ever will, ever again." My breath stuttered as he lifted the stinger. The powering whine cut through the air. "You know what this weapon can do, Beryl. Throw me the jewels, or..."

I didn't have a nanosecond to react. Sully snatched the bag from me and hurled it at Rasmussen's head. His aim was off. It nailed the man in the chest. Sully moved to pounce on him when Agent Knight burst from out of nowhere and tackled Rasmussen like Ohio State's entire offensive line on a rampage. Rasmussen banged to the ground with an undignified screech.

Still in hero mode, Knight leapt up, stomped on Rasmussen's wrist to free the stinger from his grip, then kicked the weapon my way.

"Thank you," I said. I may have gushed a little, but seriously, I was never more grateful to see anyone in my life. I plucked the stinger out of the sand and glanced at Sully. He looked mighty disappointed someone else got to take down the bad guy, but he was alive and unharmed. "Thank you for everything."

Knight *your welcomed* with a majorly grouchy, "Don't let that zapper out of your sight again." He bent down and hauled Rasmussen to his feet none-too-gently. "I'm afraid this is the end of the line, my friend."

Rasmussen glared at him then his gaze dipped to the bag of loot sitting in the sand. "Let me get a look at them before you take them away," he begged, his eyes glimmering. "You owe me that, after all this time."

"He owes you *nothing*," I said. "Slap the cuffs on, Agent Knight. He just confessed to murdering Brian Murphy."

"Agent Knight?" Rasmussen laughed. A loud, long, and supremely delighted cackle that ended in a snort. Entirely too gleeful for a man about to be hauled off to jail for both murder and robbery. "Is *that* what you're calling yourself these days?"

I frowned, confused. Did Agent Knight go by an alias?

The man in question glanced my way with an unsettled expression. "Sullivan, get her out of here," he ordered. "She's in danger every minute you stand here."

"She's more in danger from you, my friend." Rasmussen let out a bitter laugh. "You have a habit of leaving dead girls in your wake."

A ball of dread grew in my belly. They weren't talking about a jewel robbery. This was an old battle, going way back. Sully thought the same thing. His eyebrows went into confused mode as his gaze bopped back and forth between the two men.

"Uh, Agent Knight, what does he mean?" I asked, not sure I wanted to hear the answer.

Rasmussen giggled again, a sound I could grow to despise.

"Oh Beryl, you really are the most gullible girl," he said. "Haven't you figured it out yet? Don't you know your so-called Agent Knight is a time traveler?"

Wait. What was happening right now?

I gaped at Knight. Sully had said something seemed off about him. I'd noticed odd things but hadn't put them together. The way he recited details of the jewel heist as if reading from a newspaper. Last night, when I'd suggested calling nine-one-one, Sully and Millie had gone all *nine-one-what?* but he hadn't blinked. The familiar scent that clung to him that I couldn't quite place—the smell of sulfur. And seconds ago, he'd called my stinger a *zapper* and kicked it straight to me, as if he knew what it was and who it belonged to.

Cold chills of avalanche proportions rushed down my spine. "Who are you?"

He eyed me warily, holding up both hands as if to stop a speeding truck. "Beryl, please. It's complicated."

"It's not complicated at all," Rasmussen said. "Why don't you tell her the truth?" He looked at me and a hard, unforgiving note of steel invaded his voice. "Beryl Blue, may I introduce you to one of my oldest and dearest friends, Oliver Bishop."

19

liver Bishop.

O The man who'd killed my parents. The man I'd been searching for all this time. The man who'd taken my family from me.

That Oliver Bishop?

My head spun and my feet seemed to have left the ground. A giant wave could've risen up and dragged us all out to sea right now and I wouldn't have noticed. Agent Knight was Oliver Bishop. The goofy guy who'd lectured me and huffed at me in frustration and even gazed at me with a hint of affection. The man whose pleasant Jimmy Stewart face and kind manner hid the heart of a cold-blooded killer.

Rasmussen watched me with a dark and gloating gleam in his eyes. I turned to Sully. He shook his head, his expression anguished.

Bishop looked even more upset. "Beryl I—"

"Shut up. You don't get to talk to me, Mr. Bishop. Or

Knight, or whatever your name is. Like pieces on a chess-board. What name is next? Rook? King?" Tears misted my eyes and clogged my voice. "Will you change chess pieces each time you murder some innocent pawn?"

Not what I'd meant to say. I'd practiced my Inigo Montoya speech for nearly two years. *You killed my parents, prepare to die.* I'd steeled myself for the moment I came face-to-face with this man. Now the moment had arrived, and I'd forgotten my lines. Every damned question I needed him to answer flew from my head. I forgot everything except my blind rage and the bloodlust that raced through my veins. The man I hated more than anything in the world stood before me.

The man I'd vowed to kill on sight.

I lifted the stinger and aimed between his eyes. Everyone fell silent. Even the wind and the rush of the estuary's tide seemed to still. Bishop's agonized expression turned to fear.

"I can explain," he said softly, coaxing. "It wasn't me. It was him. He killed your parents. He would've killed you too if he'd seen you in the car. I've been protecting you. I didn't kill them. I didn't kill anyone. What you've heard about me is a lie."

I swiped the tears from my eyes. "Is this the part where you monologue about how you're really the hero of the story? How you couldn't hurt a fly. Well, I don't care about that, or whatever little secrets you think you have."

I armed the weapon. My finger hovered over the *kill* button.

I felt Sully's warmth as he moved in close to me. His solid presence cocooned me.

"Don't, Beryl," he murmured, his voice as deep as the ocean and as comforting as a cloud. "You're better than this. You're not a killer."

"You sure?" Wasn't that what Time Scope wanted from me? The reason they'd taken me on. Me and my untraceable DNA. To be used as they saw fit, deployed like a stealth weapon to take down the company's enemies. I looked into the man formerly known as Knight's fear-filled blue eyes. To destroy people like *him*.

"Beryl. Sweetheart." Sully rested his hand on my forearm holding the weapon, a tender but firm touch intended to cool the vengeful fire racing through my veins. "He's not worth it. Take it from me. He's not worth the regret or the guilt. There's another way besides pulling the trigger—"

The *bang* of a gunshot suddenly rang out. Everybody ducked. Sully tried to grab me, but Bishop got there first. He threw me to the ground and covered me. I lost my grip on the stinger and it bounced away.

"Don't anybody move," Dorella shouted from the top of the dune. Dressed like she'd just stepped into the gunfight at OK Corral in a wide-brimmed hat, checkered shirt, and Western-style skirt, she gripped a small pistol, pointed straight up. "That was a warning. Next time I shoot to kill."

She scampered down the hillside followed by Lester. They shot toward Rasmussen, both demanding, "How'd you get here so fast?" No answer as Rasmussen snatched up the bag and they launched into a three-way tug of war over the jewels.

Lester's burly minions flew down the dune next and

made a beeline for Sully. I lay sprawled on the ground with my nose in the sand and Bishop spooning me like a mother hen, but I could see Sully, putting his fists to work, taking on all three goons at once.

He held his own in the fight, but for how long? Spitting sand out of my mouth, I pushed Bishop off me and sprang to my feet. Bishop and I both dove for my stinger. He won the race. He snatched it up and I braced for a jolt.

"I'm *not* going to hurt you," he said. "Never was. I've been following you, trying to protect you. What you heard about me is a lie. A mistake. He killed your parents. He killed several others. And he'll kill both of us if he gets the chance."

He held my gaze, his expression pleading. I hesitated, uncertainty pushing through the rage in my brain. Could what he said be true? Was Jake mistaken about what he'd seen? Could Rasmussen be the true culprit? Recent evidence pointed to yes. He'd killed Murphy, had threatened to kill Sully.

Dorella let out a frustrated shriek that carried across the dunes and all the way to Boston. Bishop and I both swung to look. Dorella had snatched the bag from Rasmussen's grip but lost her hold. The bag sailed up, flipped over, and the contents spilled out as it hit the ground. Contents that would interest no one but the seagulls—a mismatched collection of seashells, stones, and colorful sea glass of all sizes. No jewels, just another one of Murphy's tricks to throw treasure hunters off the scent.

"Junk!" Dorella cried. "It's all junk."

Lester swore a blue streak. Rasmussen gazed around

the beach with a defeated expression. Then he froze. His face lit up in surprise and he laughed. A heartbeat later he scooped up Dorella's gun and took off down to the estuary at top speed.

"Beryl, stay here," Bishop ordered. "If you value your life, stay here." He shoved the stinger into my hand and tore off after Rasmussen. He splashed into the knee-deep water. The man he chased had already reached the other side and burst along the beach like a sprinter going for the gold.

Or, like a thief going for the jewels.

Damn. How could I have missed it? How did I not figure it out? The clue had been there on the postcard. Or rather, *not* there on the postcard. Not in a picture of the beach area in 1910 anyway.

"Sully!" I thrust the stinger into my pocket and rushed up to him and tugged on his sleeve.

"What is it?" He delivered a stinging uppercut, decking the biggest of Lester's goons. He swung to the next in line, his cheeks as red as cherries and his eyes sparkling. "I'm kinda busy here."

"The jewels. I know where Murph hid them. For real this time. They're over there."

He took down another one of his opponents and followed my gaze. Rasmussen ran full tilt down the strip of beach across the estuary and had almost reached the foot of the cliff. Bishop raced after him.

"Look up, Sully. At the lookout post." The sun beamed down on the squat building's chalky concrete, visible through the trees. "Kilroy is *there.*"

He let out an astonished laugh. "Son of a bitch."

"Rasmussen's gone after them, with Bishop on his tail. Rasmussen's got a gun. Bishop's unarmed. He's a sitting duck." A shudder ran through me, and I attempted to swallow a large lump in my throat with little success. *I could've killed him. If not for Sully, I might have.* "I've wanted Bishop dead for so long, but not this way. I have to stop him."

"*We'll* stop him."

A thousand arguments flashed through my mind, discarded all at once as he took my hand and we raced down the beach to the water. My mind raced just as fast. This had been a hell of a weekend for stunning revelations, and none more gob smacking than what I'd just heard. Bishop's desperate words, *I didn't kill them. I'm trying to protect you. He killed them.*

Oliver Bishop hadn't killed my parents. Rasmussen had.

Last night at Chaisson's, Rasmussen had filled my ears with lies. He'd played victim with the conviction of an Oscar-winning actor. I'd been so blinded by my hatred for Bishop I'd willingly bought the ticket and gone back to see the performance again and again. I hadn't seen the holes in the plot, or the way he'd manipulated me, though the clues were there. His temper and his greed and his professed love of shiny things. His anger over his co-worker Lexie's death.

And his confession. Rasmussen had murdered Murphy without a blink. He'd murdered everyone, including my parents. He'd nearly murdered me. Shame rose up and clutched my throat, joined by remorse and anger. I hadn't seen any of it.

"Hey, you!" Dorella broke away from her important

task of yelling at Lester to chase us to the water's edge. "Where are you going? Where are the jewels?"

"Screw the jewels," Sully said, tugging me along. "We're going to catch a killer."

To catch a killer, and to right a terrible wrong.

20

———

Sully and I sloshed steadily toward the estuary's opposite side. We picked our way across slick stones, seaweed, and other hazards on the seabed. Frigid water swirled around my legs, soaking my shoes and my skirt, biting into my skin. I'd forgotten how cold the Atlantic Ocean could be, even in summer. The tide rushed outward. The current pulled at my legs and threatened to sweep me off balance. Only Sully's strong grip kept me from falling.

"Don't let them get away!" Dorella shouted from behind us.

I looked back to see Lester and his one minion still conscious hurry down the beach to join her at the water's edge, but they screeched to a halt before stepping in.

"What are you doing?" Dorella hollered at them. "Go after them."

Tony, the goon who'd gut-punched Sully in the alley yesterday, vigorously shook his head. "I can't swim."

"Three years in the Navy and you can't swim?" Dorella nailed him with a contemptuous glare then swung on Lester. "I suppose you can't swim either?" He threw up his hands and Dorella swore. "You want a job done right…"

She tore off her oxford shoes and tied the laces together, then slung them around her neck and splashed into the stream. I didn't check on her progress again because we'd reached the shore on the other side. We squished through soft sand to more solid ground. Ahead, Rasmussen had made it to the Prow and disappeared into the shrubbery bordering the path to the top. Bishop wasn't far behind.

We followed their tracks at a run. Well, sort of a run. Three steps into our pursuit I cursed myself for not being as smart as Dorella and keeping my shoes dry. Water squished out of the sides like a broken pump and sand stuck to the soles with each step.

Despite that, we soon reached the base of the cliff. We paused for breath and for me to knock a mound of wet grit off my shoes. Behind us, Dorella still struggled through the water. I looked up and caught a flash of Rasmussen's golden hair through the scrubby bushes high on the rise. I shuddered. The top of the hill seemed miles away. I quaked at the height.

"Rest time's over," Sully said.

I wrestled my pumps back onto my feet. I could swear the shoe leather had shrunk. Steeling myself, I stepped onto the path. I barely bleated when Sully pushed ahead and took the lead. The narrow track wound upward, an uneven patch of packed earth made even more treacherous by the roots and rocks poking out of the ground. Several areas had been eroded by weather and gave way under our feet, tripping us up and sending mini avalanches down the hill.

We climbed higher and higher. The vegetation thinned out. The terrain became rockier. My blouse clung to my back and my sodden skirt stuck to my legs, chilling me despite the heat and the exertion warming my skin. I did my best to ignore the increasing elevation and focused on my endgame, as Jake and Time Scope had taught me. Get to the top. Get Rasmussen. Keep him from killing Bishop and complete my mission at the same time. A win-win for all.

Focusing helped keep my fear of heights at bay until I forgot the cardinal rule of acrophobia—don't look down. I looked down. Breaking waves pounded the jagged rocks below. Rocks that seemed to both zoom in and stretch far away, like a disorienting shot in a horror movie. An invisible hand wrapped around my chest and squeezed tight. I sucked in a breath between my teeth and forced myself forward, centering my gaze on Sully's broad back.

I soon fell behind, thanks to my jitters and his long strides. He pulled up and looked back. His face crinkled in concern, and he made his way down to me.

"What's wrong?" he asked, his scowl achingly tender.

"Nothing. Well, something. It's so ridiculous." I flashed a panicky glance behind me. "It's a long way down."

Our gazes connected and he nodded. "Let me help you."

He held out his hand and I saw him in uniform again, the gruff young sergeant I'd met in 1943, who'd put his life on the line to help me stop what he thought was an assassin. I remembered him not much older in Belgium in 1944, a hell of a lot more cynical, but still the first one to reach out to help.

I closed my hand over his. His palm was a little sweaty but his grip as solid as granite. He gave me a tug and we started to move.

"It's okay. It's okay," he murmured over and over, while urging me on. "You can do this, sweetheart. Just keep moving. One more step. One more breath. One foot in front of the other. Eyes front. Keep going. You'll get through it."

I let his calming voice and steady hand guide me. Soon, my fear and panic receded like the tide going out and I motored up that path with the sure step of a seasoned mountain goat.

I watched him move, his legs strong, his hair lit by the sun, and my throat tickled with emotion. Millie had been so right about him. Whenever anyone needed help, Sully would be there, like Tom Joad in *The Grapes of Wrath*. On the side of good and right. And on my side. No matter what. To help me.

Even if it killed him.

WE KEPT MOVING. An occasional shriek or curse carried on the wind from below as Dorella wended upward, slipping, stumbling, and getting caught on branches as we had. We closed in on the summit. At the top of the path, we paused at a narrow space between a tangle of bushes that led into a large clearing, with the lookout post at the center.

"I don't see Rasmussen," I said. The area was deserted and quiet, except for some cheeping birds and the sound of the pounding surf in the distance. "Maybe they went that way." I gestured to a dirt road that led off to the right, just wide enough for a jeep or other small military vehicle.

"Listen." Sully tipped his head. The wind had picked up, gusting across the open area and sending dust and leaves flying around. Indistinct voices carried on the breeze from the other side of the building.

I tugged his arm, and we crouched low as we crept into the clearing. The ground had been packed down from years of pacing boots. The lookout post filled most of the space. A square concrete block with a flat roof, the bunker had a slitted rectangular window in the front that looked out to sea, and in the back, a broader opening for people to come and go. Weeds and other flora had grown up around its base and I imagined the structure would be all *Life After People* in a few years, swallowed up by nature.

We approached the back of the building. I peeped around the corner to see Rasmussen and Oliver Bishop, standing about twenty feet apart, chatting like neighbors at the backyard fence. Bishop had his back to us. Rasmussen stood closer to the cliff's edge, clutching Dorella's gun and a large burlap bag identical to the seed bag I'd found in the brush. The bag bulged and I caught something sparkly peeping out of the top.

The jewels. Niels Rasmussen had found his treasure at last.

"...How did you find me?" he was saying.

"Getting your picture taken was sloppy," Bishop said. "You should've known we'd pick up on that."

"That was a mistake. I didn't see the cameraman. Seeing Mabel's daughter distracted me." Rasmussen frowned. "Fate's funny, isn't it? I missed her all those times, and all I had to do was wait for her to drop into my lap."

Bishop snorted. "You missed her because we moved her. Every time you got close, we took her away. To protect her."

We? That pronoun haunted me. *We* moved her. The *her* in that declaration had to be me, even someone as freaked out as I was at the moment could get that. Bishop claimed he'd been protecting me and apparently, he had help. But who? Jake? Glo? Someone else at Time Scope? Whoever *we* could be, I guess that proved I really was Special-with-a-capital-*S*.

A malignant smile touched Rasmussen's lips. "So noble of you, my friend, and a change of pace. You usually kill young women, not protect them."

I couldn't see his face, but Bishop's posture went as rigid as stone. "Lexie's death was an accident, Niels. Why can't you get that through your head? An accident caused by *your* risk-taking. If you hadn't pushed us to use the tech before it was ready—"

"If I hadn't pushed you, there would be no Time Scope. There'd be no temporal tech at all. What did I get for my labors? Lexie dead. Cut out of the profits. Everything taken from me." He hugged the bag of jewels to his chest. "And *you* chasing me through time."

"I had no choice. We have to stop you. You've already

done so much damage. That's over now. You're coming with me."

"There's where you're wrong, my friend." Rasmussen centered his gaze—and the pistol—on Bishop. His voice turned bitter cold. "I'm leaving, but this is the end for you."

"He'll kill him," I said in an urgent whisper. I grabbed the stinger from my skirt pocket. "I'm going out there."

"Too dangerous," Sully said, barely audible.

I frowned. Was he pulling a Jake on me? Trying to protect me when all I wanted to do was keep these two men from killing each other.

Sully dropped his voice even lower. "We need a *plan* before we act."

He gestured and mimed the way military types did in the movies, building a scenario I mostly understood. He'd creep along the other side of the lookout bunker. I'd create a diversion, giving him the chance to spring on Rasmussen, taking him down with either a karate chop or a bust in the mouth, I couldn't tell.

Not an ideal plan. Far from it. I opened my mouth to alert Sully to that fact when he slipped away as silent as a ghost. I watched him disappear around the corner of the building and an anxiety ball coated with fear took form in my belly. He and Rasmussen were as far apart as two men could be, but they shared something ferocious and fatal in common.

Both men liked to take risks. Too many risks.

I armed my stinger, hoping the gusty wind and the crash of the waves below would cover the powering whine. I peered out at the two men still facing off, took a breath, and, crossing my fingers that Sully had gotten into position by now, I darted into the open.

"Freeze, both of you," I ordered, like a detective in a '70s cop show, only more frantic.

"Beryl," Bishop growled, turning to glare at me. "Get the *hell* out of here."

"No, stay." Rasmussen swung his aim toward me. His smile turned ugly, full of teeth and satisfaction. "It's time I finish the job I started."

He cocked the pistol and the next moments whisked by in a terrifying blur. Sully launched himself at Rasmussen like a grizzly on the attack as I squeezed the stinger's trigger. The zapper shivered and a vigorous stream of juice shot out. The blast hit Rasmussen in the leg, too low to do anything but make him howl. Sully reached him, but too late to keep him from firing. The pistol exploded with a boom that bounced off the building and echoed across the water.

"No!" Bishop cried and leapt in front of me. His body jerked. He smacked against the bunker's wall, then slammed to the ground. His suitcoat fell open and a dark red stain spread across his white shirt like spilled wine.

Gritting his teeth, Sully swung and punched Rasmussen in the jaw with the force of an asteroid pounding the earth. Rasmussen snapped back and lurched closer to the cliff's edge. He struggled to keep his hold on his treasure and the pistol but couldn't hang onto both. The gun dropped. It *tinged* off a rock then bounced up and spun end over end like a pinwheel before it plunged downward into a watery grave.

Off balance, Rasmussen teetered on the precipice, clutching the bag of jewels for dear life. Sully grabbed for the man's collar to keep him from toppling over the edge. He got a fistful of his dog tags instead and tore them from his throat. Rasmussen clawed at Sully's arm and yanked him toward him as he lost his battle to hold steady. He plummeted backward, taking Sully with him.

Both men fell.

Over the cliff.

21

———

his. Isn't. Happening.

    I stared numbly at the spot where Sully had fallen. Gone. He was gone. Terror stilled my blood. Horror, blazing rage, and unimaginable grief shook me to the core. *Sully will die, saving you.* The deadly words banged on my brain.

Fate, that ironic bitch, had gotten its due.

With a soundless scream on my lips, I shot to the cliff's edge and fell to my knees. I peered over the side and down at the crashing surf. I blinked away tears to bring Sully into focus, dreading the sight of his broken body sprawled on the rocks below.

Every ounce of breath left my lungs when I saw him.

Alive.

He dangled in midair with both arms wrapped around the trunk of a scrawny tree sticking out from the cliffside. He kicked his legs like a bucking bronco, trying to reach the rocks and find a foothold. An effort hindered by his passenger. Still clutching his bag of loot, Rasmussen had hooked his free arm around Sully's waist and held on tight. The little tree trembled and sagged under the weight of the two men.

"A little help?" Sully said, looking up at me, his voice strained.

Relief sliced through me, followed by a burst of adrenaline. Fear of heights forgotten, I threw myself to the ground and scooted on my belly as close to the edge as I dared. Something sharp jabbed into my shin. Rasmussen's dog tags, torn off his neck when Sully tried to stop him from falling. I shoved the chain away and leaned over the side. I reached down, desperate to grab Sully's collar or wrist or hair, anything I could get hold of.

My breath seized. My arm couldn't stretch far enough. Not even close.

Sully held my eyes, his expression agonized. His arms trembled from exertion. He weakened. Rasmussen weighed him down. The tree supporting both men shuddered. Small stones and bits of soil around the roots broke loose. The debris ticked against the cliff's façade as it fell. Below, the ocean churned and pounded the jagged rocks like a ravenous beast.

"Fuck." If any situation called for a loud and furious F-bomb, this was it. Fuck Rasmussen. Fuck those fucking jewels. And most of all, fuck fate and its malicious hunger for a good man like Sully to die.

I reached down with both arms, willing them to grow longer. The TDC on my wrist caught the sunlight. Hope flared, and so did an idea. Could I break the rules? Could I take Sully's destiny into my time-traveling hands? Go back ten or twenty seconds and save him. Save Bishop too. Would it work? Or create a time-shattering paradox?

Before I could act, Sully doubled his effort to reach safety. He swung forward. His feet scraped the ragged rocks and fell away. More dirt came loose. The tree's roots snapped and tore from the soil. Sully swung again and his body bashed the cliff with a force that made him yowl, but he finally found a foothold.

The movement jolted Rasmussen's tenuous hold on Sully's waist and shook him loose. He dropped toward the water at rocket speed. He scrambled to reach his TDC so he could time skip but the bulging sack of gems got in the way. With a frustrated wince, he let go. The bag upended and a host of shiny things spilled out like a sparkling rain. Necklaces, earrings, loose diamonds, emeralds, and sapphires as blue as Sully's eyes showered down into the sea.

A beat later, a blue tornado whipped up and swallowed Rasmussen whole, within inches of smashing into the rocks below.

Relieved of his burden, Sully could move with more ease. His foot found a narrow ledge to balance on. I let out my breath—I could reach him now. I grabbed his arm with both hands and put two years of physical training and a million-and-one bicep curls to good use, pulling with all my strength. With my help and a mighty roar, he scrambled upward and swung himself over the cliff's edge, onto solid ground.

He collapsed onto his back next to me and for a moment we lay there, panting, stunned. He'd made it. He'd survived. My heart swelled with relief and gratitude and a zillion other emotions but especially love, so much love for this amazing man.

I rolled over and kissed him.

"Never a dull moment with you, Beryl Blue," he said, smiling into my eyes.

"Beryl…" Bishop called, his voice weak, thready.

Sully got to his feet, a little shaky, and helped me up. We rushed over to Bishop. He'd dragged himself to the lookout building and sat with his back against the wall. His face had paled to an ashen color, and he barely clung to life. Rasmussen's bullet had caught him in the chest, or maybe the stomach. So much blood soaked what had once been a white shirt, I couldn't tell.

I knelt beside him. "I'll get help." I tapped my junior's watch face to activate it, hoping I could connect with the 1946 version of an EMT.

Bishop tried to shake his head. "It's too late."

"Don't say that. You'll be okay."

His head lolled as he focused his gaze on me. "Did you get him? Is he dead?"

"No. He time skipped." My throat burned with regret, and from the look of defeat in Bishop's eyes.

He groaned which turned into a cough that brought up blood. Sully crouched down and wiped Bishop's mouth with a handkerchief he pulled from his pocket.

"Stay with us, soldier," Sully said, then sliced me a glance. He shook his head. Solemn acknowledgement from a man who'd seen this kind of wound before and knew the truth.

My belly roiled. How was that for bitter irony? All this time I'd wanted to kill Oliver Bishop. Now he was dying, and it shattered me.

"Beryl." His fingers fluttered and I took his hand, cold and clammy and sticky with blood. "I need to know... need you to believe me. I didn't kill them. Ras... He did."

I'd pretty much pieced the whole sordid tale together from his frantic explanations earlier, and from what I'd overheard. "I believe you, Oliver."

He gave a feeble nod. "Your parents... friends of mine. Your mother... pregnant with you. They knew they had to run. I found out about Ras, tried to warn them, but too late." He spoke slowly, his voice raspy and strained. "I chased him from the car. He would've killed you if he'd known you were alive. A... man came along before I could rescue you. Knew he'd help you." He coughed again, bringing up more blood. "I went after... Ras. Been chasing him since. Finally found him."

And Rasmussen had found Bishop. My throat closed up, filled with so many emotions I couldn't begin to name them.

"We kept watch over you. Moved you if he got too close..." He took a ragged breath. "The last time, we arranged ex... extraction."

I shivered. *Extraction.* As in, moved me from 2015. This was what Jake and Glo had kept from me. The truth about why they'd upended my life so thoroughly. I wasn't supposed to die from hitting my head. They moved me to keep a time-traveling killer from finding me.

"Now you know." Bishop took another breath, shallow and wheezy. "Stop him. Protect the others. Bring him home. To justice."

"I will. I promise."

He sighed, his pleasant features relaxed, and his hand holding mine let go.

"He's gone," Sully murmured. I looked away as he reached over and closed Bishop's eyes.

Sully helped me to stand and put his arms around me. I wiped my eyes, holding back the tears. I didn't want to cry. Not now. I would later when I had a chance to process. When I had a moment to grieve properly.

Dorella shoved into the clearing and around the corner of the lookout building a moment later. "Where is he?" she cried. Her wet skirt had been torn to pieces and leaves and twigs were tangled in her hair. "Where are the jewels?"

While I wondered which question to answer first, Sully stepped in. "They're at the bottom of the sea, Mrs. Murphy. Along with your friend Rasmussen."

She stamped her foot. "We went through all of that for nothing."

I disagreed. Not nothing. A whole lot of something. This mission had been an emotional journey full of stunning revelations that had taken me to a whole new place of joy—and sorrow. I'd learned the story of my parents, learned about my own past. I gazed at Bishop's body and grief washed through me. I'd discovered the true story of Oliver Bishop. A good man, a guardian angel I didn't know I had, but lost before I had a chance to get to know him.

I leaned into Sully's embrace. And I'd found him again. My one true love. The man who'd saved me so many times and in so many ways. The man fate had discovered was exceedingly hard to kill. The man who'd beat that ironic bitch's curse and stood here with me now, holding me in his strong, sturdy arms.

I gazed into his eyes and kissed him as the sound of police sirens filled the air.

22

We sat together on the small step at the front of the lookout post, in the shade and several feet from the edge of the cliff. We'd both had enough of that bit of geography for one day. The cool concrete felt good on my back. So did Sully's arm around me, holding me close as we gazed out at the horizon. I rested my head on his shoulder, happy to be with him, even if the moment wouldn't last.

Dorella had shrewdly skulked away before the police arrived. Sully had provided them with her address, so I had faith she wouldn't be a free woman for long. I also suspected she'd rat out Lester and his burly friends the minute the cops slapped the handcuffs on her.

Rasmussen had gotten away, as he had for all his other crimes. A frustrating state of affairs I was determined to correct. I'd start with a long talk with Jake, find out if he knew what Bishop had meant by *we kept watch over you*. I'd find out everything Jake knew if I had to drag each and every detail out of his secretive mouth word by word.

We'd spoken to Lieutenant Gunderson briefly. Sully had done most of the talking, giving him a largely factual account of what had happened and how we'd gotten tangled up with jewel thieves, minus the time travel. Gunderson announced his intention to search the area around the base of the cliff for Rasmussen's body and the jewels. I wished him luck. The alleged dead man had vanished in time, and unless an unusually vigorous tide swept the gems ashore, I doubted they would ever be found.

"What do you want to do about Mr. Bishop?" Sully asked, leaning close and gently kissing my temple. "Gunderson will figure out pretty quick there's no Aloysius Knight with Army CID and he'll have a John Doe on his hands."

I sighed. "I'm not exactly sure." I'd watched the police remove Bishop's body, filled with grief and remorse, wondering what would happen next. "I suppose I should see what the gang at C level wants to do. This is above my pay grade."

"In English, sweetheart."

"I'll ask my boss to check with the company's head office." Or maybe not. I figured Rasmussen's accusations about corporate negligence had been lies fueled by his bitterness, but I still wasn't sure I could fully trust Time Scope's powers that be. "Oliver Bishop should be brought home to his own time period. He must have someone who'll mourn him."

Besides me. And whoever had been directing him to

keep watch over me. Was it the same person who'd sent Jake to protect my parents?

Something sparkled by the edge of the cliff. I darted toward it, by which I mean I crept slowly forward, keeping my eyes on the shiny thing and didn't look down. I found a diamond earring, caught in a gully on a rock's bumpy surface. A bell dinged in my head. The fifth and final item to be placed in my suitcase had been found.

I laughed. Not really amused. A bittersweet sort of laugh. Who knew the person who'd put the items in my suitcase would turn out to be me?

I strolled back to the stoop and sat down. Sully enfolded me in his arms again. I cherished the feel of him, and the moment. We embraced the now. Our motto.

"What you got there?" he asked.

I showed him the earring, then placed it on the step next to me with Rasmussen's dog tags. "I'm going to put these in my suitcase, together with a few other things that may look random to you but are pretty important to me. Then I'm going to ask you to do me a favor."

Sully listened patiently as I unpacked the suitcase tale. His left eyebrow rose higher and higher. "Let me get this straight. I go to the Ballard Springs library, put the suitcase in storage, and you find it two hundred years from now."

"Yes," I said, hiding a smile. I knew where this was going.

"Then you bring the bag back here, and we do it all over again."

"Yes."

He tugged on his ear. "That makes no sense. It's... it's..."

"Confusing. Headache making. Ridiculously repetitive. Haven't I told you not to waste your brain cells trying to figure out any of that time travel stuff?"

He scowled. "I like puzzles, but this is a real head-scratcher. How do I convince the librarian to take the bag and store it? Those ladies can be a crabby bunch sometimes."

"Sully!" I pulled out of his embrace. "On behalf of librarians everywhere and in any time period, and I say this lovingly... How dare you!" He chuckled and I snuggled up to him again. "You'll figure something out. I'll get the suitcase to you before..." Before we said goodbye. Again. "When are you leaving?"

He took a moment before answering. "I'm staying in town a day or two more. Hadn't planned to. Mill and I were supposed to take the afternoon train home today." He shifted. "But I'll stick around and take care of arrangements for Murph. He's got no one left."

"You're a good man, Sully. I don't think I've told you that today." He brushed that off with a grunt. "And I love you."

He kissed the top of my head. "I know."

"Wait." I swiveled to look at him again. "Did you just Han Solo me?"

He chuckled. "I never have any idea what you're talking about." He slipped a hand under my chin and tipped my head back, his eyes meeting mine. "But I love you anyway, Beryl Blue. Always."

He kissed me, a deep, lingering kiss. A kiss I added to my memory file to keep with me for a long, long time. For always. After we parted, I leaned back against his chest, with his arms around me, safe and secure in his hold.

We sat like that for some time, gazing out at the sea. The ocean swells rose and fell in a steady rhythm. The late-day sun sparkled like diamonds on the water's surface but couldn't penetrate the blue-green depths or reveal the mysteries underneath. The surf beat against the rocks below, the sound of each breaking wave like thunderous snowflakes, no two alike. Eternal and fleeting all at once. Like Sully and me.

"Do you think they'll ever find the jewels?" I asked.

"I think they're in some shark's stomach by now. Those things eat anything."

I could almost hear the *Jaws* music as he said that. I nuzzled his neck. "You know I've got to leave."

His arms tightened around me. "I guess."

"I won't be back."

"You guess." He kissed me below the ear, in that tender spot that sent shivers dancing over my skin. "Do you have to go right now? Can't you stay a while longer?"

I leaned into his touch and melted, putty in his extremely skilled hands. And his expert lips. They burned a trail of fire as he kissed my neck and back up to my mouth. I sighed and he grinned. He knew he'd won. Sully would always win.

Until he didn't.

I didn't want to think about that now. All I wanted to think about was him and these precious moments we had together.

"I suppose I can stay, for just a little while longer," I said, my voice no more than a whisper. A sexy, aching whisper of desire. For this man, this moment, this now. "Let's go back to my place."

"My place first. I need clean clothes." His lips touched mine again. "I might have a couple condoms there, too."

"Why Sergeant Sullivan." I shivered from head to toe. "You are, and I mean this in the best possible way, a real piece of work."

EPILOGUE

"Complete chaos if the computers interpreted the double zeros in the code as the year 1900, not 2000. That's what the hysteria was about. The average person didn't understand the complexity of coding and the limitations of such primitive computing systems in those days and..."

Eric from Research droned on. And on and on. He'd heard about my Montpelier Y2K adventure and, since late twentieth-century history was his specialty, he'd cornered me on the pretext of wanting to hear all about it. In reality, he saw it as his chance to do what he did best. *Mansplain.* Fun fact, mansplaining was still a thing in the 2100s, and probably would be until the end of time.

But really, lecturing me, a nineties kid who'd cuddled a Furby and tickled an Elmo when I was growing up, about the Y2K drama? I'd lived through it. Though, to be fair, Eric didn't know that. No one knew but a select few, and even them I wondered how much. My brief stay in 1946 had exposed an entirely new chapter in the book of my life, a book that demanded a sequel to explore the whole story properly. Perhaps even a trilogy.

"Well, how about that?" I offered, Grandma Blue's way of telling a serial yackker to shut the hell up. Eric failed to notice the metric ton of sarcasm in those words and kept going.

He'd buttonholed me the second I'd arrived at the party at Glo's place. A party she'd planned to celebrate my two-year anniversary of becoming a time cop, but between us, really a celebration of Sully. And the fact that he'd cheated fate and survived an encounter with me.

A tornado of energy suddenly whipped up around Eric and me. No, not someone time skipping into the party via temporal oscillator. While that would be quite an entrance, it would also be against company rules, not to mention exceedingly rude. This whirlwind comprised a trio of distinct and vibrant forms of energy—Ethel, Myrtle, and Gladys, Alice and her wife Wendy's three daughters.

"Auntie Beryl," Ethel cried, grabbing my arm and shaking it to get my attention. "We want some cake."

Wendy watched from across the room. I shot her a silent thank you for sending in the rescue squad, then abandoned Eric mid "well actually..." and let Ethel and her sisters tug me to the dessert table.

"Are you really a time cop?" Myrtle asked, gazing up at me with wide eyes. She was seven, or maybe four.

"Momma says you stop the bad guys from wrecking time," Gladys said, who clocked in at somewhere between six and nine. Couldn't be sure. I'd never spent much time around kids, so my age recognition technology didn't get much practice.

"Yup, I'm a time cop and I get the bad guys," I said. Or tried to, with varying degrees of success. "But I couldn't find any of them without your momma telling me where to find them. Now, how many pieces of cake do you want?"

"Beryl, you have a second?" Jake called after I sent the girls off with copious amounts of cake and other sugary treats. They plonked on the floor at the feet of Glo's significant other, Wesley, who strummed a guitar for an appreciative audience. A bald, brown-skinned man as tall and as broad-shouldered as Sully, Wesley and Glo had been together forever and a day.

Jake sat in a cozy alcove, with a fireplace, a sofa and a couple of armchairs, tables dotted with knickknacks, and a tall bookshelf packed with books. He held his commpad. Did that guy ever *not* work?

I wandered over and took the chair next to him, one of those plush, comfy things you sink into five miles deep and can't ever get out of.

He put his commpad on the coffee table and gave me a tight smile. Not a dimple in sight. "This is a fun party."

Said the guy sitting in a corner with his work computer. "Mm-hm. Sure."

He looked around the alcove, gathering his thoughts. Reason #154 why we shouldn't be together. The man always thought things through before he spoke. An admirable trait, but those long pauses would've driven me bonkers in the long run. As would my tendency to speak first and ask questions later for Jake.

While he wool-gathered, I looked around too, scanning the bookcase, and checking out the photos and holopix arranged all about. Pictures of Glo's family members, a stunning array of gorgeous Black people with impressive bone structure going back several generations. With the exception of that one white guy in a fuzzy black-and-white photo from way back when. I could tell he was Glo's great-great-whatever by the man's determined jawline, the same as hers. He wore a Sully-era suit and stood in front of a Christmas tree with his arm around a woman as petite and fierce-looking as Glo.

"You did a good job," Jake said finally. "Your mission was a success."

I shifted, sinking lower into the chair. "I doubt Devon sees it that way. I messed up royally. Lost the jewels, lost Rasmussen." I hesitated. "Lost Bishop. A good man, turns out."

Jake grunted, sounding a lot like Sully, reluctant to admit he'd made a mistake. "You found out the truth, that's the most important thing." He paused and the silence seemed to stretch into next week. "Thought you'd like to know I've made arrangements to have his body returned here. We can put him to rest."

"Thank you."

He nodded. "Alice is searching for any family he may have left behind, but she doesn't have much hope. Seems like he had no one."

I swallowed a sudden lump of emotion. Oliver Bishop had me, at least. The man who'd occupied my brain for nearly two years, now held a space in my heart. He'd protected me. Watched over me. Saved me that fateful day and had gotten blamed for it for so many years.

"We'll adjust the official records on Bishop," Jake added. "We'll focus our search on Rasmussen instead. He temporal skipped from '46. Glo says there's a remote chance the oscillation will leave an echo in time wherever he landed. Alice's team is already tracking that. If the tech security team picks up his DNA off your stinger, that'll make finding him even easier. It's only a matter of time before we catch up to him." He looked me in the eye. "Because of you."

Way to put a positive spin on all the mistakes I'd made along the way. I mean, Rasmussen's DNA wouldn't have gotten anywhere near my zapper if I hadn't dropped it. But if that meant we caught him sooner rather than later, then yay, me. Bishop's last words repeated in my mind. *Protect the others*. That meant there were others who'd fled into time. To where, no one knew. Not even Rasmussen—yet. If we could collar him before he found any of them, then my bobbles and missteps would be worth it.

"Jake, are we gonna be okay?" I said, shifting gears. "I mean, after everything, I need for us to be okay. I want us to be friends." A clunky, awkward line, but necessary. I wanted to stamp *the end* on the story of us, the us that never was, but I didn't want to lose the friendship we'd built. "We can do that, can't we?"

He hesitated then released a heavy breath. "We'll be okay. In time. Once..."

Once he got over the idea of me. Once I put my baggage behind me too.

"I want to apologize." He put his commpad aside. "I pushed you. Used you to replace something I lost."

I nodded. The feelings I imagined I had for him were the same. "Will you tell me about her? Now that so much is in the open, will you tell me? And about Grandma

Blue? The whole story. The *true* story about both of them."

He smiled, a genuine smile this time and I got my first glimpse of dimples since I'd returned. "I will. But not now. This is a party for you."

Again, this from the guy who talked about work at a party for me.

"I need to ask you something else, and I want you to be straight with me." A Sully phrase, a straightforward request for the truth and nothing but. "Before he died, Oliver told me you and Glo extracted me because you saw some ripples that indicated he was close to me. We now know the threat didn't come from Bishop, but Rasmussen. How did you find out I was in danger and needed to be moved from 2015? Where did that information come from?"

He chewed that over a while before giving me a terse, "From above."

"Above? Who above? Who sent you to move me? Who sent you to protect my parents?"

"Glo."

Okay. Getting somewhere, at least. "Who told Glo to send you?"

"It's complicated."

My temples began to throb. "Don't do that. Please."

He sighed. "It's classified." A look of fear flashed over his face. Maybe from the ballistic, *I'm going to commit Jake-icide* glower I aimed at him. "I'm not trying to put you off, Beryl. I truly don't know. It's classified. Above my pay grade, as you would say. I don't have a clue."

My eyebrows popped up in surprise. Something Jake didn't know? Will wonders never cease.

"All I know is the man I thought was Bishop got close to you in 2015," he said. "Too close. We were ordered to get you out of there. Not so easy. Try convincing someone like you a time-traveling assassin is after them, and, by the way, we're gonna move you to a new time period." Another smile touched his lips. "We came up with a plan, not a great plan, but it had to do. Bring you here. Convince everyone we wanted you as an untraceable. The only way we could get approval to do that was the test."

"The test." And the beginning of the lies. "I'll venture to guess that whole me being a DNA ghost thing is fiction."

"Not to Devon it isn't. Not to me. You can't even begin to know the value you bring to the team."

Hooray for me, employee of the month. Give me a gold star. Or at least Jake made it sound that way.

"Okay then, why Sully?" Every conversation about the how and why of my past circled back to that question. Why had they chosen to push me into Sully's arms? I'd never gotten a satisfactory answer. "And don't give me that bull about fate and destiny wanting us together. There had to be a reason you chose to put me with Sully, out of all the people in all of time."

He clammed up. "That's not my story to tell."

"Then, whose is it?"

Glo poked her head around the corner before he could answer. "Alice has something to show us. Come with me." Blunt and to the point as always. She didn't dance around.

I stood. Well, Jake helped me to stand since that comfy chair didn't seem to want to let me go. We wended through the partygoers and joined both women by Glo's office door.

"Jake, did you tell her?" Alice asked, practically bouncing on her toes. She held a commpad, the source, I suspected, of her excitement.

"I was waiting for you."

"Hey, this is a party, we are *not* having a work meeting," I said coolly, though my pulse thrummed with curiosity.

"This is about you, Beryl." Glo ushered us inside her cluttered home office with a picture window overlooking a leafy park. My curiosity popped even more, and when she closed and locked the door, it went into overdrive.

Alice slipped the commpad out from under her arm and placed it on the desk against the wall. She tapped the screen and the device blinked to life. So did a ton of holographic images. The same image, actually, flashing a number of times. It wavered, came into focus, then faded away. A newspaper article from the *Ballard Springs Gazette* with a fuzzy headline and unreadable text.

Only the picture was clear. *Sully*. A black-and-white photograph of him wearing his policeman's uniform, his hat with its stiff brim low on his forehead. He gazed straight at the camera with his famous scowl. Underneath the photo, his name, Thomas M. Sullivan.

My heart squeezed and my belly spun like a ballerina pirouetting out of control. And, um, his middle initial was M? I had no idea. A smile touched my lips. It probably stood for Michael or Melvin or something boring, but to me that M would always mean Mule. As in, as stubborn as.

"I had a hit on this news article, earlier today, while

watching the kids at soccer." Alice spoke in a hushed voice. "The picture is from 1946, when Sullivan joined the Ballard Springs police." She handed me the device. Moving it shook the 3-D image as if caught in an earthquake. "I'm sorry, Beryl, but at least this lets us pinpoint a time period for Sullivan's... you know."

Okay, now the ballerina in my belly leapt so high it smashed into my throat. I suddenly couldn't breathe. *I'm sorry* and *Sullivan* in the same sentence couldn't be good. Not at all.

I gripped the commpad tightly. Alice and Glo flanked me, while Jake peered over my shoulder. I focused on the fluctuating images. The dates changed each time the picture faded then reconfigured... 1947, 1950, 1954. I squinted at the story's headline, willing the fuzzy letters to come into focus.

And then they did.

Police Sergeant Falls in Line of Duty.

The ballerina in my belly curled up and died. My eyes clouded and my ears buzzed. Little pins tickled my scalp. I was not a fainting woman, but swooning seemed a definite possibility. I'd known for two years this would be Sully's fate. I'd feared it the entire time we'd been together on my mission. But seeing his picture and that headline, and the news of his death written so starkly made it far too real.

Alice and Glo moved in and steered me to the desk chair, encouraging me to sit. I didn't resist.

"Good find, Alice," Jake said, all business. "Now we have something concrete."

"Keep your chin up, Beryl." Alice accessorized her plucky suggestion with an equally *can-do* grin. "At least we narrowed things down to a specific time frame. Forty-seven to fifty-four. We can keep you out of that era, keep you off the East Coast as much as possible and keep him safe."

Jake nodded like that was the best plan ever devised. Glo activated her poker face. She knew as well as I did that destiny might not cooperate. Fate would always get its way. It had gotten its way my whole life. Took my parents, took the woman I'd known as Grandma Blue far too young. Took her brother, my uncle Augie, during the Battle of the Bulge and there wasn't a damned thing I could do about it. Nothing Sully could've done, either.

I reached out and touched Sully's picture. Or tried to. I'd forgotten it was a hologram. My finger went right up his nose. I laughed, and I knew Sully would laugh too. Then he'd kiss me and call me a real piece of work. And tell me to come back to him, no matter what.

My heart swelled. A solid determination straightened my spine. So did Sully's scowl. It gave me strength and filled me with resolve.

I *would* go back to him. I wasn't going to stay away. I wasn't going to hide from time and hope that would avoid his destiny. Fate had kicked my ass long enough. Time for Beryl Blue to do a little ass kicking of her own. When we met again—and I had no doubt the celestial powers-that-be would make sure we would—I was going to save him. To hell with the temporal rules.

I *would* see Sully again. Despite fate or because of it. And I would find a way to defeat it at its own game.

I handed Alice back her commpad and stood. "Come on, my friends. Let's go have a drink."

Synthetic alcohol that tasted like gross cough medicine, but what the hell. I'd drink a toast to my friends. I'd drink a toast to Oliver Bishop's memory. I'd drink to Sully's future.

And I'd raise my glass high and toast to fate, that ironic bitch, and the battle yet to come.

Thank you for reading *It's Been A Long, Long Time*!

I hope you enjoyed Beryl and Sully's second adventure in time. If you did, please help others find this story by leaving a review.

Don't forget to sign up for my newsletter for the latest news on the next book in the Beryl Blue, Time Cop series, Every Time We Say Goodbye, as well as my other stories, plus exclusive content, free books, and all kinds of other goodies. Just stop by my website to join the fun!

WWW.JANETRAYESTEVENS.COM

Beryl and Sully's Story Continues in...

EVERY TIME WE SAY GOODBYE

Some days, it just doesn't pay to get out of your century...
Beryl has buckled down at work, hunting for both the man who murdered her parents and a way to keep Sully from meeting his destiny. She's also searching for some answers to her convoluted past, answers that may not be what she expects when she lands in her beloved hometown of Ballard Springs in 1947—and finds herself back in Sully's arms. This time she's not letting go, no matter what fate has in store.

ACKNOWLEDGMENTS

Beryl Blue's journey from shelving books in her library to skipping about in time would never have been possible without the help and support of so many others—writers, friends, and especially my family. A huge thank you for your time and talents to Suzanne Tierney, Jeanne Oates Estridge, Fenley Grant, Christine Gunderson, and the rest of the Sunday Accountability Group, Reina Williams at Rickrack Books, cover designer extraordinaire Elizabeth Turner Stokes, Melissa–The Literary Assistant, and an extra shoutout to Kari Lemor.

ABOUT THE AUTHOR

Meet author Janet Raye Stevens – mom, reader, tea-drinker (okay, tea guzzler), and author of smart, stealthily romantic adventures. Derringer and Silver Falchion Award finalist and winner of RWA's Golden Heart® and Daphne du Maurier awards, Janet writes mystery, time travel, paranormal, and the occasional Christmas romance, all with humor, heart, and a dash of suspense. She lives in New England with her family.

www.janetrayestevens.com

www.ingramcontent.com/pod-product-compliance
Lightning Source LLC
Chambersburg PA
CBHW061657190726
48289CB00006B/1920